trapped in her dreams

IN HER DREAMS SERIES BOOK TWO

JOANNA REEDER

REED IT & WEEP

also by joanna reeder

DREAMWALKER WORLD:

In Her Dreams

Trapped In Her Dreams

Purpose In Her Dreams

In Her Dreams Trilogy Boxset

Dream Walker Academy:

Remember (Tessa)

Control (Sebastien)

Belong (Meg)

LEARN ABOUT JOANNA'S OTHER BOOKS AT:

joannareeder.com

Reed It & Weep

Trapped In Her Dreams
Copyright © 2018 Joanna Reeder
joannareeder.com

Cover Art by Angel Leya
angeleya.com

Edited by Katrina Beckstrand
editsbykb.com

For Emily
You've got this!
(And Uh... someone kinda important is named after you!)

CHAPTER 1

glitter and balloons

Birthdays made me jittery.

"Emily!" Arianna squealed as I opened the door, wrapping me in a death-trap hug. "Happy Birthday!"

Let me specify. *My* birthday made me jittery.

"*Seventeen!* I can't believe you're seventeen! Seventeen!"

"Yep, it's the age that comes after sixteen," I sang, holding back an eye roll as I followed her down my front porch steps toward her silver car. Actually it was her sister Carly's car. The sister I once saved, *literally*, from suicide. Actually saving her was the reason Ari was even here picking me up today. In the alternate version of my life, the one where Carly died, Ari and I weren't friends anymore.

A lot had changed since then.

"Promise me, no surprise parties?" I had made my parents pinky swear the same request over my favorite breakfast food that morning—fried scones dripping in honey butter and brown sugar–coated bacon.

"I promise." Ari held her right hand to the square as she pulled out of my driveway.

"No parties at all?"

"Just ice cream at Nelson's after school. That's it."

No parties. No surprises. I finally relaxed into the leather seat.

Nothing traumatizing had ever happened on my birthday—that wasn't why I didn't like it. All of my birthdays had actually been pretty good, albeit mundane and typical. One year I got a bike. When I turned eight, I got an American Girl doll.

But in the five years since the dreams started, I had experienced exactly one hundred and seventy-nine birthdays. At least half of those could be easily lumped into the five- to ten-year-old classics of cake and piñatas and magicians. A few featured bounce houses. Even fewer involved fictional princesses. As most dead people predated the current princess-birthday mania, seeing something as familiar as birthday princesses in a memory-dream was a special sort of tragic. I didn't like to be reminded that there were people my age who were already dead.

Some of the dream birthdays were the milestone ones. Turning sixteen and getting a driver's license—that was pretty great. (Especially since I was only thirteen at the time.) Turning eighteen and being old enough to buy cigarettes—*yuck*. Turning twenty-one... well, twenty-first–birthday dreams were usually pretty short—the birthday girl gets plastered, then crashes early. I'd done that enough times to know I was never going to touch a drop of alcohol.

Seriously, it was a good thing I had a therapist.

But some birthdays I had the privilege of playing guardian angel to—as Grandma Grace used to call it—were painful. The horrible parents who forgot. Or, even worse, decided that their kid's special day was the perfect time to announce Mom and Dad were separating. It was a reminder of why I did what I did. To be with those kids when they needed someone most. When they felt the most alone. I was there, and I liked to think they felt a little less alone, even if they never knew where that feeling came from.

There was the surprise birthday party when I walked in on the birthday girl's boyfriend cheating on her with her sister; the much anticipated roller skating party no one showed up to; the cancer diagnosis; the abusive father who just *had* to see his little girl; the spoiled princess whose cake was chocolate flavored and not *double* chocolate flavored. (Okay, so that last one was more annoying than painful. But really annoying. Like painfully so.)

Or the worst one of all. Her name was Emily, like mine. It was her twelfth birthday, and her father, who had been deployed overseas for nine months, was flying home early to surprise her on her birthday. He'd survived raids and bombs only to die in a car crash on the way home from the airport. I cried for days after that one. Especially after I learned that Emily had died in a crash three years later—and it all happened just a few years ago. It explained why her walk had felt more modern. Because it was. Like I said, special sort of tragic.

I groaned when I saw my locker.

"Surprise!" Arianna said, waving her hands theatrically like a TV–game show model. She presented to me a poster she'd obviously made with glitter and stickers, featuring two purple and two pink balloons taped to the corners. "Do you *love* it?!"

"It's great!" I feigned joy. The *happy birthday Emily*s I heard from my peers walking by made me want to punch the wall. All thanks to the glittering, sparkling, might-as-well-have-had-a-spotlight-shining-right-at-it sign. What happened to no surprises? It was going to be a long day. "Thanks, Ari."

"What are best friends for?"

Quicker than usual, I grabbed my books so I could get to class and far away from Ari's advertisement. Maybe if people didn't see it, they wouldn't feel the need to congratulate me on being born.

"Happy Birthday, Emily," said Duncan, my ex-boyfriend catching up to me as I parted from Ari. His voice was the only one that sounded sympathetic, like he felt bad for me that it was my birthday. It was endearing. Like he knew me that well. Better than my best friend Arianna anyway.

I hated that I'd hurt him.

Last fall Duncan had suddenly appeared out of nowhere. Like literally. I'd saved someone in one of my memory walks, and BOOM! *Hi, my name's Duncan. We met in kindergarten.* He knew me and everyone else knew him, but *I* didn't know him. In the alternate version of my life, it hadn't been a big deal. Apparently we'd never been more than acquaintances. So when Duncan suddenly flashed into existence, we became friends, then more than friends. But when I saved Carly, Duncan suddenly transformed from object of budding romance to my boyfriend of six months. He had all these memories of how great we were together, and all I had was a complete blank.

It was one of many things that changed when I saved Carly. I got my best friend back (Arianna) *and* instant boyfriend (Duncan). Things were good but... weird.

Anyway, the pressure of him knowing so much about me and me not remembering any of our time together was a big part of why I broke things off with him. It was too complicated.

The breakup also might have had something to do with a certain tall, dark, and handsome guy with chestnut-colored eyes—literally the man of my dreams. But I rarely admitted that fact, even to myself. Although Andrew was safely tucked away in my memory dreams, it hadn't felt fair to Duncan. I couldn't keep pretending. It was too bad Andrew hadn't suddenly appeared in my life one day as an instant boyfriend. Or that I felt for Duncan what I felt for Andrew.

"Thanks," I muttered.

He shrugged. "Hey, and heads up, I think Ari has another plan up her sleeve."

I felt sick. "Really? Do you know what it is?"

"Not exactly. It'll be after school though."

"Thanks, Duncan," I said, truly grateful for the warning. Why couldn't I be in love with him? He was here. He was sweet. And it didn't hurt that he was very easy on the eyes too. So why not him?

I shook my head, banishing the idea from my mind, and braced myself for the day.

MY EYES DARTED AROUND THE ICE CREAM SHOP EVERY few seconds. I was trying to be covert, but I couldn't help but feel nervous for whatever Arianna had planned. Rain drops streamed down the windows in erratic patterns, making it difficult to see anything in the parking lot or on the sidewalk.

Rain was weird for January. I might've preferred snow. Snow would have left the windows clear. Which would have at least given me a heads-up on suspects carrying offensive birthday balloons, or a crowd of suspiciously happy people, just waiting to overwhelm the capacity of the ice cream shop. I couldn't ever remember it raining on my birthday before.

"Why so jumpy, Em?" Arianna asked. Her smile only confirmed that I was right to be worried.

"Duncan said you had another surprise planned."

"Oh?" She played dumb.

"Come on, Ari. He said it was probably happening after school, so I figured *now* might be *when*."

"Well, you're wrong," she sang. "It's just you and me."

Yeah, for now.

We finished our ice cream without incident. Our yummy, creamy, chocolate-and-caramel-swirled marshmallow goodness. Okay, so maybe the ice cream made up for the glitter-and-balloon-decorated locker.

As we got up to leave, I sighed. I was home free now. Mom and Dad had made dinner plans, so I knew there was nothing else Arianna could do. Duncan was wrong. Telling him would be fun.

I smiled and pushed open the double glass doors only to be met with a stream of water right in the face.

And it wasn't rain.

"Ha-appy Birthday, Emily-eee!" sang two male voices.

I sputtered and choked on the water, grateful I'd had the foresight to wear my glasses today. At least my eyes were dry. Arianna laughed hysterically beside me but was soon cut off. She held her palms up in a weak attempt to block the water stream aimed at her.

We had nothing in our defense against the two football players with Super Soakers. I looked at Ari with an is-this-seriously-what-you-had-planned? look. She ignored it and clicked open her trunk to reveal two more water cannons. Grabbing them before the guys could, she handed me one and began a counter-offensive.

"Water fight in January?" I asked incredulously.

"C'mon!" Scott O'Neil said, pumping another stream of water at me that I ducked easily. "It's not that cold!"

I aimed and shot back at him, missing his face, but soaking him square in the chest. Scott was one of Duncan's teammates on the football team. I didn't follow the sport well, but I did remember that Scott had been the quarterback for our school before I saved Carly. Somehow saving her also saved Duncan from a game-ending injury. Duncan was the better player and therefore the current quarterback... in my current reality.

Sometimes it was hard to keep the different versions of history straight.

Brian Nash, Arianna's boyfriend, was the other attacker. He and Ari shot at each other until Brian ran out of water, then he tried to grab her waist while she continued to pummel him with streams, pumping the soaker with vigor.

It was mostly moot though. It was still raining, so we were all drenched within seconds anyway. Arianna giggled uncontrollably, and I couldn't help but laugh too as we exchanged shots back and forth. It was insane and ridiculous... and crazy fun. It felt like I hadn't laughed that hard in years. Sad but probably true.

Too bad Duncan hadn't come. But he knew I didn't like my birthday or surprises. Maybe he thought I'd hate it and didn't want to be a part of something I might not like.

Since it was January, it was cold, if not freezing. So the fight only lasted about five minutes before we threw our weapons back into Ari's trunk and ducked into her car with the heat blasting.

"See?" she asked as we pulled out of the parking lot. "Aren't surprises on your birthday fun sometimes?"

My grin was still wide from the adrenaline rush of the water fight. "You win! That was pretty fun."

"And be honest," she sobered slightly. "Having fun in your *real* life is way better than anything that can happen in a dream, right?"

I sobered too. "Sometimes dreams are fun," I said. "But I suppose I could never feel that rush so organically if I weren't... well, just me?"

"Exactly." She seemed satisfied. "You will remember this birthday the rest of your life and the next part too."

My heart sunk. "Next part?"

"Yeah, the part where you waltz into dinner looking like a drowned rat."

I laughed as genuinely as possible, grasping for that light feeling I'd felt only seconds earlier. But it felt like grasping at thin air as I fell off a cliff. I understood her meaning completely. She wanted me to be happy and live only in the present—aka take my meds to stop having dreams.

I couldn't blame her for wanting that for me, but she didn't really understand all of the reasons I couldn't ever do that. I just wouldn't be me if I weren't spending my nights dream walking with other people. I helped them. They needed me. And as tragic as it sounded, being what Grams called a guardian angel defined me.

"Oh and, Emily?" Ari asked before I closed her car door in front of my house.

"Yeah?"

"Try to top that for my birthday next week."

"Just you wait." I winked at her but had no idea how.

unnecessary change

"Charles, I am so happy!"

His sky-blue eyes smile, though his lips do not as they meet mine in a gentle, barely whisper of a kiss.

"As am I, my dearest Lucy."

"Aunt Penelope and Uncle Harry will be glad we have finally set upon a date."

"So will Miss Hannah," he says, winking, then gently squeezing my fingers.

I fight the reaction to wince, and Charles jerks back, suddenly remembering my lingering injuries.

"I am all right," I say softly.

"Of course you are." It is what he always says, every time he wishes to end the conversation—which he does every time we talk about my injuries.

He is trying to appease me, but I can see the truth hiding behind his eyes: he thinks I am broken. Sometimes I fear that he will call off the wedding altogether. What use is a wife who cannot use her hands or fingers without extreme pain?

"Which part of the celebration will Miss Hannah plan first?" he asks.

"The dresses, of course." I smile.

"Ah, yes. She must get fitted at the dressmaker immediately," he says in his mock-business tone.

"What could be more important?" I laugh but want to cry. I turn my head as if to admire the neighbors' roses as we pass by in the carriage, holding back the tears that threaten to spill.

He loves you. A thought jumps into my head.

Emily.

It does not startle me anymore when she speaks to my mind, she is so familiar. Much like a sister.

Yes, and we have set a date. I say to her, my spirits bolstered just by her presence.

I heard. June eighteenth?

Yes. It is even a Wednesday! I am particularly excited about that part.

A Wednesday...? she says strangely. It is hard to detect the tone in her thought. *And that's a good thing? Having it on a Wednesday?*

Yes, the rhyme! 'Wednesday the best day of all.' She must know that rhyme. Everyone knows the rhyme.

Nope. Not familiar with that one.

Remember it goes: 'Marry on Monday for health, Tuesday for wealth, Wednesday the best day of all.' I pause, giving her memory time. When she does not respond I continue, *'Thursday for crosses, Friday for losses, and Saturday for no luck at all.'*

What about Sundays? Emily asks.

Sundays are out of the question. No one gets married on the Sabbath.

Right, Emily says. She does not sound convinced.

I cannot believe you have never heard the rhyme.

Different times, Lucy.

Yes, but you must have kept some traditions?

Sure, most brides wear white dresses, spend exorbitant amounts of money on flowers, and send fancy invitations that no one RSVPs to. Oh and the bridesmaids wear hideous dresses. Then everyone dances the chicken dance and light sparklers or blow bubbles as the happy couple leaves for their honeymoon.

That sounds horrible. Well some of it, I amend. *Do all brides wear white?*

All except the eccentric ones. Are you wearing white?

Yes. I considered wearing blue... because of recent happenings. But the color chosen is supposed to determine your future life, and white is 'chosen right.'

What does blue mean?

'Love will be true.'

Are you concerned about that? Emily asks.

I... sometimes I worry that he might... that after what happened in the fire... I cannot finish my sentence and merely look down at my damaged hands.

He doesn't see you as broken, she says.

A sob unexpectedly bursts from my lips.

"Lucy!" Charles panics. "What is the matter?"

Now I am in hysterics.

Emily takes the reigns. "I am just so happy," she says through my tears. I am amazed at how quickly she can calm my emotions. How she can take over and save me with an unknown strength I know I do not possess.

Just as she saved me from the fire. The fire that I surely would have perished in if not for her... and Andrew.

Andrew.

Charles's cousin. Emily is in love with him, and he with her, though she will not admit it.

"I—I know I should have died in that fire," she continues for me, still a bit weepy, "but I didn't—I did not." She corrects her strange speech. Emily has excelled at sounding like me over these many months, but she still occasionally falls into her different accent and colloquial speech. "And I am so happy that we can finally plan our wedding!"

She feels some guilt over the fire, though I do not know why. Tessa's death perhaps?

"What a blessing it is that you survived," Charles says softly, clearly conflicted—relieved by my survival and grieved by his cousin's death.

"Yes... a blessing," I say.

We sit in silence, a bittersweet, peaceful silence, until the house comes into view.

The northern side—the damaged side—is still in repair. Sheets drape off sections to keep the bad air from entering the good part of the house. Cleaning crews work tirelessly to scrub and paint over the fire damage. They have not yet begun on the outside. The black-charred silhouettes of flames still stain the once light-gray stone near the windows.

"Andrew has returned!" Charles's features brighten at the sight of his favorite cousin.

"Indeed." I take over again as my emotions have calmed enough for me to speak for myself. "We can tell him the good news."

He's back? Emily speaks to me.

Yes, he's back. I repeat. *Oh! You have not seen him since—*

It's fine, she says hurriedly. *I'm fine, really.*

No! You must have a moment alone. Leave it to me.

Lucy, no, don't. You don't have to—

But I must. For her sake. She saved me after all. And she has not really spoken to him since my recovery. It is the least I can do for her.

"Andrew!" Charles booms when we are in earshot. "When did you arrive?"

He chuckles. I feel Emily's butterflies swarm. Our connection is interesting that way. We feel each other's emotions, and though I have no sort of feelings toward Andrew in that way, I feel *her* new love every time she sees him. I remember those feelings well from Charles's early courting. "Only a few hours ago," Andrew says. "I wanted to see the happy couple."

"And we have good news!" Charles says when the carriage

stops. He bounds down then offers me his hand to step down. "We have set a wedding date."

"Have you?" Andrew's happy tone falters a bit, and I know why, but Charles happily does not notice.

"Tell him, dear," Charles says to me.

"June the eighteenth," I say. "Do you think you will be able to attend?"

"I would not miss it," he says, though I don't sense any truth behind his words. I hide my observation from Emily.

"It is such a lovely day," I say. "Let us sit awhile in the garden. Then Andrew can tell us all about his travels."

"That is a grand idea," Charles says, leading the way.

"Oh, but Charles?" I stop and ask. "Would you be a dear and get my hand cream? My hands..."

"Absolutely," he says. "Where can I find it?"

"Betsy knows where I keep it."

"I will have it to you straightaway." He rushes to the house.

That was sly, Emily says.

Our heart pounds at her nervousness. Emily has not seen Andrew in so long, and I have just given her some stolen moments with him.

It was the least I could do, I say. *Hurry though. Charles will not be long.*

"How was your trip?" I ask. Emily is tongue-tied at the moment.

"Uneventful," he says almost in a snap. "Is she here?"

"She is, but she's—"

Don't say I'm nervous.

"She is here," I repeat, without elaboration.

"Please, I need to speak with her."

It's okay, I'll talk to him. She takes a deep breath. "Andrew. I'm here. It's Emily."

He watches us for a moment, gauging our honesty.

"H-How was your trip?" She cannot stand silence. I find that fact about her endearing. "I haven't seen you since—"

"The fire, yes, I know," he says. She is confused and her thoughts briefly flit to a memory of escaping bondage somewhere, which confuses me. "My trip was much needed," he continues, keeping his face neutral.

Her heart falls. She thinks he went to get away from her.

"It was good to see my sisters after Tessa's passing," he says, soberly.

She hangs my head. "I am so sorry about your sister."

"It was her choice to run in the house."

It was Emily's grandmother's choice, and he knows that, but it is gracious of him not to mention that detail. I know how much the entire situation hurts Emily. Though she hides it, I know she aches inside over the loss of her grandmother. I suspect she feels tremendous responsibility over Tessa's death as well.

Remember that Andrew also ran inside, I mention to her. *And he's still here.*

Unspoken, the topic dissolves, and Andrew's face brightens into his mischievous smile. "But there were some other things I needed to attend too as well."

She feels his meaning and bats my eyelashes at him. "Oh? What sort of things?" Her tone turns flirtatious; she has always been bolder than I.

"The sort of things you would not approve of." His sly smile widens, making her heart melt.

"What wouldn't I approve of?"

"Unnecessary change."

"Unnecessary change? Andrew, you shouldn't—"

"Lucy is grateful to be alive, you know that," he says, interrupting her. He removes his gray bowler hat and takes a step toward me. Gingerly, he removes the white lace gloves from my fingers and examines the widespread scars. My entire hand is one big scar.

"Andrew, what is going on?" she feels confused and worried.

I am glad to be alive. I tell her. I do not know what Andrew is trying to say, but I have many times felt Emily's guilt over the fire and my injuries. I feel the impulse to affirm my gratefulness.

"I know these hurt day and night." Andrew ignores Emily's question. "And I know you saw her grave, that she should have died in that fire."

My grave? Emily keeps more hidden from me than I thought.

"But even though she had to postpone her wedding," he continues, "she is grateful to be planning a wedding. Not *all* change is bad, Emily."

"Of course," she agrees. "I am glad we saved Lucy. But you said *unnecessary change*," she emphasizes but with tight lips like it is a secret. "Saving Lucy was not unnecessary."

"Wasn't it? She was supposed to die." He pauses for effect. "So would you not agree that change is good?" His evasion is frustrating me almost as much as it is her. I almost take over and demand that he quit skirting the topic, but as he draws closer, she and I are both entranced.

Then he leans in.

And Charles clears his throat. "Lucy, your hand cream."

CHAPTER 3

Lies

I woke up with a smile on my face.

Partly because it was no longer my birthday, but partly because of *him*. It was just a crush, I knew that, and a very silly one at that. What hope was there for us if I only saw him in my dreams? But I couldn't help myself. Seeing him made me happy. My grin grew even bigger.

Ugh. I was so sappy sometimes.

Groaning, I rolled over and got out of bed. But I sang as I shampooed my hair and had a spring in my step as I dressed in my favorite button-down blue shirt and faded jeans.

It was such a tiny conversation, I thought as I leaned inches from the mirror in order to apply black mascara, *and inconsequential. But it was a good one.*

Emily, this is ridiculous, I chided myself, retrieving my glasses and putting them on. *He's not even real.*

Of course he's real.

But even if he's alive, he's over one hundred years old!

I should call Grandma. Then she could have this argument with me, and I wouldn't have to play both sides.

But I couldn't call her. The thought left as quickly as it came. I could never call Grandma again. She piggybacked into my dream of the fire, determined to make sure I didn't save Lucy—Grandma believed Lucy wasn't *supposed* to be saved. Grams was so adamant about it that she/Tessa followed me into the fire. But I couldn't save them all. Her heart gave out when Tessa died.

I shook off my fresh, still-painful grief over losing Grandma Grace and resumed my solo argument—if a little less enthusiastically.

Hopefully I'll have more time with Andrew now that he's back. I'm only seventeen. Can't my dream crush be the man in my dreams?

Sure. Why not? I powdered the shine out of my nose and forehead. *What's the harm?*

Exactly. And now that Lucy knows, she will let us have more time together.

Then I remembered the look on Charles' face when he saw us so close together.

My stomach dropped. Lucy's gravestone said she married Charles, but I knew better than anyone the past could change. One stolen, misinterpreted look, and Charles might call off the wedding. Lucy was already worried he would hesitate because of her injuries.

We'll just have to be more careful. Andrew and I could discuss things, figure out a way for Lucy to still have her happy ending. Just the thought of seeing him again to have that conversation put the smile back on my face. I hadn't seen him in *so* long. Why not relish in it?

I mean, I hadn't seen him in weeks. Not since the fire. Aside from that weird dream in the 60s with the kidnapped girl—I think her name was Mary? It was weird he didn't mention it... Did he not remember it? Maybe it hadn't *happened* for him yet. Ugh. My life was already complicated enough without figuring out how Andrew had memory walked into the future. I shook the thought from my head and took the stairs two at a time down to breakfast.

My smile stayed put as I grabbed a box of cereal from the cupboard and poured myself a bowl.

Mom was in the kitchen already, making eggs for her and Dad.

"Do you want some?" she asked.

The smile stayed as I turned to look at her, but before I could even get the words *no thanks* out, she interrupted and wiped it clean from my face. "Did you take your meds last night?"

"Yes, Mom." The lie came so easily. Maybe because I had said it so many times. "And no eggs for me, thanks." I took my sugary cereal and the milk to the table and pretended to be very interested in my history textbook while I ate so I wouldn't have to talk to her.

***

FORTUNATELY MY GOOD MOOD RESURFACED AS SOON AS I left the house for school. Arianna might have wanted me to focus on the present world. But she never could resist a good Andrew story. I couldn't wait to tell her that he'd returned.

"Ems!" she said when I found her near Brian's locker.

"Hey, Ari," I said, my smile returning. "I wanna talk to you."

"Oh?" She clasped my hands, leading me down the hall. "Are you and Duncan...?"

"Duncan?"

She gave me a knowing look. "I know he couldn't come to the water fight, but I figured he'd stop by last night. Did you patch things up? Are you two, you know... back together?"

"He didn't come over last night," I said, first baffled that Ari had expected him to come, then a little sad that he hadn't. "And no, we aren't back together."

"Then what?" Ari said dramatically. She had a tendency to overdramatize *everything*. "Is it about the dance? I mean, it's like *forever* away, but we could start dress shopping. Do you know who you want to ask?"

"It's not about the dance."

"Then what?"

I shrugged and felt my cheeks burn. "*Andrew* came back."

I braced myself for the squeal, for Ari to stomp her feet in excitement then and pull me into a more secluded area so we wouldn't be overheard while I related every. Single. Detail. Just like she used to.

She would love to hear about my brief conversation with Andrew: how he looked; how he smelled; what I was going to do about not messing things up for Lucy.

And oh!

I might actually be *there* when Lucy picks out her wedding dress! And at her turn-of-the-century Victorian wedding!—which was happening on a *Wednesday* no less. Ari would get a kick out of their little superstitious rhyme. And now, even with her scarred hands and a million things to do, Lucy—well, both of us, I guess —would have to juggle the man she loved and the one I preferred.

It was hard not to prefer Andrew when he was the one person, the *only* person, I had ever met awake or asleep who was cursed like me. The only person who knew the terrors and heartaches of enduring what others endured in the memory dreams. Or *walks* as Andrew called them. I was finding myself referring to them that way more and more—

"Why aren't you taking your meds?" she asked instead with *that* look on her face.

"Ari..."

"Do your parents know that you are having the dreams again?"

"I... uh..."

"Do they know you aren't taking your meds?"

I shook my head *no* in defeat.

"Ems, they worry about you. *I* worry about you."

"I know."

"Whatever happened to loving the present? Isn't this good enough? *Fun* enough?"

I was a little shocked by the emotion behind her words. Perhaps the surprise water fight yesterday hadn't just been about my birthday. Maybe Ari was trying to make my real life more *fun*, as she put it. Maybe she thought that if I liked this life more, I wouldn't feel the need to return to the dreams.

"But, Ari—"

"Take your meds, Emily. Take them and quit lying to your parents. Tell them, or else I will."

promises and plans

"Good, you are here," Lucy says as I blink into her head. She walks briskly down the path to the side garden.

Why, what's— I stop when I see him standing near some rosebushes with budding pink and white flowers.

"Andrew," I breathe without a thought.

"Miss Lucy." He reaches for her hand and gently kisses her knuckles.

"And Emily," Lucy says with a smile.

Something passes over his features I can't name.

"I thought—" He drops her hand. "I thought we were meeting *alone*." His voice is hushed.

"You know I have no say in her comings and goings," Lucy says. Something is off in her voice, like she isn't telling the whole truth.

"Then perhaps we should speak later." He moves to leave the garden.

"Wait," I say, "what is so important for you two to discuss that I shouldn't be involved?"

"Andrew," Lucy says, "it is probably best that she know our plan."

Andrew searches my face... or maybe hers. It feels that he is trying to communicate something to Lucy that he doesn't want me to know.

"About how you two can have time together without Charles thinking..." Lucy adds, but doesn't finish.

"Right..." Andrew says, clearly playing along.

What is going on?

"I love Charles," Lucy says, "and I do not want him to ever think otherwise."

"Of course," Andrew and I say at the same time.

"I think it is best if the two of you do not talk to each other when Charles is around," she says. I feel her guilt over limiting our time together. But I can read between the words, since her thoughts float around mine. When Charles came back and caught Andrew so close to her, he had looked so upset that Lucy thought he would call off the wedding that very day. I wince at her memory of it.

"Don't feel guilty, Lucy," I say. "I completely understand." Maybe I should just leave. I know *how* to leave a dream. I've done it before. Once. I just need to remember the worst moment of my life, something truly excruciating. It's unpleasant, but possible. "I don't even know why I'm here. I'm supposed to be helping people and instead I'm messing everything up. I should go. For good."

"No!" Andrew says harshly.

"No, Emily," Lucy repeats. "You saved my life, I will not ban you from... *visiting.*"

"But it's dangerous for you. You *want* me to stop coming," I say. "Everyone at home wants me to stop coming. I keep lying to my parents, saying that I am taking my meds. Maybe I should be." But a chill runs up my spine even as I suggest it. The dreams wouldn't stop. The medication only blocks my memory of them. Maybe if I take them long enough the dreams really will stop. But until then? The sensation of not remembering what I'd been through, of waking up screaming with no understanding... It's even worse than the dreams. I close my eyes, blocking out the feeling. Maybe that isn't the answer. Lucy's shoulders shudder slightly despite the day's warmth.

"No!" Andrew's tone is somehow even more firm. "Lucy," he says, softer, "I do not want Charles to think there is anything untoward going on between you and I. And if you both just give me some time, I have…" He pauses then steps back, and in one swift motion, he flicks his wrist, plucking a budding pink rose. "I have a plan." He speaks at barely a whisper. "If it works, we will all have everything we want."

My heart thuds loudly when his eyes meet mine.

He hands me the rose.

"For now," he continues, "we will be careful. Emily and I will only speak to each other when Charles is away, as Lucy wishes."

"Thank you," Lucy breathes. "Charles is not expected until this evening, so I will give you both a moment."

Without another word, she steps back.

I twist the rose in my hand, plucking the thorns from the stem. Nervous, I am afraid to meet his eyes again because I am so torn between needing to leave because it's the right thing to do and not wanting to leave because I want to see him so badly.

He visibly relaxes upon her departure. Like some weight has been lifted, but he is clearly still carrying much of his heavy burden.

"I shouldn't have come," I say.

"Nonsense," he says. "I did not mean that I am unhappy you are here. I just—" He pauses.

"Maybe this isn't a good idea," I say, when he doesn't elaborate. "I saw the look on Charles's face when he saw you and Lucy…"

"Not *Lucy*. You. *Emily*."

"Charles doesn't know that *Emily* exists." I turn away.

"Well, yes, we must be careful," he says. "Charles would never forgive me if he thought Lucy and I…"

"It would destroy her," I add. "She loves him. She wants to marry *him*. She doesn't love you."

Somehow my words cause him pain.

"And you still love her." I voice what he won't. "I really should go."

"No! It is not her," he says. "I mean, at first I thought I loved her—"

"No, this is really too complicated," I interrupt. "I am only seventeen! I'm just a teenager who likes to live in her dreams." I really shouldn't be having conversations with dream guys I have feelings for. This is just a crush. It's just a crush, and I could mess up *history* by breaking up Lucy and Charles. "Coming was a mistake."

"You forget that I have the same types of dreams," he reminds me. "When was the last time you had a dream *other* than Lucy?" His tone has turned sober, and I sense some anger behind it.

"I don't dream her every night," I say as my thoughts flit to Mary's recent kidnapping, or rather her escape from kidnappers... with Andrew's help. But I don't know whether or not he'd experienced it yet, so I keep quiet.

"But most nights." He turns on his heel and paces with his hands behind his back. "At least recently, most nights you get to live in the mind of this beautiful girl who is kind and has a comfortable life with people surrounding her who care about her."

A lump forms in my throat. All I can do is swallow hard and nod.

He stops his pacing to look me in the eye. "I was *murdered* last night. Have you ever been *murdered?*"

I lower my head. "Yes. Twenty-three times." My voice is so small I wonder if he even hears it.

"The night before, I was a small boy being beaten by his parents."

I feel sick. Those are some of the worst.

"And the night before that I was crushed under a stagecoach. I cannot even number how many bones were broken in that accident."

"But you know how to wake up," I say. "You know how to make it end."

"Yes, I do, but I never do it."

"Why not?"

He flashes his knowing smile. "Why did you stay with Lucy during the fire?"

I wonder if she listens even when she steps back. If she is listening now.

"Fire is painful," he continues. "I have been burned a few times. It. Is. Painful."

I still don't respond.

"So why did you stay with her?" He waits. "You've told me before. Just say it."

I sigh. "Because she needed me."

"Exactly. Those boys, those men, *need* me. So I stay."

"Why are you telling me this?" I ask, my voice stronger now. "I know what it's like. I know what you go through. I've been through it too."

"Because you keep threatening to leave." He takes large steps until his face is inches from mine. "We need each other. We are good for each other, but you have some magic pills, and you keep threatening to never walk Lucy again."

"I know, but—"

"Do you not realize how lucky you are to have this reprieve? That when you go to sleep you are most likely to be with Lucy? Safe and happy... and engaged to Charles?"

"What do you want me to say?" My eyes fill with frustrated tears.

"I want you to promise to never take those pills. Ever."

Easy. "I promise."

"Trust me." His eyes squint with his smile. "I have a plan for us to be together without hurting Lucy."

Okay, so maybe I *don't* want to stop walking with Lucy just yet. I hate how quickly he has changed my mind.

Andrew has a plan. I can wait.

great friends

I snuck out of the house early to avoid Arianna. As I dialed her number to tell her not to come get me, I practiced my disappointed-but-pretending-to-be-happy face. Even though I was just happy.

"Ari?" I said when her phone picked up.

"She's in the shower." It was Carly. "Can I give her a message?"

"Just tell her I don't need a ride today."

"Emily?" Her tone flipped, and it put me on edge. "Is everything okay?"

"It's fine!" I said, my voice pitched. "I'm fine. Really."

"Look." I imagined her switching the phone from one ear to the other. "Ari told me about you not taking your meds."

"She did?" *Oh no...*

"She's worried about you, and I totally get that."

"I know. Did she tell you she threatened to tell my parents I wasn't taking them?"

"Yes."

"Are *you* going to tell my parents?"

"No..." She paused. "In fact, I don't think you should take them."

That was unexpected. "You don't?"

"I know we only talked about it that one time, but you're kind of the reason I'm here today. Like literally."

She wasn't wrong.

"So, I think if you want to continue having the dreams, you should keep having the dreams. I won't tell."

I breathed a sigh of relief. "Thank you."

"You help people, Emily. I know you can't save everyone. I mean, I'm not uber-familiar with your other clients, but I get it. But at least if you're with them. They're not alone. And that means a lot."

My voice caught in my throat. "I wish Ari could see it that way."

"I'll work on her. See if I can bring her to our side."

Our side. Carly was on *my side.* Those two little words warmed me more than she would ever know.

"You're leaving early so you don't have to see her, aren't you?"

Man, she was good. "Yeah, I had another dream, and I don't want her to see it on my face. I need time—"

"I get it. I'll tell her you're in the computer lab."

"Okay..." I wasn't following.

"While you head somewhere else."

"Right." I sure was thick sometimes. "Thanks, Carly. Oh and maybe hint that you aren't supposed to know, but I'm working on something for her birthday." Then she really won't try to find me."

"That's perfect," she said. "Hey, and if you ever need to talk to someone about a dream, call me."

"Wow. Thank you!" I may have saved her, but Carly felt like a big sister to me in a lot of ways. I looked up to her. She was in college, and yet here she was, talking to her sister's lowly high school friend.

"Don't sound so surprised. You're a rock star in my book." She hung up.

Taking Carly's advice, I steered clear of the computer lab in case Ari came looking for me and instead buried myself in the library.

I tried to finish my homework, but my mind wasn't in it. Instead, I racked my brain for some fantastically epic way to celebrate Ari's upcoming birthday, but it didn't take long for my thoughts to drift.

As much as I didn't want to cause problems for Lucy, I couldn't bear giving up my dreams with her until I figured out what Andrew was up to. He was so cryptic about the *plans* he was concocting. I replayed my last couple of Lucy walks in my head. *What wouldn't I approve of?*

I had an inkling that it had something to do with unnecessary changes, but I had no idea what those were. I wasn't angry. In fact, it felt good that he finally knew *me*, that he wanted to talk to *me*, that he was worried that the things he was doing were not approved by *me*.

Although he still had no idea what I looked like, I was pretty sure he *got it*, understood where Lucy ended and I began. I could tell he still had lingering, albeit mostly unconscious, feelings for Lucy, but I could ignore that.

One thing was for certain. I would not take the pills and stop the dreams. No matter what my parents or Dr. Shew or Arianna said. So, for now, I'd just be careful in my Lucy dreams and avoid Ari when I woke up from one. She could always tell when I had dreamed of Andr—

"Emily?"

I was yanked from my thoughts.

"Duncan!" My voice came out too sharp and cheery. "Hey," I spoke slower. "How are you?" I lowered my tone too.

"I'm good," he said with a half-croak.

"Sit." I motioned for him to join me in my not-studying.

He hesitated a moment, then unslung his heavy worn blue backpack onto the floor and slowly pulled out the wooden chair across from me and gingerly sat. He had dark circles underneath his eyes, and his honey-brown hair was unusually disheveled.

"You okay?" I asked.

"I'm okay," he croaked again, then cleared his throat. It sounded like he was getting over a cold. Or getting one. He coughed a couple of times, adding fuel to my hunch.

"Thanks for the heads-up on my birthday. Have you ever been attacked by Super Soakers in January in the rain?"

He laughed. "Can't say that I have."

"Well, you're missing out." I smiled. "It was actually pretty wonderful, albeit not the healthiest environment. I'll probably end up sounding like you do. Maybe it's best you weren't there." Although I really wish he had been.

We were silent for several moments. Several *awkward* moments.

"How were your holidays?" *Lame*, but I couldn't think of anything else. Other than our brief conversation the other day, we hadn't talked... *at all* since the breakup. Whenever I saw him in the halls before winter break, he would turn and walk the other way, or make himself actively engaged in a conversation with someone else. I got the hint pretty quickly that he didn't want to talk to me. And I hated it. I felt like he was my only real, genuine friend. Especially because he was my only friend in the alternate history, before I saved Carly. Saving her had changed my social status from loner loser to popular girlfriend of Duncan Stewart and best friend of Arianna Schwartz literally overnight. But he'd been my friend even before that.

After being away from school and away from each other for a few weeks, maybe we could get a fresh start.

"They were um... fine," he said. "My brothers came home from college, and Tara and Jake brought the new baby."

"Aw..." I said and realized how much I still didn't know about Duncan. I assumed Tara was his sister, but I had no clue about the names of his brothers. I'm sure the version of Emily he remembered met them all, but *this* Emily didn't know the first thing about them. "What did they name the baby?" I asked, assuming it was information he hadn't already told me.

"Tommy. Well… they named him Thomas, but we all call him Tommy."

"Cute!" I said and meant it, but I didn't know how to continue the conversation.

"How are you?" Duncan asked tentatively.

"I'm okay." I said, trying to sound blasé. For some reason I wasn't worried about him knowing I wasn't taking my meds. But things were very complicated. It might hurt him if I told him about Andrew. "No offense, but you don't look so good. It was probably best that you didn't join in on my ambush."

"Eh," he said, sniffing once. "It's just a cold." His tone was deep and nasally. "Ari said you haven't been talking your medication lately." He turned the focus back to me.

"She told you?" My voice became high-pitched again.

"Whoa," he held his hands up in surrender. "Don't worry, I didn't tell anyone else."

"But *still*," I said, managing to lower my voice again. "It's not really *her* business whether or not I take them."

He shrugged. "She worries about you."

I rolled my eyes but said, "I know."

We sat in comfortable silence for several moments. I studied my cuticles and twisted the pretty silver ring on my finger. The pretty ring with intricate vines and leaves surrounding tiny diamonds. The ring I'd worn since the day Duncan gave it to me. The ring I should probably give back. With much hesitation, I took the ring off and looked at it for a few more seconds before setting it lightly on the table between us and slid it closer to him. "I should give this back to you," I said, not hiding the regret in my voice well at all. I hadn't planned to give it back, but I didn't feel right keeping it.

Duncan was taken by surprise, "N-no, you should keep it." He attempted a half smile and waved a hand at the antique ring.

"Duncan," I said, steadily. "It belongs to your family. It's a *Harker* heirloom. I can't keep it. I'm no longer…" I couldn't finish the sentence.

He glanced at it but didn't pick it up.

The first bell rang.

"I should go—" I rose from my chair and started to say.

But he interrupted me, "Have you had any bad memory-dreams lately?"

I nodded and sat back down. "But you already know that. Since Ari told you I'm not taking my meds," I said bitterly and stared at the dark wood grain in the table.

"Hey," he said softly and reached across to lift my chin and meet his eyes.

My first instinct was to push his hand away for touching me in such an intimate way, but meeting his eyes, I saw how sincere he was. And behind it, he still masked a deep pain. I didn't know if it was my guilt over hurting him or my desperation to keep him in my life, but I kept my hands firmly planted and the push never happened.

"For whatever reason,"—he let go of my face self-consciously—"you don't want to take the meds and stop the dreams, right?"

I nodded again.

"Even though some of them are pretty bad?"

I bobbed my head only once this time. I couldn't tell him that the majority of my dreams were tucked safely with a blonde-haired girl surrounded by people and events that would never hurt her... well, minus the fire. And my recent kidnapping.

"Then your secret's safe with me," he said.

"Really?" I was floored. "You aren't going to threaten to tell my parents?"

"No." There was no hesitation. "If you don't want to take them, I don't think that you should take them. You experience those memories for a reason, and taking chemicals to stop what is natural doesn't seem like the right thing to do."

I liked the way he put it. Of course my reasons weren't *quite* that noble. A big part of my reasons might be connected to a certain dark-haired dreamboat. But I appreciated Duncan being on my side. "Thank you, Duncan."

"We're friends, Em," he said. "Even if we're no longer..." He trailed off.

"Of course we're friends," I said and reached across the table once more to squeeze his hand. "We're great friends."

Duncan stood to leave without taking the ring.

"Hey," I stopped him. "You forgot something."

"Oh right." He hesitated, his hand jerking with what I wanted to imagine was regret, the same way mine had done when I had placed the ring there. But he picked it up and carefully tucked it away in a small pocket on the side of his backpack before heading to class.

CHAPTER 6

french class

I can see the white corner of a folded note jammed partway into my locker from halfway down the hall.

I wonder who it's from, I think as I take the last few steps a bit quicker.

Pulling it out before opening my locker, I'm even more excited when I see my name, *Jenny*—written in curly letters with tiny blue hearts drawn all around it.

I study the handwriting. *It's definitely not from my BFF in the whole world, Sarah.* She always crosses the *J* and uses her favorite purple pen. The *J* on my note is definitely not crossed and is written in a generic blue ballpoint pen. And her notes are always folded into a triangle. This is a regular rectangle.

But I only have about a minute left until the tardy bell rings, so I quickly dial in the combination for my locker and switch out my Algebra textbook for my French one and jam both the book and the note into my bag.

Skipping down the hall to my class, I actually arrive and slide into my seat up front with time to spare. A thoughtful student, I organize my textbook, notebook, and number two pencil—white with the pink flowers—on my desk.

But Mademoiselle Parry isn't in the classroom yet. *Maybe I can read my note before she gets here.* I look around again, and once I'm certain the coast is clear, I retrieve it and quickly unfold it.

Jenny, it reads in the same blue curly letters. I skip to the bottom of the page before reading the rest to see who it's from. It's from Maddie. The same tiny blue hearts that bordered my name on the outside of the note dot the *i* in her name. It's cute. Maddie and I aren't super great friends. We share a common friend in Sarah, but that's pretty much it. I keep hoping we'll become better friends, but it's hard for me to reach out. I'm too shy and quiet. *Maybe this is Maddie's way of reaching out,* I think just as I notice the phrase above her signature at the bottom: *Just the messenger.*

Not worrying what that means, I dive in.

Jenny,

I hate to be the one to tell you this, but Sarah and I don't have time to be friends with you anymore.

My heart drops, and I scan the room again to make sure Mademoiselle Parry still hasn't arrived. She hasn't, so I keep reading.

Since Sarah and I both made the cheerleading squad and you didn't, we have to focus on our practices, and it's important that we become best friends with the girls in our squad.

The blue words *cheerleading squad* are double underlined with blue pen.

I'm sure you understand.

. . .

Tears prick my eyes. I wish I could talk to Sarah right now. There's no way she would agree to this!

Sarah didn't know how to tell you this, but the cheer girls won't want to be our friends if Sarah's still being friends with you.

I hastily wipe an escaped tear before my classmates can see it.

Sarah is getting really popular. She can't have someone like you messing it up for her. You know, you are kinda a downer sometimes about your mom and all, and people don't really like being around you.

Sarah really doesn't want to talk to you about this, and she's hoping that Matt will finally ask her out after school, so if you could just take this hint and not try to talk to us anymore, that would be great.

Mademoiselle Parry trots into the classroom, so I hurry and skim to the end.

Sarah might make cheer captain! Isn't that exciting! All the boys will want to hang out with us if she does.
   I'm sure Rebecca will still be your friend.
   *Go-o Mustangs! *high kick**
   Just the messenger,
   Maddie

. . .

"Bonjour, class!" Mademoiselle Parry says in her cheery voice.

"Bonjour, Mademoiselle Parry," all of my classmates say in unison. All I can do is mouth the words, so that a sob doesn't escape when I use my voice.

Why is Sarah doing this to me? I wonder as Mademoiselle Parry calls the roll. *And why did she have Maddie write this note?* My thoughts darken. *If she really didn't want to be friends anymore, why didn't Sarah tell me herself? I mean, I get that I am sad sometimes.* My thoughts turn to my mom and all of the chemo treatments she's had over the past few months. *Maybe I shouldn't have talked about my mom so much. Maybe I should have been more happy and upbeat.*

I want to cry. I want to hang my head as soon as I leave the classroom and crawl into a dark hole.

You can't let them get to you. You can't let them see how much this hurts, something inside me says. It's me, but *not* me at the same time.

They want you to be upset about this. Don't give them the satisfaction. I deliberately wipe my eyes and plaster a fake smile on my face at the front of the classroom and say "Here!" when my name is called, as if I hadn't just read the worst note in my life. *Just pretend like it doesn't bother you at all.*

I grit my teeth hard, pushing my emotions back. A hard lump in my throat hurts, but I force it down. I keep my smile broad and let it reach my eyes until I honestly chuckle at Mademoiselle Parry's lame joke that I'm only half paying attention to.

I won't let this affect me. I won't let this affect me. I repeat the phrase to myself over and over throughout class so that when the bell finally rings and it's time for lunch, I walk out with my head held high. Ready to face the eighth-grade.

unfamiliar hands

I felt immediate relief when I woke up. I was so glad to be back to myself again. I stretched under my sheets, then sat up, reaching over to turn off my alarm that was set to go off in five minutes. I swung my legs around and stood groggily on my cool rug.

Oh man, that really sucked for her, I thought as I rummaged through my closet for something to wear. I knew how Jenny felt in a way, and though it wasn't my life, the nightmare was very real for her. I knew what it felt like to have a friend stop being a friend. Seriously, girls could really be so shallow and mean. When Arianna stopped being my friend, at least it was because she thought I was sullying her dead sister's reputation by suggesting that her death was a suicide. (Spoiler: it was.) At least it wasn't because she thought she had better chances at popularity without me.

Arianna would never do that. The thought was comforting. I dressed and walked to the bathroom. Even though I remembered the alternate world where Arianna stopped being my friend, she was way more loyal than Jenny's stupid friends, Maddie and Sarah.

As I combed through my dark nest of tangled bed-head hair, I pushed back the fact that after so many in a row, I'd dreamed of someone *other* than Lucy. It was a bit disconcerting, even though it was what I wanted. Sort of. Actually not really, but it was what I *wanted* to want. I'd been debating all week whether to end my dreams with Lucy, whether I should push myself out the next time I dreamed of her. Maybe my Lucy dreams were coming to an end anyway. Maybe it didn't matter if I wanted them to continue or not. That was a depressing thought. Would I get the chance to say goodbye?

On the other hand, Jenny's devastating moment in French class reminded me of the most important reason why I shouldn't be having Lucy dreams anymore. Jenny needed me. Lucy didn't. It was my purpose in experiencing the dreams. To be there for them even if I wasn't aware of myself.

Others needed me.

"Would you like some oatmeal, Emily?" Mom asked, stealing me from my thoughts. I nodded and went to the fridge to grab the milk carton.

I wasn't ready yet, but it was time. I had to be done with Lucy walks. I had to stop them, to push myself out whenever I showed up there. I just hoped I could say goodbye first. I didn't so much think the words as feel them. I poured myself a glass of milk and sat idly while Mom prepared my breakfast over the stove.

My thoughts turned back to Jenny, mostly to mask the sudden dark cloud that had descended over me at the thought of leaving Lucy. It felt so good to help someone again, even though I wasn't aware of myself. *Part of me must have been aware though*, I thought, *because something gave her the idea to buck up and pretend that catty note didn't bother her.*

Something—or me, I guess—made her feel enough self-worth to leave the classroom ready to face life, regardless of what Sarah and Maddie had done. A small part of me wanted to go back and help Jenny with whatever came next for her. I'd done that once with Lucy—I had sort of *thought* my way into the fire that second time. But somehow I knew I couldn't replicate it. Whatever was going on with Lucy, whatever was bringing me back to her night after night, she was the exception to the rule.

Dreaming of someone's life for one night and never seeing them again, that was how the dreams worked. I was just *there* in the pivotal moment of someone's life. I never got the chance to see what came next. Not knowing the outcomes used to cause me a lot of stress. But sometimes a little ambiguity was better—the only unambiguous ones were deaths. So I reminded myself to be grateful Jenny's dream hadn't ended *that* way. Getting a catty note was vastly better than bleeding out and dying on a frozen river like Nora.

"Did you get enough sleep last night?" Mom asked in a cheery tone but with a hand on her hip. Something was off.

I hadn't realized the steaming bowl literally under my nose. I'd been too lost in my thoughts whenever she slid it over to me. Immediately I grabbed the spoon next to my bowl and dug in. "Yup," I said before shoveling a bite and nearly scalding my tongue.

"Did you have a good dream?" Mom turned back to the stove. "Was Andrew there this time?"

"No, I was with this girl named Jenny." I blew on my spoon before taking another bite. "Her friends were horrible to her and sent this nasty note..." I trailed off, my stomach suddenly feeling sick, but I stuck another, much larger spoonful into my mouth—effectively burning my taste buds off.

Mom had already turned, and her eyebrow was raised. I was caught. "You haven't been taking your medication." It wasn't a question.

I absently chewed, pretending that my mouth wasn't on fire for several seconds—which was no small feat—before gulping it down and shaking my head. I had no response.

"You're seeing Dr. Shew. *Today.*"

"THIS IS SERIOUS, EMILY." DR SHEW'S BLONDE HAIR was piled on her head in a neat bun, not a hair out of place, as it always was. Her makeup was perfect. Her pantsuit was perfect.

"I know." I didn't actually agree, but I knew what was expected of me in these sessions.

"I'm not sure you do." She could see right through my lies. "Let me remind you about a Saturday morning not long ago when your poor mother brought you to my office and you were in an almost *catatonic* state."

I nodded. I remembered the session well. I'd just had a repeat of Nora's death on that damned frozen river, and I was almost certain that Colin hadn't made it off the ice, ending the existence of Charles. And Andrew. And maybe Duncan too. Fortunately that hadn't happened. Andrew had managed to walk his grandfather and save him, but I had very good reason for feeling the way I did that morning.

"So I don't need to remind you what continuing to have these dreams *will* do to you." She emphasized the word, like it wasn't an *if* but a *when*.

I hung my head and studied my hands, my fingers laced together and resting in my lap. They were mine, but sometimes I was surprised to see them. I wore so many different hands in my dreams. People always marveled at my long, slender fingers, told me I was born to play the piano. Relatives and strangers alike predicted it since the day I was born, but I'd only ever taken a handful of lessons when I was nine before quitting and never picking it up again. Lucy's hands were slender too, but smaller. Her fingers didn't look quite as bony as mine. And Jenny's were covered in freckles. She'd been wearing a small mood ring on her pointer finger that shifted from blue to yellow then to almost black as she read Maddie's biting note. To be honest, I had been surprised—the ring had actually sort of worked.

"But I help people," I said quietly. I didn't plan to say it, and I hadn't meant for it to come out, but it was how I felt. So I said it again louder. "I *help* people."

From my peripheral, I could see Dr. Shew lifting her pen and pointing it to the ceiling, an indication that she was about to speak. But she was at a loss for words. I looked up at her, and she lowered her pen, speechless.

I told her about Jenny. I told her that Jenny was a real girl in a real time. And although it seemed like something silly and trivial and that it wouldn't matter how her friends treated her in eighth grade when she grew up, in that moment she had needed a friend. And I was sort of that friend, even though I couldn't talk to her. In the worst moment of her life, I made things better.

When I was finished, Dr. Shew looked thoughtful. I took it as a good sign and smiled. Did she believe me? Was she going to agree that my dreams actually did some good? Maybe she'd help me. She could be a listening ear for me when I needed counseling for the particularly bad ones.

Yeah, I know, not exactly the picture of mental health. But I'm coping the best I can.

"I think we need to try a different approach." Dr. Shew grabbed her prescription pad next to her and scribbled furiously. "I am prescribing you a new medication."

"I—"

"It won't stop the dreams," she interrupted and handed me the ripped off page.

My eyebrows shot up without permission.

"I'll talk to your mother, but I want you to stop taking the other ones until further notice."

I felt the burden of lying so many days in a row fly from the knots in my shoulders.

"Take these each night before bed, and we'll see if they help."

"What are they supposed to do?"

"Let's call them a sleeping pill that won't interfere with your REM cycle."

I nodded. I wasn't lying when I said I'd try them. Once. If they did anything... *anything* to mess up the memory-dreams, I would lie about taking them too. But I promised to try one dose.

It felt good that night not having to sneak into the bathroom to toss my pill down the bathroom sink.

CHAPTER 8

trust me

Relief fills me when I again join Lucy. Then a sadness replaces my relief. I instantly hide it before she notices. I wanted a chance to say goodbye. Here it is.

"Hello, Emily," she says aloud with a smile as we walk along the cobblestone pathways in town. The trees along the street are ornamented with pink-and-white buds of new spring growth. Lucy wears gloves and a shawl against the chill in the air. And a few curls flutter against her forehead and cheeks with the gentle breeze. From the corner of Lucy's eye, I notice Matthew walking a few steps behind us, carrying some brown packages, but he doesn't look out of earshot.

Lucy? Are you aware that Matthew can probably hear you... talking to yourself? That could create an entirely new slew of issues for her.

"Do not mind him," she says. "If he hears me, he will not say a word about it. You have not visited in a while. I was beginning to suspect that you were gone for good." She feels very happy and content today, like she doesn't have a care in the world. She probably doesn't—which is more than I can say about my own life. Her happiness is slightly intoxicating.

I'm glad I'm here because I wanted to say goodbye, I say though

I want to sink into her happiness and forget about being responsible. *You don't need me anymore, Lucy. You survived the fire, you have your man, and you're planning a wedding! Your life seems pretty perfect to me.* Maybe a goodbye will be enough to prevent my return?

"I thought..." she pauses, completely shocked by the turn of conversation. "But we have a plan. You can be with Andrew without disturbing what I have with Charles." But even as she says the words, I can feel relief flood into her heart, threatening to overpower her conflicting emotions.

I'll miss you too, I say, and I'm sure tears would well in my eyes if Lucy wasn't too shocked to cry. *I can't be with Andrew, not really. He lives here. My world is far in the future. It would never work.* I almost suggest that Andrew look up Grandma Cole, my great-great-grandmother. Grandma Grace told me she had the dreams too. But I can't remember the year Grandma was born. For all I know, she could be eight or eighty-eight years old. And setting my grandmother up with my dream boyfriend could have unintended consequences... I shudder. Making Andrew my great-great-grandfather would create an entirely new slew of issues for me and my family tree.

Anyway, Andrew is technically engaged. Wow. I completely forgot about that hugely large detail. *Whatever happened to Margaret?* I ask. *You are doing all you can to help me see Andrew, but what about your friend?* What about the girl who actually could have him?

Lucy twists the fingers of her gloves, her thoughts a jumbled mess.

What is it, Lucy? I can tell she is trying hard not to cry. Matthew certainly might think something is up if she breaks down right here on the street in the middle of what looks like a pleasant shopping day.

"I feel so guilty about that," she laments. She moves to sit on a nearby bench, convincing Matthew that she merely needs a reprieve. He thankfully walks out of earshot.

About what? I ask.

"About helping you two. About betraying my friend who is busily planning her own wedding. It is a small miracle that you have not been present the last few times I have seen her."

I don't know how to respond.

"She is so happy, Emily, and I can see that she loves him very much. He has not given her any reason to suspect that he cares for someone else. He is everything cordial and charming to her, but whenever you are here… He melts around you, Emily. He loves you. It is obvious."

Hearing that warms my heart, but the fact that he has not broken off the wedding and is leading Margaret along is a little infuriating. At the same time it makes perfect sense. Andrew knows he and I could never be together. So why call things off with Margaret? Why not settle down with a girl from his own time?

I guess I don't understand why you are doing it. Why are you helping me see him?

"Because you saved me."

Oh. She feels like she owes me. That's the motivation behind these secret plans and covert meetings. All this heartache just so Andrew and I can have a few stolen moments together? *Hearing that makes me all kinds of warm and fuzzy,* I think bitterly, but hope she doesn't hear my sarcasm. I want to crawl into a hole right now. I should bail.

"And because you are my friend too," she adds. "I cannot see your face, but I have a very good impression that you also love him. I feel it in my breast whenever you see him."

All the more reason for me to leave and never return, I say, more determined than I have ever felt. I metaphorically take a deep breath, bracing myself for my final goodbye to Lucy.

Luc—

"Miss Lucy?" The voice I most want to hear and never want to hear again interrupts my thoughts.

"Andrew!" Lucy says, standing. Her heart is a flutter—or maybe that's mine since neither of us saw him approach.

Well...I guess I can say goodbye to him too.

"Emily is here," Lucy says in a rush, leaning toward him.

His eyes widen and a familiar figure peers out from behind him and slips a hand in the crook of his arm.

"Lucy!" Margaret says.

My heart sinks. She looks so happy and in love. Andrew squirms next to her.

Lucy smiles sweetly at her, which is good because if I were running the show, I probably would be sporting a nasty look even though the whole situation isn't technically Margaret's fault. Okay, so the nasty look would be for Andrew.

"What brings you out on such a fine morning?" Lucy asks. The cordiality in her tone amazes me. I can't tell if because she's had so much practice at niceties or because she actually has fond feelings for both of them. Probably the latter.

"I wanted a new hat, so I drug Andrew along with me." She squeezes Andrew's arm. "Join us?"

"I am afraid I have another engagement and must trek back home soon."

Margaret frowns slightly, but it is clear that she isn't too disappointed to keep her fiancé to herself today. I wonder if Lucy feels my churning, darkening thoughts.

"It is actually fortunate that we've run into one another," Lucy says, without even a hint of sourness in her tone. She's good. I know how my moods can affect her. I'm amazed at how well she's hiding them.

"Oh?" Margaret asks, and Andrew's face brightens.

"Could I borrow Andrew for a few moments?" she asks. "It is about Charles. Would you mind terribly, Margaret?"

"Mind? Not at all. But what secret do you have that you cannot discuss with both of us?"

That's odd. Or not. Her suspicion makes me curious if

Margaret suspects anything of the two of them. She hasn't caught us in any situation like Charles has, but I wonder...

"All right, I lied," Lucy says, widening her smile. "I am planning a surprise for you, my dear friend." Lucy winks at her. "So, by all means stay if you want all my careful plans spoiled."

That reminds me of the surprise I'm supposed to be concocting for my own friend, Arianna, in my waking life. One issue at a time. That one can wait until I wake up in the morning.

Margaret cocks her head and flashes a wry look. "Very well, Andrew darling. I will continue on to the hat shop. Meet me there?"

"As you wish, my dear," Andrew responds, and we watch her scoot past us, her heels clicking on the cobblestone as she walks away.

"I assume this has nothing to do with Charles or Margaret."

"You assume correctly," Lucy says.

"Can I also assume it involves our mutual friend?" His expression is hopeful.

Lucy smiles again and steps back.

Okay, Emily, you can do this. You can tell him goodbye... forever. It's not really a big thing, saying goodbye forever and knowing that you'll never see him again. Ever. Not in the supermarket. Not at the movies. Not on a cruise ship when you're both old and wrinkly with your lives behind you. Not ever.

"Emily?" he asks, softly. His tone could melt butter it's so creamy and rich.

You can do this. "Andrew, I need to tell you something."

"Great! I have news too!" He is giddy. Like schoolboy giddy. If I weren't absolutely enamored by him, I might be seriously creeped out.

But either way it's sparked my curiosity, and I'm all about putting off what I don't want to do. "You seem excited. Why don't you go first?"

He takes a step toward me and reaches out as if to grasp my hands, but being on a busy street with potential eyes watching, he stops himself. "I have been working on something, for lack of words."

My lips narrow with my eyes. "Like unnecessary changes, working on something?"

"Well, yes and no." His energy is bouncy and light. If I didn't know better, I'd think he needed to use a toilet. "Those plans are more... long-term."

"Cryptic much?"

His expression flashes with confusion, but he shakes it off to continue. "I have come up with a solution to our Lucy-and-Charles problem."

"And your Margaret problem?" I whisper, hearing the venom in my tone.

"Yes, and that," he agrees, but his face suggests that Margaret is *not* a problem at all. Strange. "I have found a way for us to... have time with one another... with absolutely zero consequences for Lucy."

"How?" My tone matches my skepticism.

"Well, I don't know if it will work, but I am hopeful. I have the time and place narrowed so it is finally time to make an attempt."

I raise an eyebrow at him. He has answered nothing and only left me with more questions.

He flashes his sly smile. "Wait and see."

Trust me. Wait and see. It could go on forever, with him singing the same old song. I'm starting to doubt whether he actually has a plan. "Yeah, you've said that before." Just rip the band aid off quickly. Tell him goodbye. "Look, Andrew I think we need to call this as it is."

"Call what?"

"I think we need to say goodbye. I need to stop being with Lucy."

"But—"

"Andrew," I cut him off. "There's nothing we can do. You are making this so much harder." I didn't expect to, but I begin to cry.

Immediately he pulls me into his arms, not caring that we're out in the open on the street. "Do not say goodbye, not yet, my —" He stops abruptly.

My what? *My darling? My friend? My dear?* The last is what he called Margaret so I hope I'm not lumped into the same category as her.

My love?

How could I say no? "Okay," I murmur into his shoulder.

He pulls back and smiles at me with that mischievous, heart-shattering, knee-weakening smile. "*Trust* me." He whispers.

"Lucy?" It's Charles. None of us expected to see him here on the street. "Andrew?" His tone turns more to surprise than hurt.

Before I can jerk away from him to save Lucy's reputation, Andrew looks me square in the eyes, jaw set, and takes my hand in his ring-adorned one. "Go," he commands.

And I'm gone.

isabella

I close my eyes when we arrive at the dock, the breeze lifting stray locks of hair free from my bonnet. I can almost smell and taste the salt of the sea, standing so close to it. The assault on my senses is so palpable as to be painful. The collection of tears beneath my closed lids threaten to trace each conflicting emotion down my face.

We are really leaving. The first tear escapes. We are really leaving the only home I have ever known. My birthplace. My parents' birthplace. Their parents' birthplace. It felt final when we sold the house my great-great-grandparents built. When we left more than half of our possessions behind. When we rose over that hill, breaching the boundary of the furthest I had ever ventured from home. But all of that was nothing compared to how final this felt.

Our new home will be better. The second tear falls. We will be free to worship how we wish. We will be free from the persecutions we have faced. We will be free from a country that wants to dictate how we live.

We will be free.

Nerves twist in my stomach as I contemplate the long journey ahead. More than two weeks on a ship, then many more by train and wagon. But the day is finally here.

We sail today.

When I open my eyes, the world is noisy once more. Deckhands and workers and other passengers rush past me, heading in all directions, toward the ships, away from the ships, past the ships, right and left, back and forth, their boots and heels clanking and clomping against the cobblestone with each hurried step. They're gathering luggage and hauling cargo, laughing and crying and shouting.

A huddled group of loved ones hug and kiss and say their goodbyes. The sight of them makes me smile, but also makes me grateful because my whole family is leaving together. Mama and Papa, Rachel and me.

No one left behind.

"Isabella!" Papa jerks me from my daydream. His voice is stern, but when I look at him, a huge grin splits across his beard. He is as excited as the rest of us. "Let's not miss our ride!" he says with a wink. He motions with his head toward our ship down the dock.

I pause to glance once more at our trunks lined up next to each other, stacked two and three high.

"We were instructed to leave them here, Izzy," Papa says. "Someone will carry our things on board."

I place a hand on one of our trunks, the one with Mama's beautiful hand-painted china and silverware inside. Journeying to the new world is exciting, but a little scary too. In the past weeks, I have assured Rachel more times than I could count that if we get homesick at Christmastime in the new world, we will close the curtains, eat Christmas dinner on Mama's china, and pretend like we were back in England, and it will feel just like home.

"They'll be careful with them, right?" I ask catching up with Papa. "Mama will be devastated if her china is crushed."

"I'm sure they'll be careful," he assures me, knowing I am not thinking of merely Mama's feelings.

Papa keeps an arm around my shoulder as we make our way to where we board. I can tell he's trying to walk casual, but I can feel his excitement as his fingers grip the edge of my coat. He wants to sprint as much as I do.

"What'll it be like, Papa?" I ask when we reach the line of travelers waiting to board.

"You forget, baby girl," he says with a twinkle in his eye. "I have never seen America. We'll find out together."

I smile and a warm feeling blossoms in my chest. The boardwalk we hike up to enter the ship sways gently with the movement of the waves against the hull, but Papa steadies me, and we are soon on deck, reconnecting with Mama and my sister already onboard.

Rachel and I squeeze between an Irish family and a small, dark-haired girl standing close to her father, and steal one last glance. We do not know a single face in the crowd on the dock, but we raise our hands and wave anyway. We are not bidding goodbye to any one person, but to our motherland.

"Excuse me, miss?"

I turn at the voice and tap on my shoulder. A young man, close to my age, with curly black hair and brilliant green eyes holds a white handkerchief out to me.

"I believe you dropped this."

I look at the white cloth and recognize it as my favorite, embroidered with blue and yellow flowers. "Thank you!" I take the handkerchief from his hand. "I didn't realize I had dropped it!"

His hand twitches when our fingers meet, like a lightning shock, and his eyes widen.

"Thank you for bringing it back to me," I say.

He nods quickly, snapping from his spell. "It fell from your pocket before you boarded, back near the luggage drop."

"All of the way back there?" I am touched at the gesture. "And you followed me all of this way to return it? How kind of you..." I prompt for a name.

"Nathan." He bows his head slightly, eying me strangely. It is slightly unnerving. "And you are?"

"My name is Isabella. Are you traveling to America too?" I ask wondering if he is even a passenger or if he boarded merely to return my property.

He appears to be lost in thought for a moment, then nods.

"Well, then I suppose I'll see you again."

"I suppose you will," he says, and his cordial manner immediately dispels any discomfort I feel toward him. He appears resolved about something, and then he walks away after saying a friendly hello to the girl next to us by name.

"He's handsome," Rachel hisses in my ear once he is lost in the crowd of people. "What did he want?"

I held up my handkerchief. "I dropped it back by our trunks," I say, "and he came all of this way to return it. Isn't that the sweetest thing?"

"And he's traveling on our ship?"

"He is!"

We give each other knowing smiles that quickly turn to giggles.

CHAPTER 10

frustrations and bad timing

How'd it go? I ask the instant I'm back with her. *What happened?*

She doesn't answer right away. She's embroidering something, or trying to. I can feel the stiffness and numbness in her fingers, and the chronic, sick-to-your-stomach kind of pain in her hands. Her project looks like it's supposed to be some type of bluebird, but the stitching is jagged, and I can feel her defeat, almost to the point of tears. She knows she can't make something as beautiful as she once did.

I also feel her rolling waves of anger and hurt and frustration over the scene in town the other day. I have to know what happened after I left. Or rather, after Andrew pushed me out.

What did Charles say? What did you say?

"Andrew told him that I had something in my eye."

Facepalm. *He seriously used that line?*

She doesn't answer, and instead floods my mind with the memory:

CHARLES IS HURT. I CAN TELL BY HIS CLENCHED SQUARE *jaw and the pleading in his light-blue eyes as they search mine for any sort of explanation. He is thinking the worst. And he has no reason not to. Andrew's proximity to Emily—and by default to me —suggests intimacy. What was he thinking? Out here on the street?*

"Charles!" Andrew says without hesitation. "The wind!" His tone is innocent, selling the idea that nothing is going on between he and I. "Poor Miss Lucy here nearly lost her right eye!"

"Yes." To add emphasis I cup a hand over my phantom injury. "Andrew helped me get it out as I could not see the mote myself."

Charles's eyebrow rises, but he seems to buy the story. Or he dismisses it because he trusts me so implicitly.

Lying to him causes a sharp pang in my chest. In a way, it hurts more than the burns on my hands.

"Does that answer your question?" Lucy asks. She is the only one in the room, so talking aloud isn't an issue.

Although that has never stopped her before. Which worries me.

She puts her needlework down and twists the tight skin on her fingers, almost massaging it, stretching it.

He bought the story? I ask, though I know her opinion on the matter.

"Who is Isabella?" she changes the subject.

Isabella? It's strange that I have to rack my brain for more than a second, because I just came from being her and have not been—well, me—in a while. I was Lucy before Isabella, and now I'm Lucy again. All in one night. Strange.

Oh, she's a girl I walked, I say. *Actually, it was just before I came back to you. How did you know about her?* Was I thinking about her when I popped back into Lucy's head?

"Andrew barged in first thing this morning." She says this casually, as if it is normal for him to barge in first thing in the morning. "He was going on and on, asking why I did not know myself as Isabella." She ends with a sigh. "When he realized it was just me and *you* were not here, he left as quickly as he came."

How did he know about Isabella? I ask, even though I know she doesn't have an answer.

"He made me promise to send for him the second you arrived." She sounds angry and rightfully so.

Look, you don't have to do that, I say, though I desperately want her to. I'm dying to know how he knew about my very recent walk. *He is clearly overstepping his bounds,* I say with regret. I feel the truth of my admission.

"No, I want to," she says, but I can feel the lie. Before I can protest, she rings a bell on the wall and gives Betsy the message to send for Mr. Andrew Harker as soon as he is available to call. She sends for Charles too in order to divert any suspicion from her servant, but her thoughts betray her. She knows Charles is away in town today so he will be delayed. Which means that Andrew and I will have time to talk without restraint or needing to speak cryptically.

Lucy sits again as if to return to her needlework, but she merely stares at it. She is conflicted, almost in a daze. She is trying to hide her thoughts from me, so I suspect a big portion of her concern has to do with me. She's probably worried about the way Andrew has been pushing the limits lately. I don't know what to say, so I remain quiet and leave her alone a while.

SURPRISINGLY, A FULL HOUR PASSES BEFORE LUCY'S butler, Mr. Drake, enters the sitting room to announce Andrew's arrival.

"Let him in," Lucy says with forced cheer. She does not stand to welcome him.

He strides into the sitting room with speed. His bowler hat is clutched tightly in his left hand as the other one combs hastily through his hair, mussing it and causing it to stick in several different directions. "Emily," he breathes, rushing to my side.

Lucy immediately backs away for me to take the lead and I instantly raise an eyebrow. "That's kinda rude."

"Rude?" he says the word like its foreign.

"It's not polite to barge in here, into *Lucy's* house and not even say hi... er, greet her."

Emily, it is fine, she says to me.

"It's not fine," I say aloud in reply. It's the first time we've switched roles this way, and it feels strange. Like I really am taking over her life. I don't like the feeling, especially because she doesn't really need me here. And though she won't admit it, she doesn't really want me here either.

"Lucy, I—" Andrew stammers. "How are you this afternoon?"

"Enough with the pleasantries," Lucy says. "Just tell Emily what you came to tell her. I also asked Charles to call, so he will be here presently."

Andrew looks shamed, either by my calling him out or Lucy's curtness, I'm not sure which. But when he opens his mouth in what I assume will be an apology, she shushes him again and backs away for me.

"Lucy said you came by this morning?" I prompt.

"Yes, I..." he pauses. "Were you there? With Isabella?"

Even though Lucy mentioned that Isabella is the reason he came bursting in that morning, I still can't fathom how he would know about her.

"How do you know about Isabella?"

"You were there," he says with excitement. He looks relieved too. "You were there." He says again mostly to himself. "But you were not self-aware?" he asks, sliding onto the settee next to me.

"No," I say, standing up to distance myself from him. I'd hate for Charles to walk in on another sketchy situation. "How did you know?"

He waves a hand at himself. "Nathan."

"Nathan?" It can't be true. It's too crazy a coincidence. But how else would he know about Isabella? About Nathan? "You were Nathan?" I whisper, still not believing the words as I say them. "How is that possible?" I ask when he nods slightly.

He smiles, stands, and closes the gap between us taking my hands in his. I'm too stunned by everything to pull away again. His fingers are warm and gently squeeze my/Lucy's scarred ones. "I brought you with me," he says, his eyes willing mine to meet his. Like a moth to a porch light, my eyes meet his chestnut ones. The flecks of amber in them dancing. Though he means for me to look at him, he almost seems surprised that I do, and in an instant, his lips lock with mine. His kiss is soft and gentle and tentative. When I eagerly respond, his kiss deepens. But when the word *forbidden* slips across my mind we break apart instantly. We *both* break apart. Almost as if Andrew heard the word too.

"We can't," I say, returning to where Lucy sat.

He nods without looking at me. "In the dream, in the walk, you were not aware of yourself?"

"No." I shake my head once. Half of me is grateful, the other half regretful that the forbidden kiss is over.

"You need a talisman." Andrew twists his silver ring and then pulling it off, he hands it to me. "Like this."

I take the ring and study it. He has worn it every time I've seen him. I've never touched it except that one time I—well, actually Lucy—stopped it from spinning on the dining table and I, *Emily*, was finally aware. Was this *talisman*, as he called it, the reason I became aware?

The ring is thick with intricate lines etched into the metal in a crisscrossing pattern. Two more lines border each edge of the ring.

"When I wear this," he continues, "I become aware of myself in every walk, almost immediately. Sometimes a mental block of the person I walk prevents it from happening quickly, but at some point before I wake up, I know I am Andrew Harker walking with someone else."

The ring and its powers remind me of the ring Grandma Grace wore to piggyback into some of my Lucy dreams. Where on earth did she get it?

Shoot! How could I be so stupid? Duncan gave me an antique silver ring that he said was a family heirloom. A *Harker* family heirloom.

"I think I had one."

"*Had?*" Andrew sounds alarmed.

"I gave it back," I say, "but I don't know if that's what it actually was. How would I know?"

"Did you ever wear it?"

"All the time," I say softly, the memory of my breakup with Duncan fresh in my thoughts.

"Did you always know you were Emily in your walks when you wore it?"

"I guess..." I couldn't exactly remember. "But I've had plenty of walks where I became self-aware anyway."

He paces the floor, thinking for another moment. "Have you ever thought about Lucy before you fell asleep and then immediately walked Lucy?"

Possibly. I do walk Lucy an awful lot lately. But it's not *Lucy* I'm thinking about every night before I fall asleep. Someone talk, dark, and handsome regularly features in my thoughts as I drift off to sleep. Lucy's cheeks start to burn. Ugh, this is so embarrassing. "Maybe, um, I often think about... her." My lie is pathetic, but he doesn't seem to notice.

Then I remember just before I dreamed the fire the second time, how I lay down on my bed and *willed* myself to dream of the fire. Like I believed I could control it. "Wait, maybe... I might have."

He continues to pace. He walks back and forth only two or three times before he stops and holds a finger up and his face lights up. "Ha!" he says. "You have had repeat dreams?"

"I told you I have." What is he getting at?

"This is important, Emily. Think harder. Were you thinking about your friend's sister before you fell asleep that night?"

"I dunno," I say, slightly cowed by the sight of Andrew's increasing frustration.

He slows his pacing and sits next to me. I allow him this time. "That is another way it works," he says, "You can direct who you will walk by thinking about them before you sleep."

"What? My repeat dreams are only recent. Before that I dreamt a different person every night. Aren't we supposed to be helping those we dream about? How would we know who needs us?" My thoughts turn to Jenny and the fact that I most likely will never walk her again like so many others before her.

By Andrew's expression, I can tell the thought hadn't occurred to him before now, but his determined look immediately returns as if he's decided none of that matters. "Can you get the ring back?"

"I..." *How could I possibly ask Duncan to give it back?*

"Can you get it back?" Andrew asks again when I hesitate too long.

Reluctantly, I nod.

His eyes soften, and he gently takes my face in both of his hands before saying, "It is all part of my plan." Andrew's softer tone makes my knees turn to butter.

"The elusive plan." I intend my words to come out laced with sarcasm, but they sound more dreamy than anything.

He winks, then leans in to kiss me once more, but before our lips touch another voice causes us to jerk away.

"Lucy?" His voice is so quiet and filled with hurt. I wonder how long Charles has been standing in the doorway.

Not again. Charles seriously has the worst timing.

CHAPTER 11

goodbye... for real

*N*o, *no, no!* I shove past Emily and take over instantly. "Charles!" I call out to him louder than necessary, especially considering he has not left the room.

Charles's eyes are trained on Andrew. His mouth a thin line as he keeps his emotions under control. "Could I have a moment alone with my *fiancée*, Cousin Andrew?" he says through gritted teeth.

Emily notes that Andrew does not look regretful, though I barely give him a glance and keep my eyes focused on my beloved as Andrew walks from the room.

I am already on my feet, but I do not know if I should rush to Charles or wait for him to come to me. My heart bursts beneath my corset, and I am ready to fall to my knees if that is what it takes to keep Charles.

In what feels like hours, Charles slowly walks to stand in front of me and gently takes my hands in his. An eternity passes as he absently rubs his thumbs on the backs of my hands in circles, his eyes refusing to meet mine.

"I know," he starts, his tone unreadable, "I have been otherwise occupied and away from you more than anticipated as of late." He still will not look at me. "And I know that Andr—that my cousin's endless hours of leisure have been eagerly filled with the precise task of keeping you company in my absence."

"It is not—"

"I also understand," he cuts me off, but continues to speak evenly, "that you did not become acquainted with *my cousin* until after our engagement."

"I..." I begin, but immediately stop when his blue eyes snap up to finally gaze into mine. His stare is so intense and hardened to block his hurt that it feels as though I am looking into the eyes of a stranger. A stranger who does not love me. I choke on the horrible thought as traitorous tears fill my eyes.

"If you wish to break our engagement," he says, his expression unchanged though he surely sees the tears that begin to trail down my cheeks. "If you *love*—if you want to be with *my cousin*..." He won't even say Andrew's name.

A sob escapes my lips. I am unable to speak.

He takes it as truth. "Then I will not stand in your way." Charles releases my hands immediately and walks away.

No! I want to scream, but I am too overcome with emotion, I cannot find my voice.

"Stop!" Emily finally says through my tears. In my anguish, I had not known she was still present. "Charles, you are mistaken!" she says, still emotional but once again she manages to muster more control than I can.

Charles stops walking, but does not turn and stares at the floor. "Then what did I just witness?"

Emily rushes to where he stands and turns to face him again. With my hands, she slowly reaches up to lift his lowered chin, forcing him to meet my eyes. She does not bother to wipe my tears and lets them continue to flow. "In a way, you are right," she says, struggling to mimic my lilting speech, "Mr. Harker and I have spent much time together." She uses Andrew's formal name, distancing her own feelings—which are potent—in her attempt to sound convincing to Charles. "And I am afraid that he has mistaken my *friendship*." Emily speaks slowly, choosing each word carefully. She lowers my head and twists my hands together.

"He is in love with you," Charles says, though his tone has changed. Is that hope I hear? My heart leaps at the possibility.

"I think he is," she says, "but I do not feel the same." She lifts my head slowly, and our eyes meet again.

My heart nearly stops. Thoughts of every happy memory race through my head at the look of absolute adoration and love shining through his sky-colored eyes. It is like seeing sunbeams splitting dark clouds. *He believes her!* I am grateful once again for the guardian angel who has saved me. A tiny pit of regret stabs at my gut as I remember my recent irritation toward her. But she has saved me again.

"I am afraid I have let things go too far," Emily continues, either ignoring my sudden emotion or not noticing it in her determination to make things right between Charles and I. "I was just about to tell him that we shouldn't see one another until after I am married to you." She emphasizes the word. "And I believe he was going to attempt to kiss me when you walked in." She breathes a quiet sigh of relief for effect.

Clearly her words and the way she tilts my head is an invitation, and Charles takes the opportunity to lean down and quickly brush a kiss across my lips. She closes my eyes in response and makes a happy noise in my throat that I am not entirely sure came only from her.

When we pull apart and my eyes open again, a small smile lifts the corners of Charles's lips. "I will talk to him," he says but does not make a move to leave.

She holds my hand up to his chest. "Let me," she says. "Or better yet, let me pen him a letter." She reaches up to kiss him again, making me blush at her forwardness. "You can read it before I seal it." She smiles for me, even though I am quite able to do it myself by now.

I'll take over now, I say to Emily, as we leave Charles near the door and make our way to the writing desk in the corner of the room.

Not yet, she says to me. *Let me write the letter.*

You do not have to do that, I say, I can only imagine how painful such a letter will be for her.

It needs to be me, she says. *I'll show it to Charles before I sign it, but it needs to read from me. Emily.*

No! You do not need—

Lucy! If this is not real, if Andrew thinks it's only to appease Charles, he'll keep stepping over the line. He'll ruin things for you. Let me do this for you.

I did not realize she was this serious. *You are really saying goodbye to him?*

I am really saying goodbye.

really, really bad idea

I can't believe I did that. My thoughts were consumed with everything that had happened in my dreams as I got ready for school. *She was so upset and she had every right to be.*

Wash face.

Straighten hair.

Apply mascara.

Andrew was really taking things too far. Taking things too far because of me—that part made me smile—but still taking things too far. And all in pursuit of this master plan of his.

"Emily, after school..." Mom said when I entered the kitchen to grab the piece of toast she'd prepared for me.

I mean, he figured out how to get us both in a walk together! It boggled my mind! Andrew and I were *together* walking Isabella and Nathan. Sure, I hadn't realized who I was at the time, but still! And now I had a way to make sure I *would* know I was Emily in the next one.

I had to get that ring back.

"Emily!" Mom's voice was stern this time.

"Hmmm?" I replied with mouthful of raspberry jelly and butter spread on the warm crunchy wheat toast.

Mom had a hand on her hip... and she looked angry. "Did you hear a word I just said?"

I finished chewing and swallowed as I thought hard about what she wanted to hear.

"You said something about after school?" I honestly couldn't remember if she said anything after that.

"Have you been taking your meds?" she asked. "Or are you still skipping away to la la land each night until you have another traumatic night terror and become catatonic again?" Her voice caught at the end.

"I've been taking my meds," I said, though I had to think. Last night I took the new meds the doc gave me, so at least I wasn't lying. Still, I kept eye contact to sell it. "I just have a test this morning, and I was thinking about the test when you were talking to me. I'm sorry, Mom."

But what was I really sorry for? That I hadn't listened? That I had lied about it? Or that I *had* escaped to la la land? But as quickly as I apologized, my thoughts headed back to oh-so-dreamy la la land. Could Andrew and I finally be together? I couldn't see him in Lucy's world anymore. That was clear. But that didn't mean we couldn't dream together.

I loved this new master plan!

It was perfect. After we'd helped Isabella and Nathan through whatever was coming, we could find another couple to walk. And another. And another.

But I had to get that ring back from Duncan. It would never work if I didn't know myself in my dreams.

I began to concoct a plan to get that ring today. I had to.

"So you'll do it?" Mom asked.

Whoops! I tuned out again. Fortunately my mouth was full of toast so I merely nodded.

"Thank you," she said, finally smiling and turning back to whatever she was preparing. "Your dad really needs the help with this new system."

I wasn't sure what I'd just agreed to, but I'd figure it out later. She mentioned "after school," so I had time.

———

"CARLY, I NEED YOUR ADVICE," I SAID THROUGH MY phone as I walked up the steps to school. "Call me back. School doesn't start for ten more minutes. So if you get this quickly, call me!" My voice was more excited than urgent. It made me giddy that I had a mission in my actual waking life. And it had a time limit. I wanted to get that ring back today.

"Ems!" Ari sounded a bit breathless as she caught up to me before I entered the school.

"Oh hey," I said.

"I heard you and Duncan finally talked." She attempted to sound sympathetic about me having a conversation with my ex, but there was a twinkle in her eye as she said it. Ari was still convinced we'd get back together eventually.

"Yeah," I said, thinking about our conversation in the library. "It was okay." I tried to sound at least a little morose about it even though my insides were flipping with anticipation and happiness. "I think we're still friends." I added, slightly more cheery.

"Well, that's good," she said as my phone began to ring. It was Carly. I hid my screen from Ari. "But don't stick him in the friendzone too long—"

"I've got to take this," I interrupted.

"Ooo! Who is it?"

"Um... it's for your birthday surprise," I lied and waved her away.

She took the hint and giggled before strutting away. I made a mental note to actually plan something for her birthday surprise. And soon.

I turned away to hit *accept* before Carly hung up. "Hey!" I walked toward the school trophy case so I wouldn't be overheard.

"Do you have any idea what time it is?" she asked, but she didn't sound actually annoyed.

"Um..." Maybe it was a mistake to call? "Almost eight," I said, then chuckled. "It's not like I called you at four in the morning."

"Why not? I was up at four," she teased. "What was so important that you made me get out of my nice, warm bed?"

"Don't you have class?"

"Not until eleven. What's up?"

"So, I don't know what to do and I need your advice," I started. "I need a talisman..." I gave her the CliffsNotes version of how Grandma used her ring to piggy back into my dreams.

"Why would you need that if you actually have the dreams?"

"Right. Well, there's this other ring and I used to have it, but I gave it back, and it's supposed to make it so that I am self-aware in a walk." I rambled quickly.

There was a pause on the other line.

"It might even let me choose *who* to walk," I continued.

"Who did you give the ring back to?"

"Duncan," I said quietly for fear of my classmates overhearing the name.

"Your boyfriend?"

"My *ex*-boyfriend," I corrected.

"Ah... so you can't just ask for it back?"

"I, uh... gave it back because we broke up," I said. "It was kinda a family heirloom, so I thought that since we weren't together anymore..."

"I see..." she said and clucked her tongue. "Could you get back together and ask for it back?" She was only half-teasing this time.

"That doesn't seem fair to him," I said though the idea had crossed my mind. But I couldn't do that. I couldn't use a person like that.

"You're right," she agreed quickly. "Is there another ring like it?"

"Possibly, but I'd have no idea how to get one."

"Right..." She clucked her tongue again. "Why don't you steal it back?"

"Carly!" I hissed into the phone as the first bell rang, I only had a few minutes to get to class. But I was already convincing myself that it was either the best way, or a really, really bad idea.

"I mean it, if it's that important, figure out where he's put it and take it back."

My heart thudded loudly. I'd never so much as stolen a piece of candy from the store. Though I suppose I was just *borrowing* it... *Why did I ever give it back in the first place?* I lamented to myself. "Do you think it's at his house?"

"Check his room," she said.

"When?"

"He's at school, right?"

"Yeah..."

"March over there right now. Give his parents an excuse to check his bedroom. It's not like you're asking to get inside a bank vault."

My heart beat even faster as adrenaline began to pump. Granted, I wasn't knocking over a bank or anything, but I was still about to *skip school* to *steal something*.

"Ok. Wish me luck, and don't tell your sister."

"You know I won't. Good luck. And remember it's not like his parents are the FBI or something. You've got this. I'm going back to bed," she said and hung up.

I shoved my phone in my back pocket and walked back out the front door right as the final bell rang.

I can't believe I'm about to do this.

contradictions and complications

Last year, my English teacher had this quote on the wall by one of her favorite science fiction authors, Joan D. Vinge. It read, *"The contradictions are what make human behavior so maddening and yet so fascinating, all at the same time."*

Yeah, I memorized it because I was a bit obsessed by its meaning. I was by no means a literary genius, but I kinda felt like that was a novelist's excuse to have contradictions in their characters and not just fix those contradictions so the characters were truer. That is until I realized that actual, real people do too. Then I figured that saying people are full of contradictions was just an excuse for people to do bad things when they normally wouldn't. Like justifying it in a way.

I'd never stolen anything in my entire life. But this was important. A contradiction of character, I know. But this was important. And maybe it was worse that I was stealing from my friend.

But this was important.

It took me forever long to walk to Duncan's house, because of the back and forth in my head. To distract myself, I instead rehearsed what I'd say if anyone answered the door. That helped silence my nerves. Someone being home and actually letting me in was preferable, really. Breaking in sounded worse, and I had no idea how to do it.

So, I hoped one of Duncan's parents was at home and tried not to berate myself too much over the fact that I didn't know what his parents did for a living or if either of them happened to work from home.

"Emily!"

My smile was genuine, mostly with relief, when Duncan's mom answered my knock cheerfully. *She's not the FBI,* I reminded myself.

"Aren't you supposed to be in school?" she asked teasingly, wagging a finger at me.

I let some of my real guilt show through and shrugged. "I left one of my textbooks in Duncan's room," I said, reciting the excuse I'd rehearsed. "Could I come in and grab it?" *I'm not asking to get inside a bank vault,* I calmly assured myself. Hopefully my expression was equally calm and assuring.

"Of course!" She moved aside for me to enter the house. "Just wait here a minute while I see if Duncan is decent." Then she winked at me.

Wait... "He's here?" I asked. The words flew from my mouth before I could stop them. I hoped I sounded more surprised than panicked. Frantically, I tried to remember a reason why he wasn't in class right now. "Isn't he supposed to be in school?" I mimicked what she'd just said to me, lamely. *Stupid. Stupid.*

"He's home sick. We thought it was just a head-cold, but it turned out to be the flu," she said, then walked down the hall, leaving me to wait in the entry.

Crap! What do I do now? I wondered. I'd been banking on the fact that Duncan's mom would probably just let me into his bedroom alone to look for the ring—well, textbook as far as she knew. How could I look for it and potentially steal it with Duncan *in* his bedroom?

"Come on back, Emily," his mom said a few seconds later from Duncan's doorway. "He's clothed." She smiled in amusement, almost like she wasn't expecting him to be presentable for visitors.

"Great!" I said, feigning enthusiasm and trying not to seem hesitant as I walked to Duncan's bedroom.

"You can go to work, Mom," Duncan said when I stopped at his open doorway. His voice sounded nasally. "Really, I'm not five. I can take care of myself for a few hours."

She seemed to consider that for a few seconds. "Okay, but let me go pick up that soup for you first," she said. Then turning to me, she added, "Just let yourself out when you find your book, Emily."

I nodded.

"I'll be back in a bit, sweetie," she said to Duncan, then walked back down the hall.

"Thanks, Mom," Duncan croaked too loud, causing a coughing fit.

It strangely reminded me of when Lucy was sick. She could hardly get a word out without nearly coughing up a lung.

"This must be what it felt like for..." Duncan paused like he couldn't remember who he was talking about. "For Matteo, when he was sick last week."

Slowly, I stepped into his bedroom. I couldn't ever remember actually being in his bedroom... although that didn't mean that I hadn't. After all, there were several memories lost in the shuffle of changing the past.

Duncan's room was as expected. Clearly a boy's room: gray-blue painted walls covered with several sports posters, all hung crookedly and secured with scotch tape. An old brown dresser against one wall with the paint chipping in places, a matching brown desk underneath the window, covered in neat stacks of textbooks and notebooks, and his bed—opposite the dresser—against the other wall with a blue-gray bedspread and Duncan lounging in it. Some sort of gaming system with a green case lay next to him on the bed, the screen still lit up. He'd obviously been playing it until I walked in.

"What'cha playing?" I asked pointing to the video game, not sure what to say now that I was actually here. My plan was clearly thwarted.

Duncan lifted the console at the corner and pressed a button at the top that caused the screen to go black.

"Madden NFL," he said, then smirked at me. "Football," he clarified.

"Ah... fun!" I said, still standing awkwardly in the doorway. "H-how are you feeling?"

He ran a hand through his slightly greasy hair, spiking it in places. He had dark circles underneath his eyes and his nose was red, probably from extensive use of tissues. An orange metal trash-can, probably the most brightly colored thing in his room, over-flowed with used tissues. Some were scattered on the floor around it.

Once again, I felt absolutely dumb for asking the obvious question.

"I've been better," he said, smiling. He could see my unease. "You can come in." He gestured to his desk chair. "Sit there if you're worried about getting sick."

Hesitantly, I obeyed and tripped my way to the chair and sat with my hands folded over my backpack I'd placed on my lap.

"Ditching school, huh?" he asked with a wink, then coughed several times.

"I, uh... I thought I left one of my textbooks here," I said and looked at his desk next to me as if it might actually be there. None of my books were piled with his, but there was a loose picture of Duncan and me partially hidden beneath some papers. Absently, I wondered where it was taken before looking back at him. I knew the *when* of the photo, it was sometime during the alternate past of my current reality that I didn't remember. We looked happy.

He raised an eyebrow slightly, but pushed it back down. "Which one do you think you left here?" His eyes turned to the top of his dresser when he said it, but quickly shifted back to look at me.

There weren't any books there, but my gaze automatically flitted to where he looked.

And there it was. Laying smack-dab, right in the middle of his dresser—my silver ring. Well...not *my* silver ring.

But soon to be mine. Hopefully.

And in the worst location possible! There was no way Duncan wouldn't notice if I lifted it.

"My history book, I think?" I turned to the stack of books next to me again, pretending to look for my American history textbook, but knowing full well it was actually in my bag. I stood and dropped my backpack to the floor. *What now?* I wondered, strangely wishing someone was walking my life and could give me some guidance, speaking to my thoughts or taking over. "Could I get a glass of water?"

Duncan's face showed amusement, and I was almost certain he was reading my thoughts, but he waved and hand and said, "Be my guest."

I walked to the kitchen, wishing it would have made sense to ask him to get water for me. But I wasn't about to ask someone who had the flu to play host to me.

I opened several cupboards until I found the one that housed the glasses, then turned on the tap for a few seconds until it ran cold to fill my glass partway.

"Mind getting me one too?"

I nearly jumped from my skin hearing his voice behind me.

"Sure," I said, trying to keep my voice steady. Then I retrieved and filled another one for Duncan and slid it across the counter to him.

"You okay?" he asked after taking a sip.

"Never better!" I said much too cheerful. *Holy lame! With a capital L!* What had gotten into me? I was clearly not cut out for actual espionage. It was just a stupid ring from my ex-boyfriend, who probably would've let me continue wearing it if I hadn't insisted on returning it.

Stupid. Stupid, Emily.

"I'm gonna get back to school," I said, then emptied the glass and put it in the sink.

"You could've texted me about the book instead of walking all this way," Duncan said, then chuckled, then coughed.

"Yes, but that would've been *smart,*" I said and laughed with him. He could clearly see how flustered I was, though he probably had no idea why.

"It was nice to see you anyway," he said, in that genuine good-guy way that could've meant we were just friends but could've meant that I could be his girlfriend again if I wanted to. Like perhaps the choice was all mine.

Why did everything have to be so complicated? I should choose Duncan and forget about my dreams. I should go back to walking a different girl who needed my help each night and not getting uber attached to any of them. Or their ridiculously good looking soon-to-be relatives. But that would mean a real-actual goodbye to Andrew. More than a letter, like an I'd-make-sure-to-never-walk-Isabella-or-anyone-else-who-might-be-in-the-same-location-as-Andrew type of goodbye. And to put the final nail in my coffin, I'd have to never walk Lucy again.

I couldn't do that. Not yet. As much as I told myself I needed to. As much as I attempted to do just that, in truth, I wasn't ready.

"You too," I responded. "I'll just go grab my bag and let you get back to your Maddox NHL."

"Madd-en. N-F-L," he corrected, then laughed again.

"Right," I said and laughed too, then walked back to his room to get my bag.

I continued to chuckle to myself as I entered his bedroom about the whole disastrous mission because I hadn't been able to get the ring. But as I mourned the loss, I realized Duncan wasn't following me back to his room. I cocked my head to listen for his footsteps, but heard none.

And the ring sat there on his dresser. Taunting me. Displayed like a piece in a museum or an ancient artifact—I felt like Indiana

Jones, ready to switch it out with a look alike or something that weighed the same.

Should I take it?

Moving toward the desk, I picked up my discarded backpack, and in two steps, I slung it over my shoulder and with the other hand scooped the ring and pocketed it.

My heart hammered. *That was too easy. That was too easy.* The words beat in time with my heart as I left the room and headed for the front door. Was I the maddening type of contradiction or fascinating kind? Probably the former. Good-girl turned thief was definitely maddening.

"Feel better, Duncan!" I shouted in the direction of the kitchen.

He still sat on a stool at the counter, his back toward me and raised a hand. "Thanks," he said, and I swear it sounded like he was smiling.

raspberry hot chocolate

"Carly!" I shouted as I let myself into Ari's house. Arianna was conveniently meeting with the dance committee, and she'd let slip that Carly had come home right after class for the weekend. "I got it!"

I'd been bursting with excitement through the rest of my school day. I almost successfully ignored the thought that it had been too easy to get the ring at Duncan's house that morning.

Carly rounded the corner from the back room to greet me, her brilliant red hair escaping her braid down the back. "You got the ring?" she asked in disbelief.

I closed the gap between us and pulled it from my pocket, holding it between my thumb and finger. "I got the ring." I repeated.

Her eyes widened. "You're a thief!" she said, winking at me. "How'd you do it?"

I followed her to the kitchen and sat on one of the high bar stools as she heated some water for hot chocolate—the raspberry kind that Grandma Grace only pulled out on special occasions but was Carly's go-to—and I recounted how I was able to get it back. I put it back on the finger it had been home to for so many weeks and twisted it absently as I spoke.

My phone vibrated from my bag a couple of times as we chatted and carefully sipped from our mugs, but I chose not to look at it.

"That sounded too easy," Carly said when I'd finished.

"I know," I agreed, "it felt too easy."

"Maybe he wanted you to take it back?"

"Then why not just give it back?"

One of her eyebrows lifted. "Oh, sweetie, you *broke up* with him and *returned* it. Do you really think he'd risk bruising his ego even more by offering it back again?"

"I suppose not," I said. "Do you think he knows what it is though?"

She looked at me thoughtfully for a moment, then asked, "Does he know about your dreams?"

"Yeah, the changed version of me told him... I think." I didn't have an actual memory of telling him for the first time. But he knew all about them, so we must have had a conversation about it at some point.

"Then maybe he knows what the ring does. Maybe that's why he gave it to you in the first place. To help." She sipped from her mug again, looking very convinced of her theory.

"Why not tell me from the start then?"

She shrugged. "Men are a mystery."

My phone vibrated from my bag again. I ignored it a second time.

"So what now?" Carly took my now-empty mug and put both of ours in the sink.

My heart leapt, I was almost as excited for the next part. "Now I tell Andrew I got the ring back and hopefully find out the rest of his 'master plan.'" I couldn't stop the giggle that followed. The plan so far was pretty good.

She giggled too and was still laughing when the house phone rang.

"Hello?" she answered, a smile still wrinkling her cheeks. Her face fell as she listened to the person on the line. "She's here," she said, then handed the receiver to me and whispered, "It's your mom."

I had a sinking feeling in my stomach as I took the phone and answered. "Mom?"

"Why aren't you answering your phone?" she scolded. Practically shouting.

"I, uh…"

"You promised you'd help your dad after school. You promised to go straight there!"

Shoot. I vaguely remembered promising something that morning, but I'd been so preoccupied I couldn't remember what exactly I was supposed to do. "I—I'm sorry…" I stammered. "I forgot…"

There was a heavy pause. "Your dad was counting on you," she said, her voice scarily even.

"I'll—I'll be right there," I said, then mouthed to Carly, "Could you give me a ride?"

She nodded.

"No, come straight home." Mom hung up without saying goodbye.

The happy, jovial mood I'd been in ever since getting my ring back was shooed away as Carly drove me home.

After thanking Ari's sister for the ride, I dragged my feet up the front porch. I was in no hurry to meet my mom's fury. I didn't get into trouble often, but mom sounded stressed so I was bound to be in for a big lecture.

I found her in the kitchen, typing away at her laptop.

"I'm home," I said in a small voice.

She didn't answer right away and typed for a few seconds before closing the computer slowly and swiveling to face me.

Her face was as stone, but with swirling emotion just beneath the surface. I braced myself for the yelling match. But it didn't come. Instead she began to cry.

I didn't know what to say. I just sat beside her. After a few seconds I slowly put my arm around her, but she jerked her head to look at me. "You lied to me," she said.

I furrowed my eyebrows. "I—"

"You aren't taking your medication," she interrupted. "You're still having the dreams."

"Wait...what? But Dr. Shew—"

"No, *but Dr. Shew.* Are you still having the dreams or aren't you?"

Well, yes. Dr. Shew said I probably would. But I could tell that wasn't what she wanted to hear. I tried to keep my face neutral. "They're not all bad."

"They're dangerous." Mom's face had terror written all over it. "They're dangerous for your health."

I didn't know how to respond. I was confused.

"Promise me you'll take your medication from now on."

But I am, I thought. I took the new medication last night. For once I wasn't lying to her about that.

"Promise. Please," she said when I didn't respond right away.

"I promise," I said softly.

She must've been upset by something else, I told myself. *She's still grieving Grandma's death. That must be it.* I walked upstairs to start my homework and refrained from arguing the point that I *had* taken the new medication Dr. Shew gave me last night. And I made certain to take it again before I went to bed.

CHAPTER 15

introductions and awareness

My stomach rolls again, causing me to groan. "Ugh." I lean over the side of my bed to vomit into the bucket once more.

"Izzy," Mama says quietly, "a walk on deck might do wonders for your seasickness. Go get some fresh air and look at the horizon." One of the crewmen gave the same advice a day or two ago, but so far I haven't made it out of my bed.

The idea of standing on the never-steady floor, let alone *walking* all the way up on deck makes my now-empty stomach churn sickly again. But Mama walks the deck often and seems to have less discomfort.

"All right, I'll go up." I push myself to my feet. The boards creak as I adjust my balance again and again with the rocking of the boat, one hand gripping the edge of the bed.

I have to stop several times on the way up to take deep breaths and calm my complaining stomach, but soon I reach the open air. A breeze combs through the loose strands of my hair, held only by a single ribbon, and causes the skirts of my dress to dance.

Mama was right. The fresh air is already helping my nausea, and though the rocking of the ship certainly hadn't stopped, looking out across the sea seems to steady me.

I walk to the edge of the deck so I can see the horizon without obstruction and grip the rail with both hands. The skies are mostly clear, but the waves are high today, probably from the wind gusts that certainly would steal my bonnet if I were wearing it. I watch the rolling waves, feeling the ship move smoothly over each crest, up and down. Up and down.

For a moment I close my eyes, my face wet from the mist of the waves hitting against the sides of the boat. It tastes of fish and salt, but with even the peripheral of the horizon gone from my vision, my stomach resumes its churning. I quickly open my eyes again.

"It is beautiful, isn't it?" a voice asks beside me. I turn to see the young man with the curly black hair again. Nathan.

"Hmm?"

"The sea, the waves, the sky. You can feel God in all of it."

Nathan and I have not properly been introduced, other than exchanging of first names. His forwardness in speaking to me without a proper introduction feels inappropriate. I look behind us at the other passengers mulling around. There are at least a dozen men and women on deck. The Irish family, minus the mother and baby, are only a few feet away, so I relax a bit.

I turn to examine the scenery again. The waves are a deep blue with lines of white that skitter along the top as the water breaks. The sky is full of long white clouds that stretch across the whole of it. I can only imagine what those clouds would look like drenched in the oranges and pinks of a sunset. I might have to stay above deck until then to experience it.

"You are right," I say, "it is beautiful."

I feel his eyes on me, so I turn to look at him. He watches me strangely again with those piercingly brilliant green eyes. When he doesn't release his gaze, I avert my eyes, feeling the crimson rise in my cheeks.

Looking back at the sea, I hide any sign that his actions have affected me and count the swells. From my peripheral, I note that he has also turned his head to look at the waves. And he mutters something underneath his breath.

Finally he says, "We have not yet been properly introduced minus exchanging first names. But since we are on a ship in close quarters, perhaps we can forgo social demands?"

I look at him and smile.

"My name is Nathan Sloan," he says with a sort of smirk like he hides a secret. It gives me a strange feeling in my stomach that has nothing to do with seasickness.

"Isabella Broadbent," I say quickly. "It is a pleasure to meet you."

"Glad to meet you as well, Miss Broadbent," he says. "Is everything all right?"

I look at him again. "It's just..." My eyebrows furrow as I fight the feeling to blurt it out, but the expression on his face urges me to trust him. "There's just something familiar about you. It feels as if I know you... somehow." I shake my head again.

His eyes light up, and he covers my closest hand on the rail with his own. Instinctively I want to pull it away, but I don't. Something holds it there. Something *wants* it there.

I finally pull my hand free when he doesn't speak. "I am afraid you are being too familiar, Mr. Sloan," I say, my cheeks darkening at his continued forwardness. "Remember, we have only just met."

"You don't...?" He pauses. His expression does not look rejected by my actions and words, but rather determined.

When I don't look away, he smiles, and I can see his confidence rise. He takes both of my hands from the rails and holds them in his own. When I try to pull away, he grips tighter. "Trust me, Isabella," he says, "You look lovely, as always." The words come out slowly, deliberately.

"I—" I begin, but then everything flashes purple, then blinding white.

And I know myself.

And then I vomit over the side of the ship.

Man, this seasickness is not fun. I feel immediately embarrassed. Isabella was holding it together really well through the conversation, but the wave of nausea hit me with full force when I —Emily Chandler—became aware.

"Are you all right?" He asks tentatively. "Isabella?"

Hoping my breath doesn't smell too bad, I throw my arms around his neck. "Andrew," I breathe. "I'm here. It's me, Emily," my voice is barely a whisper.

He makes a choked sound and returns the embrace, one of his hands gripping the back of my head to hold me tighter. "You are here," he repeats, relief in his voice.

After a moment, we pull away. Mostly out of awareness of where we are and that we are supposed to be strangers.

I smile slyly at him. "I got the ring."

bittersweet

"You are early," I say with a smile on my face.

Yeah, weird, Emily responds to my thoughts as always. *I don't usually pop in at the beginning of your day.*

"Well, everything about this is strange." I point a finger to my temple. "Who else has a girl visiting their head on a regular basis?"

True.

Emily fades into the background as I begin my routine. Without asking her to, Betsy plaits my hair just the way Charles prefers. My excitement jumps into my throat as I anticipate that we are planning a wedding today. *Our wedding.*

That's great, Lucy, Emily pipes in. *So things between you and Charles are better?*

"They are!" I say as I make my way downstairs to breakfast. "The wedding is still happening, and I could not be happier!"

I am happy for you, Emily says, *I feel horrible that Andrew and I almost messed everything up. Again.*

"It was not you," I say softly. "And I am sorry that a goodbye was necessary."

So... have you seen him since my letter?

"No." How to tell her? "He went back to Savannah." Though I am grateful for his departure, I am sorry for Emily.

Wow.

"Emily, I am really so sorry—"

Don't apologize, she interrupts. *He actually found a way for us to be... together. Sort of.*

"He did?" I pause with my hand on the wall before entering the room. It wouldn't do to be caught in a daze at breakfast whilst Emily recounts Andrew's plan coming to fruition.

Remember all of the talk about Isabella?

"Of course."

Well, that's his plan. He's found a way for us to be in the same dream. We can speak to each other without causing suspicion here.

"You are walking the same person?" I feel the horror on my face. One voice inside my head is difficult to come to grips with. "You are both inside Isabella's head?" I cannot imagine two voices crammed in between my own thoughts. I sometimes cannot tell my own thoughts from Emily's. The confusion would be two-fold if there were another! I shudder to think where I might be sent if anyone ever finds out about Emily.

No! Different people. Emily's words are reassuring. *Andrew is with Nathan. It's kind of unspoken, but I've only ever walked with girls and I assume he's only walked with guys.*

Right. There was a mention of someone named Nathan. I let out the breath I was holding and push the door open, seating myself to breakfast.

It's that bad having me here? Emily asks when I take my first bite.

Yes, I want to tell her. But that feels ungrateful after everything she has done for me. I was scheduled to die in that fire. She saw my gravestone with her own eyes. Because of her presence, and thanks to Andrew, I am here today. *It was unpleasant at first, but not anymore.* I do not speak aloud as I am now in the company of my family members. *Let's not speak of it again. This is not the first time it has worried you, but I really do not mind much anymore.* I am mostly truthful. A dark feeling washes over me before I say, *It makes me feel less alone sometimes.*

"Tell me more about this dream you and Andrew meet in," I ask after being excused from my meal and disappearing into the yard. The spring sunshine dissipates the darkness I felt during breakfast. The day is glorious.

It's nothing like being here. I detect a hint of sadness laced in her words.

"Are you lovers who must meet in secret because your parents have forbidden you to marry?" I inject jubilation into my voice, forcing the pair of us to brighten our moods.

But the word *forbidden* hangs between us. I wonder if she hears it as clearly as I do. My apprehension cracks open, and the darkness returns. Sometimes I am not certain if the feelings originate in her or me.

No, nothing like that.

"Your love is not forbidden then?" I must keep the conversation alive.

No, they've only just met. As far as we know, neither of them are attached to anyone else. Nothing is forbidden at this point.

I feel her meaning, and her use of the word proves to me that she heard it before. But no matter how many times I try to convince myself otherwise, I cannot help but feel that mine were the lips who declared Emily and Andrew's love forbidden. And now I fear it is too late to take it back.

My tongue sticks out between my teeth in a very unladylike fashion as I strain to hold my hand straight with the calligraphy brush.

"Mister..." I say the word slowly as I attempt a natural stroke, pushing against the stiffness of the skin on my fingers and palm.

That's the spirit, Emily says in my head. I had suspected she left shortly after lunch, so I am surprised to hear her again. *Is it necessary to make it so fancy?*

"They are wedding invitations," I say. "Do they not have weddings in the future?"

Yeah, but they use computers and mail-merge to prevent hand cramps, she says, though I only understand half of it.

"Mail. Merge?" I know what the words mean separately, but together?

Never mind. Do all brides address the wedding invitations?

"Most send them to be done professionally," I say. "But ever since Uncle Harry commissioned a tutor to teach me the art, I have always dreamed of doing them all on my own."

I'm sorry that your hands... She doesn't finish the sentence, and I cannot tell if it is because she does not want to offend me by continuing or if she has grown tired of the subject.

"Lucy?" Charles stands in the doorway.

"Charles!" I stand and greet him, taking both of his hands in mine.

"Were you speaking to someone?" he asks, looking around the room for a companion.

My stomach lurches. How much of my talking to Emily did he hear?

"I was just talking to myself," Emily takes over and says for me, she's quick to come up with explanations when my tongue is tied. "I am addressing our wedding invitations and must've been saying the names out loud."

He looks at me strangely, but shakes his head and moves further into the room, guiding me to sit next to him on the love seat.

"I wanted to speak to you about something," he says, his shoulders suddenly taut. He looks nervous.

"Is everything all right?" I ask, taking my voice back again.

"I must confess that I thought..." He pauses and stares at the elaborate Victorian rug beneath our feet.

"Yes?" I prod, though I'm not entirely sure if it was me or Emily who voiced the word.

He looks at me again. His blue eyes squint slightly as he smiles with the guilty look I have only seen a few times. "I thought that Andrew was in love with you."

Didn't you sort of go over this at one point? Emily asks. *Like, really recently?*

"He is not in love with me," I focus on letting the truth of the words match the truth in my voice.

"No, he is not." Charles smile broadens. Emily mentions something about *chick* or *chickens flick* expressions before a marriage proposal, but I tune her out. She can be confusing and distracting sometimes. Plus she knows Charles and I are already engaged. "He's been away making his own happiness... with your dear friend Margaret."

My heart twinges for Emily.

"They are engaged," I say.

"Yes, but at first I thought the engagement had something to do with not having you." Charles shakes his head. "I guess what I am trying to say is that Andrew is finally happy again after losing his sister. He spends all of his waking hours in the company of Margaret."

"Yes," I say, then per Emily's prompting I continue, "I bumped into them in town not long ago." I feel her pity for Margaret. Emily feels guilty that Andrew is keeping up appearances but possibly does not mean to marry her. I agree with her but say nothing to Charles.

"Well, she has traveled to join him in Savannah. I just received a letter from him." Charles's eyes are alight. "He apologized for the misunderstandings and promised that he only ever had eyes for Margaret. They've set a date for their wedding. One week after ours!"

"That's wonderful!" I say. Emily's emotions make it difficult but not impossible for me to express true happiness at this news.

Charles leans in to kiss me, and I feel Emily fade further back.

I am truly sorry, I say to her for the second time today before she feels completely gone.

It's for the best.
And the pain in my heart for Andrew vanishes with her.

CHAPTER 17

reasons

"Who was that man you were talking to yesterday?" Rachel asks as we eat breakfast. "Was it the same one who returned your handkerchief the day we set sail?" The gruel is a bit undercooked, but shuffling through Isabella's recent memories, I note that they had to cook the meal themselves in a shared kitchen used by most of the ship.

"Yes. His name is Nathan Sloan," Isabella says, her cheeks coloring a little. She hardly tastes her food, she's so distracted, which makes me inwardly smile. She thinks Nathan is cute! I search her thoughts on the surface. Isabella isn't attached to anyone. She isn't in love or engaged. *This could work for us*, I think and hope that Nathan is similarly unattached.

I look around the steerage area for Andrew, but have to stop myself and close my eyes to picture Nathan. Black curly hair, broad shoulders, a little bit shorter than Andrew, and a rounder face. But hopefully Andrew all the same if we are synced in our walks.

He doesn't appear to be in the room, but the ship isn't too large, so I am certain to bump into him soon. Especially if Andrew is with him. My heart soars with the thought that he might seek me out.

The waves are still strong, but all of the time spent up on deck the day before—

and the plans to head straight there after breakfast—make Isabella's stomach more settled. There is a slight queasiness, but it seems she is finally getting her sea legs.

I shovel in my last couple of bites and stand, taking my bowl with me.

"Where are you going?" Rachel asks.

"Up on deck," Isabella answers, "it helps with my seasickness." She holds a hand to her stomach. "Would you like to come?"

Rachel shakes her head, "I'll go find Papa," she says, "He promised to play a game with me."

I feel Isabella's relief at Rachel's other plans. Yes, she does want the fresh air, but mostly she is hoping to run into the tall, dark, and handsome Nathan.

Great minds think alike.

The vast expanse of the ocean leaves me breathless every time I see it. It's the first thing both Isabella and I notice when we reach the upper deck. Sure, I've seen the ocean. From the beach. But out here in the middle of it, with large white-capped rolling waves rocking the ship forcefully back and forth, powerful and wild and now a dark blue-gray color, it is beautiful.

"Miss Broadbent!" Nathan says, approaching us. His curly hair stands straight up, surrendering to the wind gusts that are nearly constant.

"Mr. Sloan." Isabella smiles sweetly at him. She itches to touch her pinned-up hair but most of it feels secure. Only a few strands escape to dance.

"The sea is active today," he says squinting up at the gray sky. "You should be safely below."

"Will it storm today?"

He shakes his head. "Crewmen said not for a couple of days, but it is coming."

"Then I want to be outside today."

Nathan's face splits into a smile, and he holds out an arm covered with a pristine light-gray coat. "Care to walk with me?" he asks, that familiar smirk hiding beneath his carefree smile.

Both mine and Isabella's hearts speed as we slip a hand through his. I want to swoon. I feel like I'm in an Austen or Bronte novel. Or a really good adaptation of one. I want to speak with Andrew, but Nathan talks before I can. "Where are you from?"

"Manchester. And yourself?"

"London."

"And what brings you to the new world?"

"Religion," Isabella says poignantly.

Nathan stops and looks at her, clearly surprised by her tone and how confidently and quickly she responded. I am surprised by her quick response too. Religion can be a loaded topic in any century. She is apprehensive about his reaction, but instantly relieved when all she sees is admiration. I hope deeply that those are Nathan's feelings, not just Andrew attempting to cover for him. This relationship will be very short-lived if Nathan takes issue with Isabella's newfound religion. I suppose Andrew could find two other people for us to walk, but I would still be really sad for Isabella.

"Why are you going to America?" Isabella asks hesitantly when Nathan doesn't answer right away despite his expression.

"Opportunity," he says like it's a less noble reason. "You couldn't have religion in England?" he asks, directing the topic back to her.

"We seek freedom to worship how we wish. America allows that. So we left."

"Did your father and mother force you to leave?"

"No, I wish to worship as I want too. I believe in our church." The wind has picked up, so we duck next to some crates to have shelter from the worst of it. The quiet and semi-privacy give an intimate air to the conversation. Isabella feels nervous, but she is passionate about the subject and is bursting to share it with someone. Specifically with him. She's hidden her feelings about Nathan deep into her subconscious, unintentionally hidden from me, but it's easy to see how her pulse quickens at the sight of him.

Again, he looks surprised by her. His expression has the same admiration as before and something else now.

She sees that he's waiting for her to explain more, so she takes a deep breath and begins, "Papa converted to the new church instantly. He said it was like he had been waiting his entire life to find a church he could agree with and he finally did."

"And you converted quickly too?" Nathan folds his arms across his chest, and she hopes it is a reaction to the weather and not her words.

"No. Mama and Rachel joined a few months after Papa, but I could not be convinced that it was any different from any other church in England."

I am just as engrossed in her story as Nathan is. Most of the time I don't get to hear stories about important events in a person's life unless I am experiencing it with them. The last time I heard a past story was when Lucy told Margaret of her engagement. And I wasn't aware of myself then, so I couldn't truly enjoy it or appreciate it until I woke up the next morning.

"But then I had an experience," Isabella continues. "The missionaries of the church were visiting for dinner one night, and one of them was reading from the scriptures. They often came for dinner, so it wasn't a particularly special occasion, but when he stopped to express his feelings about the words he had just read, he said that he knew the words were true. And that's when I felt it."

Nathan unfolds his arms, "And what was that?" he asks, leaning slightly forward as if he doesn't want to miss a single word.

She uses her hands to illustrate as she continues, "A warm, tingling sensation in my breast that affirmed to me that what the man was saying was true." She pauses, and I feel the warm feeling inside her and the smile on her face as she reminisces. "A week later I was baptized into the church. That was a year ago, and though we never planned to leave, it felt like the right thing to do. I was the first to suggest we leave our home and go to America."

In a flash of memory that encases almost a lifetime of emotion, I see, or rather feel something that she omits in her story. A deep depression. The type that stabs the heart with physical pain and makes a person never want to get out of bed. It's a familiar feeling. Not from my waking life, but I've experienced it in many dreams.

I felt it strongly in my last dream with Carly.

Nathan's enraptured face seems to fall, and I wonder if he's detected something in her expression. Then he says, "Do you have a specific destination?"

Isabella nods. "A small settlement south of Chicago." Her voice deflates slightly, but she seems oblivious of Nathan's reaction. Maybe it was nothing. "Where does opportunity await you?"

"New York." His tone is definitely laced with disappointment. They will be hundreds of miles apart when each of their journey's end. "My aunt lives there, and she's found me a job at one of the factories."

"And you left your family behind?"

"Influenza. Killed everyone but me."

"I am sorry for your loss."

He shrugs. "It wasn't your fault. Now, tell me about your family."

irresponsible

erfect. It's the first thought in my head when I wake up and am eating the same under-cooked meal near the bunks. I'm still Isabella, sitting with Rachel and their mother. *Maybe I'll actually get a chance to speak with Andrew, as myself.* As much as I loved experiencing Isabella and Nathan getting to know one another, Andrew and I haven't gotten a word in edgewise. And since I can never see him again when I am with Lucy, this is our only way to meet. Even if neither of us are... well, *us.*

Even though he's never actually met me. That would be impossible.

The porridge sloshes around Isabella's bowl in a clumpy, grayish, cement-looking sea. It makes me want to gag. Isabella doesn't seem much more interested in it than I am and stands up.

"Izzy, you really should eat more," Mama says. "It's important to keep up your strength."

"The swaying of the ship," Isabella says, exaggerating the sway with her body and planting an open palm on her stomach. "It has made the sea sickness return, and I have no appetite."

Mama nods in agreement, her own face slightly pale, and looks at Rachel, who is sallow-looking herself.

"I need to get some air," Isabella announces. "I am going up."

"Don't go near the edge," Rachel warns, a little bit of hysteria in her voice. "You might lose your balance and tumble over."

"I promise to steer clear," she assures her sister with a wink before walking away.

Isabella brushes past one of the crew on her way out. "Get back to your cabin, miss!" he shouts in our direction when we are several steps away from him. I'm pretty sure Isabella didn't hear him.

She is impatient with her awkward movements, slowed by her own unsteady feet. *Are the waves always like this?* I wonder, but she hardly notices.

When we reach the upper deck and are finally outside, I shiver. The semi warm wind from yesterday has turned cold and leaves goosebumps on Isabella's uncovered arms. The skies are stuffed with thick dark-gray clouds from horizon to horizon, and I see a flash of lightning in the distance. Isabella sees it too, but dismisses it and merely slows her walking.

She makes her way to the space near the crates where she spoke with Nathan yesterday. She reminisces about them laughing together, remembers leaning close while Nathan recounted the deaths of his parents, things I don't recall. I must have left mid-conversation. The beginning stirrings of first love are swirling and fluttering within her breast. The feeling is contagious. It makes me giddy, reminds me of my first feelings after meeting Andrew. The ones I still get whenever he steals a kiss or finds a way for us to talk together. Like this, here with Isabella and Andrew. I just hope that we can have a moment for *us*, as we walk with *them*.

It feels like standing vertical requires more effort now than before. She places a hand on a nearby crate every time the port side dips down. Absently, I wonder if it's safe to be on deck. I push away the memory of warning from the crew member, hoping that she doesn't remember it.

A storm is coming. Nathan said as much, but he also said it might not come for another day or more. I squint Isabella's eyes to focus on the distance and can see a haze not far off. It is probably rain.

She notices it too but convinces herself that she is safe. The ship is secure and will not toss her out to sea. After all, she can always rush inside if the rain reaches them.

The rolling of the waves rise, but we stand our ground, trying to predict the amount of pressure to put on each foot to stay upright. Honestly neither of us wants to leave until we see him. I realize then, hearing and analyzing her thoughts, just how alike Isabella and I are.

"Isabella!" The voice we both want to hear is near, probably staggering toward us on deck. "Emily!" (Okay, he might have said *Isabella*. A girl can dream.) Judging by Nathan's frantic tone, I am certain Andrew is with him.

My heart soars. It feels like it's been so long since I've seen or talked to him.

It takes him too long to reach us with his unsteady footing. Part of me wonders if he is inebriated when he rounds the crates into sight. It wasn't *that* hard for Isabella to walk here, even with the rolling waves.

She cocks her head in confusion, releasing the hand steadying her against the crate. She nearly topples backwards.

The waves are definitely higher. Much higher than even a few minutes ago.

She feels a pang of fear. *What was I thinking?* she wonders. I kick myself for not being smarter. Even if Andrew did have a hand in bringing me here, I am still here for Isabella. It's my job to keep her safe. "Why was I so reckless?" Isabella groans. I'm having the same thoughts myself.

This isn't like the fire. That was obviously dangerous, and since I'd seen Lucy's tombstone, I knew it was certain to kill her. Lucy knew the danger and was determined to save her sister at all costs. This is just me being stupid. *Awesome guardian angel work, Em. Really helpful.*

Nathan/Andrew reaches us finally, after his slow-motion

walk, and immediately grabs my hand and attempts to drag us back to safety.

I resist for a moment. "Andrew?" I ask, wanting to make sure he's really here too.

"Emily, what are you doing up here?" he asks, his voice a low hiss.

"I..." I don't have an answer. *We were hoping to see you,* seems like a flimsy excuse to disregard safety.

"C'mon," he says, pulling me again. "Let's get inside."

I allow him to drag us out from behind the crates and across the deck, which is now swaying violently. We concentrate on our steps to keep from falling. It's no small feat.

Right foot forward, shift weight, squeeze Nathan/Andrew's hand to keep from toppling over.

Left foot forward, shift weight back two steps. The ship dips down, giving me a feeling of free-falling, and I slam onto my knees. Luckily, many layers of petticoats, underskirts, and over skirts cushion the fall. Still, there will probably be bruises on both knees tomorrow.

Isabella whimpers in what I first assume is pain, but then I realize she's terrified.

"We can do this, Isabella," Nathan says softly to her. Or maybe he says it loudly. It's hard to tell. Gusts of wind are drowning out all other sounds.

How did I not notice the fierceness of this storm? I scold myself, but I know exactly how. Because I was too busy daydreaming about a pair of chestnut eyes, hidden behind brilliant green ones, and hoping to get half a minute to speak with him.

Nathan/Andrew glares at us, and I know it's Andrew glaring at me. The daydream stops abruptly.

With her free hand, Isabella wipes the sea spray from her stinging eyes. Damp locks of hair are plastered to her face.

"Stand up, Isabella," Nathan pleads with firmness in his tone I haven't yet heard. I don't have to wonder how much of that is influenced by Andrew. "We have to get inside."

I lift her up—it's a strange dance between us. Where Lucy and I essentially take turns with control, it's as if Isabella is already familiar with my presence, like we've been together since her birth and she is used to the back and forth between us.

Nathan and Andrew seem to be doing the same thing. Almost as if all four of us are on the deck together as individuals, aware of each other and in separate bodies.

After I get Isabella to her feet, she is able to put one step in front of the other. I sense a renewed vigor and determination. Hopefully it will be enough to get her to safety.

The boat lifts again, bringing the deck toward us, making her body feel heavy.

The door to the lower deck seems miles away, but she takes another step. And another.

The ship dips again, and on the now-slick wood, Isabella's traction-less shoes cannot grip and we slip. Nathan/Andrew's hand is ripped from our grasp, and we land on her hip hard, then slide several feet.

"Isabella!" Nathan shouts, ducking down and sliding toward us. He grabs our elbow roughly and hauls us back to our feet.

"Get a hold of her," Andrew says roughly grabbing both arms and pulling me up until we are eye-to-eye. Wind whips his borrowed black curls and makes his green eyes suddenly look as dark as the sea.

I scowl at him. "It's not like she did it on purpose," I say as my soul sings that we are finally speaking to each other.

"Yes, but I've seen you take control."

"It's different this time," I say. I want to open my mouth and explain. I want to throw my arms around him and tell him how much I've missed him and how happy I am that he found a way for us. Instead, my damn pride gets in the way. "Are you always this rude when you walk, or is today a special occasion?" I ask.

"How about we focus on not getting Isabella and Nathan killed?" he says under his breath, arrogance thickening his tone.

"That's exactly what I'm *trying* to do!" I snap, then grit my teeth to push back the tears. We've never fought like this, and I hate it. "It's not like anything will happen to us anyway." I say it, but don't mean it.

Nathan/Andrew's eyes widen then narrow, and I instantly regret my words. "Show some respect for other people's lives, *Emily*. Even if they are in the past."

"Andrew, I didn't mean it. I promise I didn't, I—" I backpedal.

"I'll get these two to safety," he says. "You should go."

And for the second time, he pushes me out.

thorns and regrets

"Ouch!" Instinctively, I jerk back at the painful prick in my arm.

"Miss Lucy?" Betsy asks, holding hordes of satin and lace. She glances at the other person in the room, an older woman with wispy, graying hair. She has several silver pins jutting out from between her teeth, which she removes gingerly with one hand and cocks her head at me.

"Are you feeling faint, miss?" she asks.

"No," Lucy moves to touch her forehead but gets another prick on the inside of her elbow and winces again. She paints one of her practiced-perfect smiles for Betsy and the woman. "I am quite all right," she assures.

The woman chomps down on the pins once again and gathers fabric at my feet; she furrows her eyebrows in concentration as Lucy wills me to hold us still.

Are you okay? Lucy asks. She sounds irritated.

I think so, I say, wanting to apologize. But since this situation isn't exactly my fault, I don't. *I was kinda shoved in.*

Shoved?

Yeah. I don't explain more, taking a moment to recollect my wits instead. I am still disoriented from leaving Isabella so abruptly—one minute I'm freezing, sliding, scared-for-her-life Isabella, and now I'm warm, standing like a statue, safe Lucy. I look down to see what exactly she is being fitted for.

Your wedding dress!? All thoughts of Isabella flee. I'm sure my voice would squeal if my words were audible.

Yes, she says. I imagine that she would bow her head to hide the flush of pleasure in her cheeks if we were normal girls having a normal conversation in two separate bodies. Like normal people.

My vantage point isn't the best, but by the layers of cream-colored lace and satin flowing from Lucy's neck to the floor, and the way the corseted bodice hugs tightly, but not uncomfortably, I can tell that a very beautiful dress is in the works.

What do you think? she asks.

What do I think? Lucy, a hundred years from now, women will still be dreaming of this dress. It's, like... epic.

She doesn't answer, but I can feel she's pleased at my words.

It's timeless, I continue, *I can't wait to see it when it's finished... and, well, in front of a mirror so I can see the whole thing.*

Me too.

I feel her urge to say more, to gush about how beautiful the dress is. But she holds back. She is surprisingly well controlled in her thoughts. We both ease into silence. I essentially allow my mind to go blank—I let my brain recharge. After a few moments, I hear Lucy's thoughts swirl with questions until she lands on one. *Where were you before? I have never felt you so... affected when you arrive.*

I ponder a few more moments before responding. *Probably because I've usually just fallen asleep when I arrive.*

Are you not asleep now? she sounds concerned.

Of course! I blurt out. *But I came straight from another dream. I was just pushed out of another walk.*

That is what you meant when you said you were shoved?

Yes. I was Isabella again. Andrew was there with Nathan.

What happened? she asks, obediently shifting as the gray-haired woman instructs her.

Did I tell you they're on a ship for America?

You did not.

I think it's the early eighteen forties, I say. I think I saw the date written somewhere. Isabella is traveling with her family for religious freedom and Nathan has lost his family and is looking for better work.

That sounds adventurous.

It wasn't at first. It was pretty boring. And the food... Inwardly I shudder. *But I wanted to see him, and for the record Isabella wanted to see Nathan too.*

For the record?

If Andrew tries to tell you... I pause. She has absolutely no desire to speak with Andrew. Possibly never again in her life. *Are you sure you want to hear this?*

I admit Andrew is not my favorite person. She arranges her thoughts for a moment. *But he matters to you, and it is very romantic that he has found a way for you two to have time together without...* She doesn't finish her thought. She doesn't need to.

I guess it is romantic. My heart swoons, and Lucy attempts to squash it, but catches herself and stops. Briefly I wonder what kind of mental trauma Lucy is enduring as a result of my continued presence.

Go on, she prods.

We went on deck to see each other, but it was stormy. Like, dangerous stormy. Like I might've been thrown overboard if I'd missed a step. In fact, I'm not totally sure Isabella made it.

"Oh!" Lucy says aloud.

All fingers stop and eyes flash to Lucy.

"I apologize," Lucy says, flushing. "I just had a thought."

I could tell that she was hoping that was explanation enough for her outburst, but the two women kept looking at her.

"I was thinking about..." I hear her scrambling for a topic.

"Charles?" Betsy asks, ducking her head.

"Yes," Lucy confirms. "I was just reminiscing about our early courtship. Certainly the wedding dress is reminding me about how I got here."

"Oh?" Betsy says. "Do tell us!"

"Tell you about... our courtship?"

"Yes," she says.

The gray-haired woman merely smiles.

"You were there," Lucy says to Betsy, "I mean, you were my maid through all of it. Certainly you know the story."

But I don't, I say. *Tell it. Please?*

"It's a story worth repeating," Betsy says.

"All right," Lucy says, a little disappointed. *I still want to hear about Isabella and Nathan,* she says silently to me before speaking. "We actually met at a wedding," Lucy starts and internally nods at me to tell my story.

Really? Okay, I say. *Well, I was being so stupid. I wanted to see him, and it didn't hurt that Isabella wanted to see Nathan too, so we went up on deck.*

Yes, you told me that part, she says to me. Then she says aloud, "It was at my cousin's wedding. I was one of her bridesmaids."

"Was the wedding in town?" the gray-haired woman asks, clearly eager to hear the story too.

"No, it was down south, on a plantation in Georgia. Charles was a friend of the groom," she says, then internally points at me again.

It wasn't raining at first, but the clouds were dark. And the ship was swaying more than usual. But, in our defense, the ship kind of sways all the time. It didn't seem like a big deal.

"I walked outside the church for some fresh air before the reception, and my dress got caught on some rosebushes. I was terrified about ripping my beautiful bridesmaid dress, so I tried to free myself, gently removing each thorn one by one."

We stood between some crates—somewhere we had spoken before —so we didn't notice that the waves were getting higher.

"After several minutes, a handsome gentleman found me—it was Charles."

Andrew—as Nathan—found us and told us it was too dangerous to be on deck.

"You wouldn't think that his large hands would be able to save lace so nimbly, but he did just that."

But by then the waves were crazy high. The ship was rocking so bad that it was really hard to walk. We tried to make our way to safety. But the wood was slick, and we kept slipping.

"He had quite a few injuries on his fingers from the thorns, but he was such a gentleman. He made no complaints as he walked me back to the reception."

Things weren't going well. Isabella fell a couple times—hard. And Andrew was angry with me for being so irresponsible with Isabella's life.

"We danced, we talked," Lucy says. She's so enraptured in her own story that I can almost feel the glimmer in her eye. "And when it was time to say goodbye, we made the happy realization that Charles and his family were moving to Harker Manor, just a few miles away from my home, to care for his ailing uncle who passed a few months later."

Then he just pushed me out.

"We courted for several months after he arrived, he proposed, and here we are."

And here I am.

The room is silent for several seconds, everyone lost in their thoughts. I wonder whether Lucy even heard my story, she was so caught up in retelling hers. But I feel a darkness, a sympathy seep in, and I know she heard it. Darkness doesn't come from a knight in shining armor saving a favorite dress. Her favorite blue one I pluck from her memory.

I am so sorry, Emily, she says after a time.

He was right, I say. *I was risking that poor girl's life because I wanted to see him. Even though she wanted to do it too, I should have stopped her.* Shame fills me. Walking other people's memories has made me lose my respect for the mortality of living things. If Isabella had died, I would be fine. Andrew and I would just find another couple to walk. Being dashed in the sea wouldn't kill us. But Isabella...

I am truly sorry that you cannot be together here, Lucy says answering my internal dialogue.

We shouldn't be together at all. I am starting to feel like a broken record.

needed

My stomach rolls when I awake. I keep my eyes shut tight and wish I could be back with Lucy immediately. I would stay in her world forever if it meant I'd never feel this sick ever again.

I hear my insides revolt, and I sit bolt upright to dash to the toilet, but I bang my head on the bunk above me. Shooting stars flash through my vision, and I vomit over the side of the bed.

When my vision clears, I realize I'm not Emily. I'm back on the ship as Isabella. I feel a teeny tiny bit of gratitude that I'd managed to get most of the mess into the bucket beside my bed, but just the glance at its contents causes me to lose the rest of whatever was left in her stomach.

I groan and lie back down, feeling the gut-twisting rocking of the ship. Is it possible that it feels worse than when I was up on deck in that storm?

"How many more days do we have?" Isabella asks the wood above her.

"Four or five, I think," a small voice replies from above. It sounds like Rachel. "Are you still feeling sick?" she asks tentatively.

"Is the storm over?"

"Yes, but Mama overheard one of the crew say they think another one's comin'"

I move to swing my legs out to go up for some fresh air—it's always helped before—but the movement sends shooting pains from my right ankle up through my leg. "Oww!" I cry out.

Rachel's face peers over the side of the bunk to look at me. Her wavy brown hair hangs down in long tangles—badly needing a combing. "Does it still hurt that bad?"

I grit my teeth to push back the tears. The pain is so intense. Gingerly, I remove the coverings from my legs to view the damage. Rachel gasps when I reveal the injury. Isabella's right ankle is swollen twice its size. Black-and-blue patches cover the entirety of it and trail down her foot. Next to the healthy pink left ankle, I can tell it's sprained or broken or shattered. Without an x-ray it's hard to know the severity.

"How?" I say aloud without thinking. I meant to silently find out from Isabella.

"You don't remember?" Rachel asks. "It was during the storm when you were trying to get back down here," she says, thankfully not questioning why her sister didn't remember such a horrible injury. "You were with that fellow, Nathan, and you slipped on the stairs coming down."

I suck in air through my teeth making a hissing sound. Even gently touching it sends deep pain shooting through the ankle.

"Luckily he was there to carry you the rest of the way down," Rachel continues. I don't respond, hoping she'll go on. And she does, though she sounds hesitant: "The doctor says it's probably broken..."

Fury at Andrew and heavy dread fills my stomach. He pushed me out when Isabella needed me most! She endured the pain of this injury and whatever followed without the help I could have given her. If it wasn't for the painful jolts snaking through poor Isabella's trashed ankle, I'd march up to him right now and give his gorgeous face—er, Nathan's face—a piece of my mind. He can't just go around pushing people out of walks whenever he feels like it.

Then the dread comes... If the doctor is right and the ankle is broken, or if the tendons or ligaments are torn, Isabella could be crippled for life. No orthopedic doctors or titanium rods in the nineteenth century. This one stupid injury could affect her entire life.

Finding someone who wants to marry a cripple is nearly impossible, Isabella says. It's half subconscious, but the fear is loud enough that I hear it.

Nothing is determined yet, I say to her, hoping that she hears me even if she thinks the idea is overly optimistic. *It might only be sprained. Maybe it just needs a few weeks to heal. Time will tell.*

The idea seems to buoy her spirits a little, but my fury reignites, realizing what she went through alone.

If I could find him...

"I think some fresh air could help my seasickness," Isabella says to Rachel. I love how we always seem to be on the same page.

"But how will you get out?"

"Could you find Papa and ask him to carry me?" she asks, "He said he would if I wanted to."

Wordlessly, Rachel climbs down and takes the mess bucket with her—plugging her nose with the other hand. Isabella smiles, feeling better than she has in days and marveling at the change. She unconsciously tries to block her unhappy memories from me, but ever since the injury, she hasn't been able to keep any food down. Even the thought of food makes her want to vomit. Her parents have been practically force feeding her to keep up her strength. I wonder if her intense pain is worsening her nausea.

While we wait for Isabella's father, her mother arrives. The thin skin below her red-rimmed eyes is a light-purple color, but despite the exhaustion etched on her face and in her expression, she is smiling with vigor.

"Mama," Isabella greets her, a smile emerging to match the

one she sees. "What's this?" she asks pointing to the package wrapped in brown paper that her mother carries.

"I came to cheer you up," she says.

"And you've brought a present?"

Mama nods, then sits on the bunk next to Isabella, handing over the gift.

"What is it?" Isabella asks, her voice barely a whisper. She can hear the young girl in her tone—giddy with anticipation like Christmas morning.

"I was going to wait until you had a young man with a question for your father." She gives a knowing look, and Isabella's thoughts flit to Nathan immediately. "And perhaps that day is not too far away, but with everything that has happened, I thought now would be appropriate."

Isabella carefully removes the string keeping the paper together and unwraps the round object.

Tears prick Isabella's eyes seeing the familiar object. A china plate with hand-painted red and blue flowers and a thick gold-leaf strip enveloping the edge.

"I thought you left this behind," Isabella whispers.

Mama's smile creases the skin around her eyes and mouth. The stress and turmoil of leaving home and the voyage has aged her. Isabella can see new gray strands framing her face. "Oh no. The entire set is packed safely away on this ship."

I feel Isabella's eyes widen. "You brought the entire set?" she asks, breathless. "For me?"

Mama nods and pulls Isabella into an embrace.

"Thank you, Mama," Isabella says as tears soak into the cotton of her mother's dress. After a moment she pulls away. "But what about Rachel?"

Mama's smile doesn't fade. "I've brought the pink set for her," she says pressing a finger against her lips. "But do not spoil the surprise. I want to wait until she is a little older before I give it to her."

Isabella hugs her mother again, squeezing her shoulders with love and gratitude. When they pull apart again, Papa is standing before them.

"Rachel says you want some fresh air," he says, hope brightening his tone. She detects guilt just beneath the surface. He searched for her during that storm, Isabella remembers. He looked everywhere, never thinking to look between those crates. He blames himself for Isabella's accident, no matter how many times she assures him that it was her fault, no one else's.

"Yes, could you take me?" Isabella asks.

Carefully, he hooks an arm underneath Isabella's knees as she holds onto his shoulders with one arm.

"Rachel, bring a blanket," Papa instructs as Rachel also arrives. He hoists her up and staggers a few steps with the rocking of the ship, then sure-footed, makes his way to the stairs that lead up. At that point, one of the deckhands lends his assistance and the two shimmy her up the steps and out into the fresh salty air.

"Smidge!" the deckhand calls over his shoulder at a burly, dark-haired man. "Get the miss a chair!" The burly man nods and disappears for a few minutes, returning with a chair from an unknown location. He places it near the starboard railing, wedged between two heavy barrels to keep it from tipping.

Papa and the deckhand lower Isabella into the chair, and Rachel immediately covers her legs with the wool blanket from Isabella's bed.

"Are you all right, then?" Papa asks after the deckhand returns to his duties.

"I'm fine, Papa," Isabella says.

"Do you want me to sit with you? Can we bring you anything?" Papa asks.

"I do not mind the solitude, but I would like something to eat."

Papa's face brightens even more. He nods before walking back below with Rachel trailing behind.

Isabella closes her eyes, feeling the wet mist on her cheeks, her stomach feeling better by the second. It rolls again, but this time in healthy hunger.

She opens her eyes to stare at the familiar waves. They aren't big and menacing and white-capped like the storm's minions. Now the deep-blue waves sparkle and flash with the sunlight as they roll up and down in a much more friendly way. Sunglasses haven't been invented yet, but despite her squints, Isabella doesn't seem to mind the bright light. After being stuck below for so many days in the dim light, it is taking her eyes some time to adjust to the brightness. I can feel how much she loves it. Her excitement for this journey is renewed, and she allows herself to daydream about her mother's gift, a certain dark-haired gentleman, and what the new world might be like.

I say nothing. The stirrings of first love are intoxicating. Even though the new world is home sweet home for me, her life will be vastly different. After all, there are almost two centuries between us.

I am convinced now more than ever that Isabella needs me. I don't know how Andrew picked Isabella and Nathan for us to walk together, but Isabella needs a guardian. Her memories of the past few days in contrast to how she feels now—with me here to help her—proves it.

first is not always best

I nearly stumble as I step back into Lucy, who is walking down a street. Expecting to crumble in pain as I shift my weight to my right foot, I hesitate, causing Lucy to misstep, but she recovers quickly.

"Hello, Emily," she says. "Everything all right?"

Um...yeah. I move to touch a hand to my head, but she resists and keeps control.

"Were you shoved again?" Her tone is light and happy. She's amused that I'm here.

No. Isabella's injured her foot. I guess I got the two of you confused. She couldn't be walking around like this.

"Do you ever wonder why you walk the people you walk?" she asks, truly curious and carefree. I suppose it's easy to do that when you're healthy and happy and in absolutely no danger.

Sometimes, I say, allowing Lucy's mood to fill me and erase my fury. Being with her—without the pain of the broken ankle—is better than morphine. *I wondered for a long time why I was with you, and why so often.*

"But it was for the fire, correct?"

That might be the reason, I say. But I often wonder why I keep coming. It probably has something to do with wearing the ring and choosing to come back. Maybe.

"How did Isabella get hurt?" she asks, slowing her steps.

That one question sends shooting threads of anger coursing through me as potent as Isabella's pain. Lucy stops in her tracks, clearly feeling the whiplash of my emotion. She doesn't move another step as she waits for my response.

Remember how I was shoved out before? When I arrived the day you were being fitted for your dress?

She nods internally.

It was during that storm, I say. *After Andrew pushed me out, Isabella slipped and fell down the stairs leading below deck. They suspect she has a broken ankle, but who knows? It might be broken. She could be crippled.*

Lucy winces.

Exactly, I say.

"And you are angry because Isabella was hurt?" she asks, guessing at the cause of my strong emotion.

I'm angry because I wasn't there for her when it happened. Or afterwards, when she was sick. Because he *pushed me out.*

"She dealt with her injury alone?" Lucy says half-dazed. I see glimpses of her memory of the fire.

Nathan and Andrew were there, but yes she was alone. And I could have helped her.

"Did you talk to him? Was Andrew there just now with Nathan?"

I don't know. I didn't see him.

"Do you want to speak to him now?" she asks. "I believe he is back at Harker Manor although I have not yet seen him."

No! I practically shout in her head. *I'm too...*

"Angry? Upset?" she guesses.

That and a lot more. He's messing things up all over the place, I blurt out, thinking about how he almost ruined the relationship between Lucy and Charles. *He used to be...* I trail off. I'm almost surprised at my anger, but he should know how important it is to be responsible when we walk. After all, he scolded me for that very reason. About being responsible.

Were you planning to go inside? I ask when we pass by the shop I suspect was her destination. *Don't change your plans because of me.*

"I am not changing them. I am delaying them," she says. "I want to tell you a story."

I will her to look back once more. *Flowers?* I ask.

"Yes," she says, not even attempting to hold back the smile. "For the wedding."

I almost insist that she turn back and pick her flowers because a story can wait, but she begins before I can protest.

"You have never met my older sister, Vera, have you?" she asks.

I think I saw you write a letter to her once. But no, I have never met her.

"She married a man named Robert Brownell two years ago."

Did I hear affection in her tone when she said the name?

"Robert is charming and handsome and kind. He is the kind of man every eligible young woman falls in love with the instant they clap eyes on him. Or the instant they receive one of his elegant compliments."

Ah... I know the type, I say, my thoughts flitting to Duncan. He always seems to have at least a dozen girls crushing on him. Fortunately I'd been spared their claws when I was Duncan's girlfriend. Or perhaps I just don't remember the catty-girl encounters. There are some benefits to not remembering all the details of my alternate past.

"I wasn't immune to his charms either," she says, surprising me. I hadn't caught her meaning or the wistfulness in her tone until now.

You liked him?

"Emily, he was the type of person who made you feel like you were the only person who mattered in the whole world. How can you blame me for falling in love with him?"

You fell in love with him? It was hard for me to imagine Lucy ever loving anyone but Charles.

"Well, I thought I did." She sighs. "But he had eyes only for my sister. I did not see it at first, but Vera was his entire world from the moment we were introduced to him.

"When they became engaged, I was devastated. I vowed to never love another. And the fact that he had chosen my *sister* was even worse because I would still be forced to see him."

But then you met Charles, I prompt.

She laughs. "I got over Robert quickly," she says. "I was young, and it was the affection of a young girl. Nothing like true love. Nothing like what I feel for Charles."

Lucy pauses for a time, lost in thoughts I can't decipher. Feelings and emotions and images of Charles flit through her mind, but also images of an older version of Lucy dressed in a wedding gown next to a sandy-haired Ken-doll-looking man. Probably Vera and Robert.

So, why did you want to tell me that story? I ask when she doesn't volunteer the information.

She hesitates. She is worried about my reaction to whatever she is shielding from me.

"I told you that story because I believe that a person's first love isn't always the best one."

You mean Andrew and me. I know that's what she means because her thoughts focus on us the instant the words leave her mouth. With it are reasons why it won't work between us. Andrew's overstepping things in his present time and in walking memories with others. His secrets. Our completely different worlds and backgrounds. And the elephant in the room, our biggest obstacle—our being born a hundred years apart.

The sooner I get over Andrew, the better. Our relationship was doomed to nothing but heartbreak the instant it began.

But of course I already knew that.

mutual feelings

"They've pulled together a violinist and a cellist! It's really going to happen," Rachel says twirling in front of me, letting her skirts flare out. She stumbles with the dip of the ship, but catches herself.

"Careful, Rachel," Mama says next to me/Isabella. She gives me a sidelong glance. "I'd hate for you to be injured too."

"She's excited, Mama," Isabella says. "Less than three days until we reach the new world and a dance to celebrate tonight? Everyone is excited."

"Excitement is no reason to disregard safety," Mama says.

"Are you excited, Izzy?" Rachel asks hesitantly, still standing, but planting her feet to hold her balance. The wind picks up tangles of her brown hair escaped from her braid.

"Absolutely, Ray." Isabella smiles wide at her to prove it. "I plan to stake out the best seat to watch." She winks at her.

Rachel claps once, then leans over to kiss her sister on the cheek before bounding off to find their father, who promised a dance lesson.

Isabella's smile falls as her sister leaves. I try to push it back up, but fail.

"Everything alright, Izzy?" Mama asks, concern pulling her eyebrows together. "Are you feeling ill?"

"No, no," Isabella assures her, but I wince at the pain in my ankle that is constant. "My foot is merely tender."

That's an understatement, I think, but Isabella doesn't answer my thoughts.

"Well... Papa has been talking to the other passengers, inquiring about a doctor we might see when we land."

"Did he get any recommendations?" I ask when Isabella suddenly seems tongue-tied.

"There's one in New York who sounds promising," Mama says.

Dark curls in my peripheral explain the sudden speed of Isabella's heart and her loss for words just now. She hears his voice behind us first—my ears are trained for another one so I don't catch it as quickly.

"Hello, Mrs. Broadbent." He nods his hat at Mama, who is halfway out of her chair.

"Mr. Sloan," she replies cordially and with a hint of a smile. "I need to find Mr. Broadbent. Would you mind sitting with Isabella for a while?"

"I would be happy to." Nathan's smile is wide. He waits until Mama has left before taking her seat.

Isabella is beaming inside. I have other feelings about him being here and hope for once that Andrew is *not* with Nathan. Either way, I plan to hang back and act like I'm not here anyway.

A strong breeze lifts Isabella's hair, whipping it across my face.

"Do you think the worst of it is over?" Nathan asks.

"The worst?"

"I suppose I merely wonder why we still come," he says. "The storm is passed."

My pulse quickens. The seemingly cryptic speech tells me Andrew is with him.

"Her foot is still broken," I point out, trying to keep my tone normal. I am still angry at him for pushing me out. But since my attitude is at odds with Isabella's toward Nathan, we are in an internal tug-o-war. She wants to bat her eyes at him and hang on to his every word.

If he weren't wearing Nathan's face, I might take a swing.

"Emily." He whispers, grasping Isabella's fingers and closing his eyes.

I jerk her hand away.

"You are angry at me for pushing you out."

"She broke her ankle!" I nearly shout, but catch myself.

He leans closer and lowers his voice. "You were being irresponsible."

"That's not the point." I grit my teeth, holding myself back from lashing out. "She needed me, and you pushed me out."

"She made it to safety." His tone turns smooth and condescending.

"You call this *making it to safety?*" I scoff. "She may never walk again."

He grasps my fingers again. I pull back, but he tightens his grip so they are trapped. "Isabella did not die. Because of me."

"Because of Nathan."

"Because of Andrew." The change in his voice shocks me. Nathan is talking to me. He took back control from Andrew and is talking to me.

I am speechless. How much does he know?

"Emily, is it?" Nathan says. "I was frozen where I stood. If it hadn't been for Andrew, here"—he gestures at himself—"we both would have been swept overboard." Nathan releases Andrew's grip.

I take back my hand and fold my arms over my chest. "You still pushed me out." I feel the venom of my anger seep out of Isabella's broken ankle, dripping all over the deck.

"I thought I was going to lose you." It's Andrew. He peels my hand away to take it again. This time I willingly let him.

"You know that isn't—"

"You understand my meaning," he cuts me off.

"You would lose me if something happened to Isabella because you are too busy in your waking life with Margaret—your fiancé—to visit Lucy and talk to me there." I did not mean for it to come out. I did not realize how much hearing Charles recount the letter Andrew sent him would affect me. I knew he was spending time with Margaret. It just felt more real when Charles gushed about his cousin's happiness with someone who wasn't... me.

Nathan's eyebrows and mouth furrow in confusion.

"Lucy told me to stay away. *You* told me to stay away." He looks truly shocked. "It was written out in the letter." His mouth twists into a scorn. "Sincerely, *Emily.*"

"I did it for Lucy. I had no choice. But then, one week later, you send a letter to Charles and announce your happiness and plans to marry Margaret?"

"I did it for Charles."

"Yes, and it's for the best. For Lucy and Charles." I don't mask my bitter tone. "I just don't understand why you are still playing this whole charade." I motion at Isabella. "I mean other than being with Nathan for whatever he needs help with."

"He is falling in love with her, Emily."

My pulse quickens again. Whether because of Isabella or Emily, I'm not sure. Could be either, could be both.

"He plans to propose, I think." He fidgets with his hand for a moment, as if trying to twist his ring that isn't there. "Not right away, but his thoughts are leaning that direction."

"Should you be telling me this while I'm with her?" I ask, disapproval coloring my tone. I can tell Isabella doesn't seem to mind though.

He shrugs. "I do not see the error in it," he says. "If two people care for one another, why keep it a secret?"

"Like how you care for Margaret?" I force down the lump in my throat that rises. "Like how you love her and want to spend the rest of your life with her? This is ridiculous, Andrew. As soon as you wake up, you'll be with her again. You're getting *married*!

And you are only here with me because Nathan loves Isabella and plans to propose at some point. Thank you for making it crystal clear. It would have been nice to have a heads-up, but I was planning to say goodbye to you too."

His head snaps to look at me. "You have no idea what you are talking about."

"Don't I?" I take my hand back again.

"Are you saying goodbye?" he asks, pain etching into Nathan's features.

"We live a century apart," I say. "It's for the best. I tried to say it in a letter, but I suppose in person leaves less room for misinterpretation."

"No need to panic," a deckhand says in a thick Irish accent, coming up behind us. "But a storm's a-brewin'. Need to get the miss below to safety."

"Is it another bad one?" Andrew or Nathan asks.

"Hard to tell, gent. Just following orders."

Nathan/Andrew nods and stands immediately.

I hold my arms up to be carried below, thinking only of Isabella. If it were me with the broken foot, I'd crawl before letting Andrew touch me. Even as he holds me in his arms, neither of us speak. I can't even stand to look at him. And I'm pretty sure the feeling's mutual.

CHAPTER 23

feeding the sea gods

"Not again. Not again," Rachel repeats as tears trail down her cheeks. She's shaking and shivering despite Isabella's attempts to hold her tight. Rachel seems years younger now, and Isabella's mind wanders to memories of summer thunderstorms back home. Safe under their roof, the loud claps terrified them both. Rachel would rush into her sister's room and press herself against her under the covers. Isabella acted brave, but was always grateful when her sister came running. She didn't want to be alone either. She remembers how she softly sung hymns to calm both of their nerves.

"*Abide with me...*" Isabella begins to sing the familiar hymn as they huddle together on Isabella's bunk. Rachel seems to relax her tense muscles at the familiar song.

"*The darkness deepens...*" The violent rocking of the ship threatens to throw them from the bed across the room. It's all Isabella can do to keep herself and her sister seated. But with each shift of weight and bracing of different muscles, fresh pain courses through her broken foot.

Sway left. Lean right with her left hand to brace them. Fall right. Lean left.

"*When other helpers fail and comforts flee...*"

The mangled foot slides out instinctively against the wood to keep Isabella from crashing out of the bunk. Her voice cracks as she cries out in pain, and with it the fleeting peace flees with the absence of the music.

Now Rachel must be the strong one as she tightly holds Isabella, who quietly whimpers into her shoulder.

A writhing, creeping darkness enters Isabella's heel and up her leg until it encases her heart with spindly tethers. It's tentative and prodding, inquiring whether she'll let it stay.

She is sinking.

"*Abide with me...*" I sing with her lips. Paralyzed by her fear and her pain, all I can do is sit and watch and experience this hopeless moment with Isabella.

As the darkness takes over, and Isabella relinquishes herself to it, I try to shove it away. But its black web is sticky and strong—too strong for me to break. I try to keep it at bay as I continue to sing the verse.

"*Help of the helpless, oh, abide with me!*" I sing and let the words hang in the air. I recognize the hymn from church. From the one place where all of my memory dream troubles vanish completely. The notes are comforting. The verses are comforting. But I don't have it memorized, so I cannot continue.

The bunk room is attacked by deckhands and passengers with hair plastered to cheekbones and foreheads, hats pouring streams of water off faces and throats and coats, dripping into puddles onto the floor. The men begin hauling trunks and barrels back to where they've come from.

I see Nathan's black curls amongst the crowd. His hat is missing, his coat matches the others. He scoots, then hefts a large trunk next to Isabella's bunk. With the help of one of the crewmen, they rock their heels and anchor their toes against beds and posts. Nathan gives us a withered look before they haul it quickly up the stairs. Before the next wave can throw them back down.

"What's going on?" Rachel whispers when most of the men have left the now cleared room.

"I do not know," Isabella says. Her curiosity overpowers the darkness and pain for a small moment.

Papa slides down the stairs and stalks firmly and purposefully toward us.

"What are you doing, Papa?" Isabella whispers when he mournfully drags a trunk. One of theirs.

He pauses only a moment, "The storm is bad," he says. "The captain thinks we'll perish in the sea if we do not lighten the ship. All nonessentials are being tossed to save us."

Isabella's heart reaches out for the web to finally conquer it. *Nonessentials.* Isabella doesn't exactly think the words so much as feel them. The thought comes almost simultaneously—*The china is nonessential.*

"Papa, that trunk is not nonessential," Isabella blurts out.

Papa pauses to glance at her. "We can purchase new pots and pans when we arrive in America."

"What does he mean, Izzy?" Rachel asks after their father has taken the trunk of cookware to throw to the sea gods.

"They are throwing everything but the food overboard."

"Mama's china?" Rachel asks, tears forming along her tiny lashes.

Isabella nods and scoots to the edge of the bed.

"What are you doing?" Rachel hisses, holding her sister's arm in a vice-like grip.

"Come on, let's save a few pieces before they toss it." Isabella steps down, trying to balance on her good foot, but the unsteadiness of the floorboards causes her to rock back and crumble when the shattered limb hits the ground. Stars flood her vision as the pain intensifies and everything around her becomes a blur. Someone scoops her up and puts her safely back in bed.

Rachel sobs beside her, rocking back and forth with tears streaming down her face.

When Isabella's vision finally clears, we both scan the room for the trunk with the precious cargo. "It is gone," she manages to whisper. The trunk filled with not only Mama's china, but also

Isabella's and Rachel's china saved for their future lives in the new world. Their tiny piece of home dashed across the waves.

"Christmas dinner," Rachel whispers as she weeps softly. She lies down and stares at the wall as the tears continue to flow.

Isabella nods as the web tightens.

Suddenly my heart speeds in panic. Isabella's feelings and actions have preventing me from doing much. And there isn't much a dream-walker can do stuck on a boat in the middle of a hurricane anyway. But when the impression enters Isabella's thoughts that she'd rather join the dishes, I am forced to do something.

Think of Nathan, I urge, unsure whether she'll even hear me.

Why bother? He's heading to New York, she says to me, although I suspect she believes she's speaking with her subconscious.

That plan could change, I argue. *It's not set in stone.*

He's not going to follow me.

Maybe he will. Maybe his plans are flexible. I wonder if she heard when Andrew mentioned Nathan plans to propose.

She shakes her head, probably wondering how her subconscious got so out of her control.

Aren't you going to New York to see a doctor about your foot first anyway? You can be together in New York for a little while. I'm sure a wedding is in the future for you two.

Who would want to marry a cripple?

it will be over soon

ho would want to marry a cripple?

Isabella's darkness squeezes tighter. I recognize it as severe depression. But there is something else behind it, something sinister. It is trying to push me out. It wants her to wallow, to embrace the darkness. I plant myself and try to resist. I can't leave her. Not now.

The feeling is jarring. I've never been attacked like this before. I thought I knew how it felt to be pushed out. But this is nothing like what Andrew does. This is so, so, so much worse. I don't know how much longer I can resist, but the thought of waking up in the twenty-first century before this crisis ends is scaring the crap out of me.

Isabella pushes herself up from the bed again and crumbles to the floor.

Rachel must have fallen asleep at some point—surprising myself and Isabella. The mere possibility, let alone reality, of sleeping through such a violent storm seems unreal. Isabella chalks it up to the exhaustion. Rachel has always been able to sleep in the strangest of places.

Isabella begins crawling across the floor toward the slick stairs that lead above. *What is she doing?* I wonder to myself. Her broken leg drags behind, her mind so focused on her forward movement that she seems to have all but forgotten about the pain. *How is that possible?*

But then the darkness digs in further until I catch the edge. I feel that she does not intend to throw herself overboard. That comforts me slightly until her true purpose reveals itself. She intends to go toward the danger and hope the ocean does it for her.

No. No, no, no, no. *Isabella!* I focus on taking control of her hands to stop. *Isabella, you can get through this!* I am still concerned about being shoved out, but I can't watch while she crawls to her imminent death and do nothing. Her hands continue to move despite my attempts. *Isabella, I'm here. My name is Emily, I have come from the future to be here with you. To help you!* Ugh, why do I have to sound so stupid! It doesn't feel right to say it that way in such a rush. If my thoughts started speaking to me that way, even *I* would think I had gone crazy.

Even with everything I know.

I don't know what else to do. I desperately wait for an idea, any idea, to pop in my head. *You can have a life after this,* I stammer. *You heard yourself, the journey is almost over. You'll see a doctor about your foot. Nathan loves you.*

Isabella shakes her head, trying to knock my thoughts out. How she manages to climb the stairs and ignore the pain is beyond me. Her determination paralyzes me. It's similar to Carly, yet different. Her head *feels* different. Carly was also determined, but I was able to take over and save her. Isabella is clenching her control as if her life depends on it, even as she wishes to toss it overboard.

Maybe I'm the problem, maybe I'm not strong enough to take over. Maybe it isn't Isabella who's changed or who is different, but me.

She shares her darkness. She passes it to me like she's sharing a bag of chips. Cool and calm and friendly darkness. I try to remind myself that I will be okay if she dies. It's the argument I had with

Andrew not long ago. So if this is what she wants I should let her have it. Right?

She slinks along the deck, hoping to remain invisible to the scrambling men as the sheeting rain and wind drench her hair and dress. I brace her against the cold and help her ignore the throbbing and shooting pain from the freezing water and her wrecked ankle so she can focus on moving her body to the edge—where the waves are big and inviting and ready to scoop us away.

It'll be over soon, I whisper to her silently between our thoughts. It's more like a feeling than actual words. Everything feels like feelings now—but the darkness takes that from us too.

I should do something. Something inside me says I should do something, but that part of me is barely a whisper now. No, less than a whisper. Just a vibration of thought. It tells me I should not let Isabella die. She might have a great life ahead of her. But I don't know. I never looked for her grave. I never checked to see if she made it to America or not. I never did that for her. I have failed her.

"Isabella!" A man with dark hair and muddled green eyes rushes to our side. He looks at us, holding our head so he can speak directly to us and shouts to keeps our eyes from closing the curtain though the show is clearly over.

"Nathan," I croak. She finally lets me hold the strings. "You should go back below." Yes, we care about his safety. He should survive.

"What is happening?" he asks, his voice high and strange. "Why aren't you down below?"

Just close them, Isabella says to me, giving me the okay to shut out the world. And I want to. I am so tired. So tired of walking with others and dealing with the hardships and trauma that have nothing to do with my real life. Why should I have to endure this? I want it to end. All of it.

"Emily," his voice growls low to match his eyebrows. "What is going on?"

I stare at him blankly. "Her name is Isabella," I correct him.

"Emily," he says again, his eyes flitting across our face right as lightning flashes. The green iris sparks the same color against the gray backdrop as certain familiar flecks shimmer against gray-blue eyes.

"Duncan?" No, that isn't right. "Andrew?" Andrew has *amber* flecks against *chestnut* eyes. Andrew has chestnut-colored eyes.

At the sound of his name, my face is immediately pressed against the soggy, cold, coat Nathan wears. His hand firmly holding Isabella's head, he rocks back for an instant, and then drags us quickly behind some heavy crates, far away from the ocean's tantrum.

He pushes me back to look into my face again. "Emily?"

"It's me, Andrew," I say, shame filling me for allowing Isabella's darkness to overpower me so much. Had I really been enabling her to kill herself? Had I really wanted to go with her and never wake up? My shoulders shake in a shudder not entirely because of the cold.

He looks at me, waiting for an explanation.

"I lost control," I say, the regret washing over me heavy like the waves Isabella wanted to be swallowed into. "She's struggling."

I still myself to evaluate her feelings now. Being held in Nathan's arms dulls the pain better than the darkness did. It's louder and more at the surface, but the comfort she feels being here, close to him, being touched by him, makes it... bearable.

Andrew or Nathan seems to sense this, "Isabella," he says, boring his eyes into mine—ours. "I've talked to your father. I'm going to join your church. Not because of you. My initial interest was to be closer to you, but now I want to join for me." He shakes his head. "But that's not the point. The point is that I want to marry you, Isabella."

"What—?"

"I do not care that you are injured," he interrupts. "The accident was my fault. Even if you never walk again, my feelings will not change."

Her heart blooms beneath her soaked clothing and skin.

He lets out a nervous laugh. "I was not going to declare myself like this, in the middle of a tempest where we very well might be dashed into the sea despite our efforts to remain afloat. I had intended to take things slower." Nathan's eyes grow serious again. "But you have to know, my life is brighter now that you're in it. Even in this hell-sent storm." He waves a hand at the angry skies. "Please do not take that away from me."

She blinks several times to see him clearly through the rain and searches his face to see the truth in it. We both see it. It's there.

Before he leans in to kiss her, I see a flash of a smirk I know all too well. I almost protest, but for her I don't.

Her grin takes over. I feel the absence of the darkness now, almost like it was never there to begin with. Like it never even existed within her.

I am relieved.

"Better?" Andrew asks me as he helps us back below to safety.

"I think she'll be okay," I say. "I assume Nathan meant what he said?"

He nods. "That look in her face terrified him."

"Me too," I say, omitting that my own thoughts most likely contributed to it. We both pause. Isabella wants to curl up next to her sister. She is so exhausted. "She wants to sleep," I say, "so I'll probably go soon. I suppose Nathan can stay, but I doubt either of them needs us for a while."

Andrew nods and smiles. "See you on the other side?" he winks and the recent argument springs to the front of my mind.

I frown and shake my head. "You don't have to pretend, Andrew. Go and see your Margaret."

insanity

"I need to speak with her now!" Andrew's voice bellows outside the garden.

Lucy holds still. We are both a little stunned to hear his voice. It has been a while since she has spoken to him. So it has been a while since I have heard his actual voice.

"What is going on?" she whispers to me, her fingers gripping the pruning shears a little tighter, causing an unpleasant tightness in the skin of her still-damaged fingers. Fortunately she had set the clipped roses on the bench near her knees, saving the fingers on her other hand from the thorns.

I just got here, I say, like it's an answer.

"Did you come directly from Isabella?" she asks.

That seems to be the latest trend, I say, like that's an answer too.

She lets out an irritated sigh, then moves to clip another blossom. "I thought you two were working things out *elsewhere.*" Clip.

I shrug her shoulders as she lays the flower next to its siblings. *I might have mentioned that he should go and be happy with Margaret.*

"And what made you think *that* was a good idea?" Clip.

"Lucy," Andrew rounds the hedge near us and stalks purposefully in a nonfriendly way to confront us. He gives us a few feet, thankfully, perhaps finally realizing that proximity to Lucy has caused trouble on more than one occasion.

I want to applaud Lucy, who doesn't even flinch or stop clipping her flowers.

"What do you want, Andrew?" she says to the roses, her tone equally nonfriendly. I want to applaud her again for not falling into her gracious, well-mannered behavior.

Clip.

He paces. Lucy still doesn't turn to look at him. "It's Emily."

My heart does a little flip. Lucy keeps her hand still. Clip. No fingers are lost.

"She persistently tells me to go and be happy with Margaret," he continues, and I realize that he doesn't know that I am present.

That makes Lucy stop, then pivot until she is facing him, and points at him with her sheers. "You are *engaged* to my friend, Andrew Harker." The fire in her tone sends shivers through me. "You are engaged to *Margaret*. This whole *Emily* situation is complicated," she says, shaking the garden tool at Andrew with each word. "Believe me, I know." She gently taps the pointed metal to her temple—directly at me. "I have stood by and have been compassionate toward your feelings up to this point, but this. Must. Stop." She clips the words as deliberately as she does her roses.

Andrew's jaw drops a fraction.

"She said goodbye, Andrew," Lucy takes advantage of his speechlessness and continues her attack. "My hand might have written that note, but *she's* the one who wrote it."

"I thought—"

"You may have found a way for you to be with her without tramping all over my relationship with Charles, but that doesn't change the fact that you are not meant to be together."

I feel sick. She was kinder when she had this conversation with me, but I feel the truth of it even as the blood within Lucy's veins rushes faster. She's right. And that reality, the reality she's pounding into Andrew at this very moment, aches as much as it did when I first came to the conclusion myself.

"Lucy?" It's Charles. Her eyes race to his face as he stands like a Roman statue near the hedge.

How much did he hear? Lucy's panicked thoughts shout at me. I want to tell her that we share the same eyes when we're together. I didn't notice him because she didn't notice him.

Charles's face is strange. For once the proximity between Lucy and Andrew isn't suggestive of anything untoward going on, and the stern tones certainly wouldn't have implied that the words between them were laced with forbidden sweet nothings. But Charles's mouth and eyebrows frown together and his posture is tight and stiff and wary.

He heard enough. I say as Lucy remains frozen and speechless at being caught speaking so strangely.

"Andrew?" Charles finally moves to look at his cousin.

Andrew, amazingly, hasn't changed his expression at all and turns to him.

"What is my beloved talking about?"

"You might as well know."

"No!" Lucy attempts to throw herself at Andrew to gouge out his eyes—the sudden impulse to violence surprises me—but for once I'm quicker and stop her in her tracks. Slamming her mouth shut after the outburst and folding her body on the bench next to her cut flowers, I lace her fingers together to keep them still in her lap. With effort, I manage to lower her head down to look at the dirt beneath her feet.

Although I don't believe the words I'm about to say, Andrew's statement has made it too late, and I can't think of anything on the spot that would explain it away without another elaborate stitching of lies. "He should know, Andrew," I say. "If we are to be happily married," I add to hopefully assuage any doubt on Charles's part about Lucy's feelings and intent to marry him, "he should know."

Out of the corner of my eye I see the confused expression on

Charles's face. What it must have looked like from the outside: Lucy lunging, then quietly sitting like she was being controlled by someone with a remote.

I guess in a way that explanation is entirely accurate, except that I control things from the source, not a small device with buttons.

I lift her head again so we can better see the interaction between the men.

"Every night, I experience the memories of other people who have died," Andrew says, twisting the ring on his finger.

Charles folds his arms across his chest and studies Andrew without making a sound.

"Not only do I experience and remember them, but my mind is essentially *walking* with them as they go about their lives."

Charles's eyes narrow. He doesn't believe a word Andrew says. It's clearly written on his tight-lipped mouth.

Andrew doesn't seem to notice. "I help them cope with painful events, sometimes even their deaths, so they do not feel alone. Like a guardian angel."

Charles's arms loosen, but he's still clearly skeptical.

"And Lucy—"

"Ha!" Charles outbursts, his arms unfolding with fists clenching at his sides. "Am I to believe—?" he stalks toward his cousin.

Lucy bounds from the bench and firmly places both hands on his chest.

He wouldn't hit him, would he? Charles doesn't seem like one to spring to violence. But neither did Lucy. What has Andrew done to the pair of them? I can't help but smile with Lucy's lips.

"Emily!" Andrew hisses, seeing the slip and obviously knowing where it came from.

Charles backs away with his hands raised, away from Lucy's touch. His arms fall to the side again. "Who's Emily?" Charles asks Andrew.

"Darling," Lucy's voice softens dramatically, like melting

butter. "What Andrew is telling you... I know it sounds like a fantasy—"

He turns to us, his blue eyes a blazing flame. "You believe this nonsense?" Charles asks incredulously with a bitter laugh.

She nods slowly.

"And am I to believe that you prance around memories too while you sleep?"

"No!" Andrew and Lucy almost shout at the same time. I remain in the background, wishing I could hit the off button. I know better than either of them how ridiculous dream-walking sounds to outsiders. I've seen Charles's expression on my own parents' faces.

"No," Andrew repeats. "A girl from the future. Emily." I don't fail to hear the tenderness in his tone when he says my name. It floods me with warmth. "Emily walks with Lucy."

Charles stares at Lucy, looking for any sign of teasing or prank. She shrugs, smiles, and takes his hands. "*Emily* saved me from the fire."

Facepalm. Though she speaks the truth, I cringe at the words as they escape her lips. I *know* how crazy it sounds.

"I thought Andrew carried you out." He is clearly uncomfortable about that fact.

"He did," she glances at him, and I can't help but soften her features when he meets her gaze. I pray Charles doesn't notice, but I know that he is watching our every move. There's no way he missed it. Lucy looks back at her fiancé. "But I would not have survived without Emily's guidance here, in my mind." She taps her temple lightly with a finger.

"And I love her, Charles," Andrew says quickly. "You should find comfort in that."

Charles stares him down and the words *if looks could kill* enter my thoughts.

"It was never Lucy I fancied, but Emily, a kindred spirit."

Charles stalks away.

k.o

I have never been so happy to be back with Isabella on this hellish ship. Anything to get away from the replaying the painful, wincing, cringing, add-a-thousand-more-awkward-adjectives conversation between Andrew, Charles, and Lucy.

After Charles walked away, Lucy sent Andrew away and hid in her room for the remainder of the day. I couldn't tell who felt more awful after the exchange, but we suffered the aftermath together, holed up and sprawled across her bed. Angry tears from both of us soaked into her down pillows. She even skipped supper, complaining of a headache and went to sleep with a grumbling stomach to avoid any other humans.

I didn't blame her.

But now the sun blazes down on the deck, and the continent sprawls north and south as far as Isabella can see. With greens and browns, hills and trees and rocks and buildings are suddenly more beautiful to her than the expanse and wildness of the blue waves.

The journey by ship is over.

The little girl with curly hair is standing near Isabella's left elbow. It's the same girl who stood next to Isabella when they left England, waving goodbye to their old lives. Her father is also next to her, same as that day. It's the perfect bookend to the voyage.

Though it's only been two weeks, Isabella's body and soul has aged years in the crossing. Seeing the little girl and remembering how she felt that first day aboard, contrasting with how she feels now, is life-altering.

I watch the little girl from the corner of Isabella's eye. She is familiar somehow. And not just from the docks in England. A woman, clearly pregnant and probably due to deliver soon, joins the little girl and her father. She is obviously the little girl's mother. The man puts his arm around her, and she pulls the little girl into her side.

A warm hand grips Isabella's as they watch the green land consume the view. Nathan's hand. Nathan whom she intends to marry by the end of the week.

Happiness fills Isabella's core with the churning and excitement of new love. It directs my focus away from the strangely familiar family next to us. The pain of Isabella's foot is deep and intense at times, but her new happiness acts as a sort of morphine, dulling it and forcing it into the background. When I focus on it with her, the natural pain relief grows even stronger.

I don't want to give her false hope if the bones are truly broken or crushed, but part of me thinks it might only be a sprain. It might heal completely in a few weeks. The lessening of the pain certainly suggests it. But I allow her to believe it's because of Nathan.

"Well, that could have gone better," Andrew says, ruining the moment.

"Not here, Andrew," I say. Isabella wants to continue holding Nathan's hand, but I pull it away.

"Charles needed to know."

"Charles did *not* need to know," I argue. "He didn't believe you anyway."

"He should feel glad! Lucy never loved me, I never loved her. It was always you."

"Except he didn't believe you." I still can't believe he did it. "All he knows is that you love the girl he plans to marry, the person underneath those blond curls. Which to him is only Lucy."

"He will feel the truth in it. Once he thinks about it and sleeps on the information, he will believe it." Andrew turns his back to lean against the rail, looking back toward the ocean.

Our little argument drew some attention. The little girl's father looks over at Andrew sternly. And his eyes widen. Mine do too because if I didn't know better I could have sworn he looked exactly like...

But Andrew smooths Nathan's features quickly, and I wonder whether I saw the surprised expression at all.

"You should go," I say staring at the growing land. "You are spoiling this perfect moment for Isabella and Nathan after they have endured so much. I wonder why you and I are even here anymore."

"You sent me away. How else can we speak to one another?"

My eyes dart to him, him and that stupid, sneaky, knowing smile. "Look, I get that these two needed us," I say. "The storm, Isabella's injury. But why are you still here? Why are we still here?"

He shrugs and nods triumphantly, like it's no big deal to intrude on people's lives, like it's no big deal to come and go as he pleases to live inside someone else's head.

I suppose I'm a hypocrite for wanting to be with Lucy so often, but now I see the *wrongness* of it. It's one thing for us to intrude when we are thrust in, when our hosts need us. But to interfere just for this? Just so he can talk to me?

A bubbling, churning, furious mass of anger builds beneath Isabella's ribcage. She feels it too, and I have to hold her back from screaming her rage at poor Nathan even as I want to do the same to Andrew.

Shaking my head and shivering with the coiled emotion beneath my skin, I ball my fists until Isabella's knuckles turn white.

She doesn't need me anymore, she has her happy ending. And Nathan doesn't need Andrew either.

Internally winding up as if to strike Nathan's poor large nose and snap his dark curls back, I steel myself and shove him palm up, square in the chest instead. Isabella's strength is only enough to push him a half step back, leaving him very unharmed. But when his green eyes flit innocently and confused, searching Isabella's, the effect is clear.

I did it.

I pushed Andrew out.

"Is everything alright, miss?" the little girl's father asks, positioning himself between Isabella and Nathan.

"Fine," I say genuinely. It's clear that Andrew is gone and the argument between us finitely over. "We are fine now, and everything is perfect." I hold my hand out for Nathan to take, and he does. Then I step back and allow Isabella to take over, fully intending to leave very soon myself.

The man studies us both with a wary expression, but seeing Isabella's happiness play on her face, he steps away to rejoin his family.

Why does he look so familiar? I wonder, stalling. *Who are they?* I watch them converse quietly amongst themselves and notice that the little girl is clearly communicating with her parents with hand motions and body language, but she doesn't say a word.

And then it finally clicks. With nostalgia overpowering me, I finally fade out of Isabella's life with a smile.

unexpected quest

And then I slink again into Lucy's head, or something to that effect. I feel guilty for everything that has happened to her because of Andrew and me.

Again.

I'm feeling guilty *again.* For the same stupid reason.

My thoughts turn to my first moment with her. Waking up, happy and newly engaged to Charles. Her only cares in the world were what kind of sandwiches to serve for luncheon and which words to best describe the exquisite happiness of her engagement.

Here we are now, a thousand memories later. Now I'm not even sure if she's still engaged.

Is the wedding still on? I ask, hesitantly but instantly regret my phrasing. We are in the sitting room. Lucy is reading a book, which normally isn't shock worthy. But I expected her to be busily about another wedding task, so it comes as a shock. A dread-filled, *guilty* shock.

Lucy puts her book down to be polite or something. Though it's just her in the room—and well, me—and isn't necessary.

"I do not know." Her voice hitches. She closes the book firmly and sets it beside her. "Charles left town without saying goodbye. I knew he planned to go with his father before..." She trails off, but being a frequent visitor within the walls of Lucy's own flesh and blood, I catch the rest of her meaning.

Maybe he needs a chance to think.

"He should not need time to think!" she shouts. "This should not be happening." Lucy raises her hand like she's ready to rip her hair out—I don't blame her—but I stop her.

I'm sorry, I say. It's my fault. My fault and Andrew's. *I promise to make things right.* And then I'll figure out a way to leave forever, I want to add. But as usual, I chicken out. I'm still not ready to leave Lucy. What's wrong with me? I'm like some kind of ghost, a disembodied spirit haunting her, desperate to see her again—even though I know my presence pains her.

"Tell me about Isabella," Lucy says. "I cannot dwell on what is going on with Charles at the moment. It was the reason I was losing myself in a book. To not think. Please, distract me."

Sure. Um... they made it, I say. *To America, I mean.* Lucy doesn't comment so I continue. *It was kind of nice, actually. Helping someone. Don't get me wrong, I love being with you, it's not terrifying or sad—well, most of the time—and I can actually talk to you.*

"You do not talk to the others?" she is truly surprised.

No. Most of them don't even know I'm there. For a while, I didn't know I was there, I say. *Isabella might have suspected, but mostly she thinks I'm just part of her subconscious. Part of her own thoughts. Mostly.*

For a moment it feels like she is about to say something along the lines of feeling sorry for me, or that it must be lonely or sad to be watching and experiencing memories without the host knowing. But instead, Lucy says, "It is probably for the best. Some might think they are losing their mind if their thoughts gave themselves a name and personality."

You understand that I am a real person, right? I ask. *I'm not your brain tricking you. I'm real.*

"Mostly I know," she says using my word. "Mostly."

I don't want to dwell on the myriad of issues that her hesitation could cause—both for her and for me—so I move the subject back to Isabella.

Isabella was badly injured in that storm, I say. *I told you about that, didn't I?*

"You did."

I still don't know whether her ankle is broken or not, whether she will ever walk again. Then she also almost died in another terrible storm.

When Lucy doesn't respond I continue.

She survived both, and I feel like I truly became what my grandmother said my calling was.

"A guardian angel," Lucy says without emotion. "The same as you were for me in the fire."

Yes, I say quietly. *It felt good to be needed.*

I feel my unasked question slip into her mind. *Why am I still here when I'm not needed?*

She answers with an unanswered answer. *I don't know. But you're like a sister to me, so I haven't tried to stop it.*

Drake enters the room, and Lucy straightens.

"Mr. Andrew Harker is here to see you, Miss Lucy," he says.

I feel her lingering hurt and anger at the sound of his name. Her pulse quickens and she clenches her fists, but she remembers her manners. "Let him in."

Andrew bounds into the room, all hair and gray suit and desperate looking before Drake exits. He's practically dripping with impatience during the seconds it takes Drake to leave.

Lucy doesn't rise to greet him, but narrows her eyes. "She is present if that is the reason for your visit," she says. The *she* meaning me. Emily.

"What's with the hair?" I ask as my heart quickens its pace for a different reason than Lucy's. Never have I seen him in such dishevelment until now.

"I would tell you that I have not slept much, but that would be a lie." His laugh afterward is a little maniacal, and he twists the hat in his hand a little too roughly. "The truth is that I have been sleeping *too* much. And of my own volition."

Lucy's right eyebrow raises and she questions me, but immediately notes that I don't have a clue to his meaning either.

"But I came, knowing Charles was absent," he continues, rushing to sit next to us, "because I wanted to speak with Lucy."

She resists the urge to back away. Most likely for my sake.

"Should I leave?" I ask with Lucy's lips.

His eyes grow wide, looking a bit panicked. "Not yet," he says. He knows something, but doesn't voice it.

"Lucy," he says, reaching for her hand, but she shies away.

Her resentment toward him is thick and hangs in the air like a noxious gas between us. She'd surely order him out of the room if it weren't for my presence. Maybe that's why he asked me not to leave?

"Lucy, I want to assure you that everything will be made right. I am determined to fix things between you and Charles, and I have a plan that will certainly work." Andrew's confidence is strong. "Once I've implemented it, there will be no questioning of your feelings for Charles and Charles only. Any thoughts that I have even a fraction of your heart will be nonexistent."

Nonexistent? I don't like the sound of that.

Lucy narrows her eyes to match her mouth. She is skeptical. No, more than skeptical. She won't believe it until he proves it. And I don't blame her.

"Emily, my sister is here to see you," he says, his tone warming, but laced with worry.

"Your sister?" I ask. My first thoughts flit to Tessa, the only one of Andrew's sisters I had ever met.

The sister who Grandma Grace walked.

The sister who Grandma Grace died with.

He stands and exits the room without speaking, then enters a moment later with a small, pixie-faced girl who shares none of Andrew's features except the color of her hair. Her curls look like they want to break free of the pins holding them together.

Lucy and I stand to greet her.

"Lucy, let me introduce my sister, Rose," Andrew says.

Rose curtsies a little stiffly, her tiny lips pursed.

"Pleasure to meet you, Rose." Lucy curtsies back. I hold back to allow Lucy's curtsy to flow.

"Emily," the girl says, "I believe someone named Carly wishes to speak with you."

CHAPTER 28

bombshell dropped

"Carly?" I ask, hoping Emily will provide an explanation. But Emily's thoughts are a mix of jumbled images that clash and collide along with bright beams of light getting closer and closer. I lift my foot slightly as a sudden cramp in my toe hinders my ability to stay standing. Taking a step back, I sit again to hide my sudden discomfort. Another image—I flinch back, feeling as though I have been struck by a locomotive. That cannot be right...

The moment is gone as quickly and instantaneous as it came.

I stiffen my spine, the muscle memory from my finishing schooling automatic and a comforting mask to hide behind.

Sorry about that, Emily says without further explanation.

Andrew eyes me with a knowing look from the corner of his eye. Did he see what happened? I cannot dwell on it as my bubbling emotions rise. All of the complications in mine and Charles's relationship are his doing. I loathe his smug smile. That smug smile that pretends to love my friend, pretends to want to *marry* her, all while pining for the girl in my head. I only tolerate him for Emily's sake, because she is also a friend. But even so, I itch for him to leave my sight as soon as he arrives. Now is no different.

I banish the feeling quickly to keep Emily from hearing. Instead I focus back on the petite woman whose mouth is twisted in a sort of way that suggests she is having trouble forming words.

"Emily?" Rose finally asks, her petite facial features pinched in something that looks a lot like awe and disbelief.

Emily nods my head. "It's me," she says a little shakily. "How?" Emily is also at a loss for words. I hear several phrases that want to escape, bumbling and overlapping each other in Emily's thoughts. Part of me feels compelled to take over and speak for her as she has done for me a dozen times, but the strange way that Andrew referred to his sister as *Rose* and then *Carly* suggests that the latter is a contemporary of Emily's world and only along for the ride with Rose.

Rose clears her throat and looks at the vacant space next to me on the settee. Without being invited, she clumsily takes several steps until she sits beside me.

Don't judge. Emily prods softly when my eyebrow hitches. *We don't sit quite so proper in my time, but you've always managed to counteract my slouching.* Her thoughts suddenly align themselves, as if Rose's faux pas calmed her.

I want to ask what in the world a *slouching* is, but Rose/Carly's expression changes, and she looks ready to speak.

With a determined confidence she says, "So, this is where you have been hiding?"

"Huh?" Emily asks. "Hiding?"

Rose/Carly looks around my sitting room, as if scrutinizing the choice of wallpaper and the color of velvet covering the armchair in the corner. She even cranes her neck a bit to look at the spine of the book I was reading moments earlier, though I do not know if she would recognize the works of Miss Austen.

"I mean, I've experienced firsthand what you can do," Rose/Carly continues. "Since you saved my life and everything. But this is a lot to take in."

You saved her life? I ask silently.

Just as I saved yours, Emily retorts. *Well, Andrew did the actual saving—at least in the version you remember.*

The version... what do you mean?

Her thoughts betray a memory of falling alone onto the back lawn instead of being carried out by Andrew, and then an alternate memory all my own of the excruciating tightness and pain of learning that... Hannah died in the fire?

You lived through the fire twice? I ask. *How did I not know that, how is that even possible?*

How is any of this possible?

"If it weren't for you, I'd be just a smear on some backwoods train tracks," Rose/Carly continues.

Emily winces with my face. Clearly she hides another memory.

"And I guess I was or am in one reality." Rose/Carly's tone lowers and hitches with a specific sound reserved for tragedy.

"As I'm sure Andrew's explained to you, I am currently with Lucy," Emily offers. "I have walked Lucy many times over the past few months." Wordlessly she remembers something and adds, "In fact, I first came here *before* I was given the second chance to save you."

Rose/Carly nods with understanding. "Arianna doesn't reveal much about what you tell her, but I've heard the name." She looks at Andrew and seems to assess him in the same manner she did a moment before when she surveyed the room. "She mentioned him too," she hooks a thumb over her shoulder in a strange gesture to point at Andrew, though clearly he is listening as intently to every word as Emily and I are. She mouths something that I don't follow, but my cheeks flush with Emily's reaction and I feel her meaning. I sense that whatever she said wasn't entirely appropriate coming from his sister's lips. But then again, even though we currently share minds and hearts, my feelings about Andrew are vastly different from Emily's.

Andrew's irritating smile and tall stance indicates that

whether or not he caught the actual words of the exchange, he certainly felt the meaning behind them.

"I really shouldn't be wasting any more time," Rose/Carly says, her tone weighted.

"What do you mean?" Emily asks. "What's going on?"

Rose/Carly takes my hands and pulls them toward her until our eyes are level. "This is very serious, Emily," she says. "A lot of people are freaking out."

"What's wrong?" Emily says, but it's barely a whisper as my heart pumps double-time with nerves.

"Emily, you've been in a coma for two weeks."

CHAPTER 29

homesick

"A coma?" My thoughts spin. "How is that...what...?" I can't even form the words. Lucy has graciously stepped back during this conversation, though I know she's paying attention to every word.

"Your parents said you never woke up one morning," Carly says with a pair of stranger's lips. Lips that have the same shape, though fuller, than the pair that stand in the corner—also listening to every word. I feel his carefree air change to a tense, panicked one. He shifts from foot to foot and has stopped spinning his ring.

"What is she talking about, Emily?" he asks, his voice low and stretched tight like it's about ready to snap.

I look to him for... anything really. "Has this ever happened to you?" I ask, not answering his question—mostly because I don't exactly know the answer to his question. But then I shake my head. Of course it's never happened to him. His memory walking is a secret to *everyone*. He only recently told Charles. And I suspect if it had happened, they would've buried him by accident.

I shudder. If I lived in a different time, *I* could be buried in a pine box, slowly suffocating while I dreamt.

"No," Andrew says.

I look back to the face Carly wears, squinting my eyes to imagine her brilliant red hair hidden underneath Rose's dark curls. Both have the same wildness to it, which makes me smile faintly.

"You were still breathing, so you were taken to the hospital where you have been ever since," Carly continues. "The doctors can't find anything wrong with you."

I stare at the ornate rug beneath Lucy's tiny feet. It occurred to me at one point that I hadn't been *me* for a while. But now I rack my brain for the last memory of my own I *can* remember.

Do you remember me mentioning anything about my life recently? I ask Lucy. Even in thought, I can hear the shaky panic in my voice.

She is thinking hard too. *We've talked about Isabella mostly,* she says. *And Andrew,* she adds.

But nothing about my parents or my... or Duncan? No one?

No. Even before you did not speak much about your life in the future. Other than a feeling that you were unhappy with some things that were going on—but that was a long time ago.

"And you wouldn't know anything was amiss anyway," I say aloud. "I don't visit every day. Sometimes I skip ahead, even if I was with you the night before."

She doesn't have to comment for me to feel her agreement.

Andrew has been pacing for several minutes, but I've tried to ignore it to keep my own anxiety from rising quicker. Lucy's stomach churns with nausea.

"Andrew, please stop," I plead. "I'm feeling sick as it is." I pause, "Or rather, *Lucy* is feeling unwell because of me. Apparently I am safely tucked in a hospital bed somewhere, probably wearing one of those pinstriped gowns that don't cover everything, hooked up to beeping monitors and drips that feed me glucose. Meanwhile, my friends and family are standing by panicking and someone has set up an account at one of the credit unions for people to donate and help my parents pay for the ever-increasing medical bills." I grimace at the look of confirmation on Rose's face.

"So every time we were with Isabella and Nathan, you came back here?" Andrew asks, "Not home—not waking up in your time?" He runs a hand through his thick hair, amazingly disheveling it even more. Sometimes I wonder if he puts some sort of product to make his hair do that, though I'm not sure what they used—if anything—in 1902.

"I guess I didn't really think about it," I say, angry at myself and embarrassed that it hadn't occurred to me that I'd been with Lucy and Isabella over and over without once being alone in my thoughts, or speaking to Arianna or my parents in between. "But no, I haven't been home in a while."

"You said you got the ring back," Andrew says, "But did you put it on?"

"Would that have stopped this from happening?"

"I don't know. Are you wearing it?" he asks again.

"I don't remember."

"Is it that tiny flowery thing?" Carly asks, jumping in.

"Yes!" Andrew and I say together. I look at him suspiciously. I don't remember ever describing it to him.

"You weren't wearing it for a while. The doctors or nurses probably took it off," Carly says matter-of-factly. "But I think Duncan got a hold of it a few days ago and slipped it back on you."

"Duncan?" Andrew and I ask together. Andrew's tone is injected with a slight jealousy, possibly because of Carly's tone when she said his name. Like he and I are close. Which is true.

But I don't dwell on Andrew's... whatever. Instead, it warms me to hear that even though I essentially broke his heart, he still cares about me enough to see me in the hospital. My feelings war with all of the possible implications that are behind the reason for slipping the ring he gave me back on my finger. Even if the gesture could very well be the thing I need to break out of being trapped in these dreams.

"It's actually how I got the idea to look for you," Carly says. "Arianna refuses to talk much about your *dreams*. She thinks your *condition* caused your coma."

"She's not wrong," I say, both aching to see and talk to my friend again and fully aware of the scolding I am going to get from *everyone* once I wake up. Did *I* do this? Did I put myself in a coma? Just to spend more time with *Andrew*? What is wrong with me?

"She was crying in her room again when I came home for the weekend," Carly says. "I forced her to talk through what you've told her about the dreams. I felt like I owed it to you after saving my life."

"You don't owe me anything," I say, "Everyone's world is better with you in it."

Carly shakes Rose's head. "Anyway, after much persuasion, she broke down and mentioned that you claimed your grandmother was able to join you in dreams, so I asked her to snoop around to find out how to do it."

Lucy's eyes widen with my shock, "And she did it?" I ask.

"Not exactly."

"Oh." My hope deflates immediately.

"So I snooped around myself," Carly says. "They're your parents, not the FBI." She winks at me. "I just told your dad that Arianna needed some things from your room for school. It was easy."

I smile at the memory of me thinking the exact same thing when I needed to get into Duncan's room to search for the ring.

"I found some old journals stacked on your desk. Your Grandma Cole's journals?"

I nod. "After Grandma died, I asked if I could have them. My aunt wanted them for family history purposes, but she said I could borrow them."

Carly smiles. "Fortunately a picture of the ring your grandmother wore was sketched in detail on one of the pages." She raises one of Rose's eyebrows up into her hair. "I found the ring in the drawer next to your bed.

I smile sheepishly. "I didn't tell anyone I took it."

She waves a hand and says, "And that's how I got here. Now let's get you home."

I take a deep breath and give Andrew one last glance. Quietly I say to Lucy, *Tell him goodbye for me?*

You are not returning? she asks. She was not expecting that.

I really don't know. The future feels so uncertain right now. What's happened to me? Will I ever come back? *Just in case?*

After a pause she says, *I will tell him.* I can feel that she wants to say goodbye, that she'll miss me. But I know she wants to get her mind back to herself, and I can't blame her for it.

"So how do I get back?" I ask.

Rose's shoulders shrug. "I don't know," she says.

"I do," Andrew says reluctantly from the corner. His pacing stopped when I asked. He's stood still as a statue in silence until this moment. He walks toward me and reaches for my hands to pull me to Lucy's feet.

"You're going to push?" I whisper.

He nods, leans forward and brushes a whisper of a kiss across Lucy's lips. She shudders beneath her skin, but stays still and resists a shout or slap for my sake.

One last eye lock, then he pushes me out.

waking up

When my eyes opened, my lids weighted and my lashes glued together with tears and eye dust, the world was fuzzy and muddled and muted. The edges of everything blurred together in the dim room. My heart felt weighted too.

It was the feeling you get in your feet after walking off a particularly spinny and twirly roller coaster, one that lifts your stomach into your throat again and again. Like gravity's trying to squash you into the pavement.

It was a depressed feeling.

I was me again, and my head was filled with just... me. There was no irritated Lucy or confused Isabella. I was completely alone in my thoughts. And that reality was lonesome and depressing.

A huge part of me didn't want to be me. It was much easier hiding behind another face and solving all of *her* problems. I wasn't ready to face mine.

Immediately I began working out in my head how I could get back. I *had* to get back to Lucy. I couldn't leave her to deal with that mess with Charles. There's no way he believed us. What if he called off the wedding? What if he sent Lucy to an insane asylum?

I'd seen the documentaries; mental wards in the early 1900s were... unspeakable.

Even through my blurry vision, I could see a television up in the corner that was on, volume low. I couldn't tell which program or channel was playing, but its familiar glow was almost comforting. Even if I didn't want to be back in the twenty-first century, it was still home.

Maybe it was comforting because it looked like the kind of show my Dad would fall asleep to. A blossoming emotion began in the center of my chest and radiated out, the ache of missing my parents, my family. My friends.

I turned my head to see if Dad was indeed sitting next to me. If he'd held vigil by my side, taking turns with Mom while I gallivanted through the lives of Lucy and Isabella. The feeling of missing everyone soured with the realization of what had happened, what I'd done. I'd been trapped inside my dreams. For two weeks. And it was quite possibly my fault.

Someone sat next to me, but even with my poor eyesight, I could tell it wasn't Dad. He was taller, his shoulders were broader, and he wore what looked like a letter jacket.

"Duncan?" My hoarse voice cracked. Probably the result of not using my vocal chords for a couple of weeks.

He jerked, but merely shifted and said something I didn't understand before breathing heavily again.

I smiled. He was asleep.

Before I could even decide whether to say his name again or let him sleep, he sat bolt upright almost in a fight-or-flight reaction, then looked at me.

"Welcome to the waking world," I teased.

A blurry finger stuck out at me, but I couldn't make out the expression on his face. "You're one to talk," he said, his tone light. "It's about time."

"So I've heard," I said but immediately wished I could take it back. Clearly no one else was in the room to clue me in about being asleep for over two weeks. I learned it from Carly who wasn't here and had managed to seek me out in my dreams to let me know. Certainly all of that wouldn't make me sound like I was delusional at *all*. "I mean, I guess so," I said, covering my slip. "How long was I out?" I asked to hopefully keep up the ruse.

"Twelve days, I think," he said, his voice was calm. But I could hear a hint of excitement in his voice. "Can I get you anything before I announce that you've woken up?" I could hear the matching tease in his tone.

"My glasses?" I asked. Being so blind made me feel like *this* was the dream.

After fumbling through what were probably my things in a bag underneath a small table, I heard the click of my glasses case—*obviously they wouldn't be next to my bed when no one knew when or if I'd ever need them again*. I shuddered at the thought as Duncan pressed the familiar frames into my palm.

Slipping them on, everything focused. The edges of the furniture and walls became straight lines again and the abstract pink-and-purple painting on the wall became very pretty, yet very generic—purple and pink and blue spring flowers.

I looked at Duncan, gauging his expression and bracing myself for a lecture. Surely after being asleep for so long, he was going to royally chew me out. He knew about the dreams. I think he supported the dreams or at least me having them and not drugging myself to forget them at one point. But after *this?* I was pushing my luck, even I knew that.

Although I had been a good girl and taken the new medication? Hadn't I?

But his expression left me speechless. He stared at my hand that wore the Harker ring for a moment before looking at me. And though I could see relief in the creases of his forehead, when one corner of his lips turned up in a sort-of smile, all I saw was...*hello*.

I cocked my head to the side.

If I weren't sitting in a hospital bed wearing... (Okay, now I was suddenly aware of wearing the thing that doesn't cover everything well. I pulled the blanket around my waist a little higher and tighter.)

If I didn't hear the beeping of the monitors or feel the pull of tubes injected into my skin... (Which hurt a little to be honest. I could feel bruises there.)

If not for the sterile smell and dry taste in my mouth, and everything else that screamed at my senses that I was in a hospital bed... by his expression Duncan might as well be picking me up from the airport after a twelve-day long European academic trip. All while wearing that pretentious letterman jacket that wasn't pretentious when he wore it.

"Thanks," I managed to squeak out in my confusion, but my eyes immediately fell to the ring on my finger. A thousand things I could say to him scrolled through my thoughts, and again I wished Lucy were in there with me to take over or at least help me sort them out for the best one to say. "Did you put this back on my finger?" I asked, then instantly wanted to shove the entire IV cord into my mouth. After all, I had technically stolen it from him.

Duncan's face split into a grin. The type of grin that warmed my insides and reminded me why I liked him. He was a good friend. "Well, you did *steal* it from my room," he said, then laughed. "I figured you might as well wear it if you like it that much."

The different type of warmth in my cheeks announced my embarrassment, but I smiled through it because he laughed harder. I almost started to apologize, but I stopped myself. I didn't regret taking it. Somehow, coincidentally, my taking it had helped me wake up.

"I would have given it back if you'd asked," he said, his voice and eyes lowered.

It didn't seem right, pining after a guy in my dreams and being with Duncan, who didn't hold my heart the same way. It wasn't fair to Duncan. And that is why I returned the ring in the first place. But here, now, in this darkened room with the horrible light, I saw something in him that I'd been blind to with my Andrew-filter on.

I wanted to hold my hand palm up, inviting him to take it, I wanted to patch things up or hint that perhaps, someday things could go back to the way they were between us. But I didn't. Instead I said, "I was afraid if I asked, you'd think it meant something it didn't." For the second time since I'd woken up, I wanted to shove something into my mouth. Like a shoe. Because it was not what I meant. It's not what I felt. But I was too stubborn to take it back, especially after seeing the look on his face after the words flew from my mouth. I couldn't tell if the words had hurt or not because his expression didn't change. His mouth didn't twitch into a frown, and he didn't meet my eyes again.

Instead he stood. "I'd better get the nurse," he said, walking toward the door. "I'll call your parents too."

He didn't come back.

dreaded questions, unhappy answers

The doctors wouldn't let me go home right away. Something about being asleep for twelve days required tests and scans and waiting.

Dr. Shew found me walking the halls a couple of days later. Actually, I was sitting in the orthopedic surgical waiting room next to a large fish tank when she found me. My legs were understandably weak from lack of use, so I walked as often as they'd let me. But it was frustrating that I couldn't go far without the need to rest. I was determined to build up my endurance again.

Her bun was perfectly smoothed and centered on her head, and her blue pantsuit pressed and tailored. I stiffened when she walked in. Her look was intimidating, but I relaxed when I saw the creases around her eyes and mouth when she smiled. She held no clipboard or file, which relaxed me even more. She wasn't there to shrink me. At least it didn't look like she was there to shrink me.

"Had enough of your room?" she asked, feeling my mood.

"I needed to walk," I said, "but then these fish caught my eye, and I couldn't resist." I hooked a thumb at the fish tank, though admittedly I hadn't been watching them and I still wasn't watching them.

"You'll regain your strength," she assured me. "Twelve days isn't twelve months. Your muscles didn't have time to atrophy too severely, and you're young. You'll be walking to school and around the cemetery in no time."

I almost smiled at how well she knew me but quickly remembered that it was her job to know me. The fuzzy feeling dissipated.

She asked me the dreaded question and I answered with the unhappy answer. I didn't try to hide my deflated tone.

Her mouth twitched like she was pleased and wanted to smile, but hearing my disappointment, she graciously pushed it down.

"Your scans from the past two nights were normal," she said, "which is good news because it means you get to go home today. Right now if you'd like."

I nodded and stood, my mood slightly improved. After being in the hospital for the past three days—ok, more than that, but that was all I remembered—I was more than ready to go home. We walked back to my room in a silence I didn't know how to fill.

I'd already rehashed everything that had happened while I was asleep. Dr. Shew had come the day I woke up to evaluate my dreams while they were still fresh in my mind. She had insisted that I tell her every detail I could remember.

Fortunately everything about Isabella was clear, but remembering my Lucy dreams was harder. I'd walked her so often before the long sleep that her memories became familiar and normal. I remembered the wedding planning, but it was like trying to recap the last twelve days of a person's life when nothing particularly exciting had happened.

The whole ordeal was mentally exhausting, and I had nothing else to add.

"Dr. Shew says you can go to school Monday if you're feeling up for it," Mom said, a little too peppy as I changed into my clothes—*my clothes* not the starchy doesn't-cover-everything hospital gown.

I didn't answer.

"Of course you can stay home a few extra days, if you're not feeling up for it," she amended, misinterpreting my silence.

"Thanks, Mom," I said, tying my shoes while she signed the last of the discharge papers.

We made our way to the parking garage across the street, stepping out into the blizzard—wow, yeah blizzard—while Mom prattled on about everyone who had cared enough to come visit me while I was in my comatose state. But my thoughts weren't on what had happened while I dreamed: while I was hurting and despairing with Isabella; while I was venting to Lucy and possibly ruining her happily-ever-after wedding; while I was growing increasingly angry with and feeling conflicted toward Andrew. My thoughts were on what happened *after* I woke up.

After driving Duncan away in those first few moments, I brainstormed everything I could do to stay off of the drugs I knew the doctors and my parents would quite literally shove down my throat if needed, or slip into my IV drip. Dr. Shew would certainly put me back on the dreaded dream-stopping ones again. But to my surprise, they concluded that drugs were not the answer.

If I only had the energy to cartwheel...

They gave me nothing that first night and prayed that if I dream-walked, I would wake the next day. Several probes were attached to my head in order to monitor my brain activity while I slept, which felt a bit intrusive, but I happily anticipated joining Lucy and helping her with her mess that night. I needed to fix things and make them right for her.

Instead of waking to a flurry of more wedding plans or the dreaded halt of wedding plans, I woke to my hair painfully stuck to the sticky leads, still lying in the depressing hospital room.

My first thought was that they had lied to me and slipped me something anyway. But when my IV was removed and I had yet another dreamless night, I began to worry.

· · ·

"ANY MORE DREAMS?" DR. SHEW ASKED THE DREADED question softly.

"No," I answered with the unhappy answer.

how do you really feel?

"I keep screwing things up with Duncan," I said with a mouthful of toothbrush and foam when Arianna barged into my bathroom. She was driving me to school my first day back.

It was Monday, and Mom said I could stay home a few more days, but since I was cleared to go, I wanted to go. It was so much worse being home and having Mom hover and panic every time I closed my eyes. It was time to be surrounded by people who either didn't know or didn't care I had been in a coma. Or at least didn't hold their breaths every time I so much as blinked.

Needless to say, it had been a long weekend.

I hadn't even been allowed visitors, so having Ari here to spring me made me slightly giddy.

"How do you figure?" Ari asked, arms crossed over her chest and leaning in the doorway. An amused smile played on the Mauve Ice gloss I'd apparently given her for her birthday last week while I was *elsewhere*. (I couldn't thank Mom and Dad enough for that.) But it wasn't enough to keep me from feeling guilty, even if being gone over her birthday wasn't exactly in my control. She'd made my birthday memorable. And I couldn't even stay awake for hers.

I rinsed my mouth, then pulled my own Apricot Glaze gloss from the drawer to apply. "I told you he was there when I woke up, right?" I asked her reflection in the mirror, then smeared the applicator across my lower lip.

She stiffened, but released her arms to let them hang by her side to hide it. Her smile didn't change. "You mentioned it a few times," she teased.

Then the top lip. "Well, I haven't heard from him since," I said, "He never came back to the hospital, and every time I text him, he doesn't answer back."

"Maybe he thinks you need to recover," she said, handing me my backpack from the floor of the hallway.

"Maybe..." I slung the bag over my shoulder. "But you'd think he'd answer a text."

"Maybe he's busy with football?" she said. I didn't fail to notice that she wasn't looking at me while she rattled off excuses for him.

"Football season is over."

"Right," she said and laughed once.

Is she lying for him? There was something she wasn't telling me.

We walked downstairs and were subjected to a kindergarten-worthy checklist from Mom—*Do you have your backpack? Coat? Gloves? Hat? Doctor's notes?* Seriously the list went on and on. I kissed her on the cheek and donned my winter coat like the dutiful daughter I was and followed Ari out the door.

She'd left her silver Prius running in the driveway, so the interior was toasty warm with the heater blasting when we got in. I had to turn the vent away from my face so it wouldn't scorch my eyebrows as we pulled onto my street.

"I'm afraid Lucy might not get married to Charles after all," I said to my unusually quiet friend. I didn't know what else to talk about. "I suppose I am partly to blame for that. But I just can't believe Andrew *told* Charles about the dreams!" I scoffed.

Ari made a similar noise, so I continued, "Who would believe that some girl from the future was hiding inside his fiancé's head? I guess I can't blame him for doubting."

"The *condition* is a bit difficult to swallow," Ari said, her voice clinical sounding. And I'd never heard her describe my dreams as a *condition*.

Ari used to be upset when I didn't share what happened in the dreams, so I shrugged and continued, "And it certainly didn't help that Charles walked in on Andrew and me... in a few compromising situations that he interpreted the way anyone with eyes would interpret it."

"*Compromising situations?*" Ari's eyebrows rose. "What were you doing?" She sounded horrified. The car unexpectedly jerked, and for a moment I worried that she might careen into a snowdrift.

"Nothing!" I blurted, then rolled in laughter. "Just being close and sometimes... kissing."

She righted the car. "That sounds like you are very much to blame, then," she said. "If you were taking Lucy over enough to be *kissing* someone who wasn't Lucy's fiancé."

"Touché," I said and smiled. "Actually, there was kissing, but I don't think Charles ever saw it," I amended, but then everything else that Andrew did caused the blood in my veins to boil. "But Andrew really did get carried away and took some things too far. Have I told you about Isabella and Nathan?"

Arianna shook her head slightly.

"Well," I said, twisting in my seat to look at her while I spoke. "Andrew came up with this elaborate plan for him and me to be together without causing more issues for Lucy. So we both went back in time even further to this guy and girl named Nathan and Isabella. And it worked! We were on a ship together. A ship that took them from England across the Atlantic to America—"

"Will the story take long?" Ari asked as we pulled into the school parking lot.

Her tone deflated my mood. She sounded irritated.

"I can tell you later, if you'd like," I offered. "Which is probably for the best because a *lot* happened to Isabella."

She pulled into an empty parking spot about halfway to the commons, but left the engine running and turned to look at me.

"What's wrong?" I asked, seeing the bubbling emotions underneath Ari's features. She looked hurt and angry and irritated all at once.

"How was your birthday, Ari?" she said in a mock-Emily voice. "It was good, except for the fact that I could barely taste the red velvet cake and vanilla bean ice cream." She paused. "And why is that?" Her mock-Emily voice cracked at the end as tears welled in her eyes. "Because my best friend was in a coma and missed all of it. Oh, but don't worry about her, she was just hanging out, kissing her dream-historical-boyfriend-whatever and saving people."

"Ari, it's not my fault. I was trapped." I almost mentioned that it was actually her sister who finally pulled me out.

"That's not the point," she said, her expensive waterproof mascara advertising just how waterproof it was—but I didn't think right then was the time to point it the quality of her beauty products. "The point is you *want* to dream. You wouldn't have cared if you'd stayed *trapped*."

I couldn't tell her how true the words were. I couldn't tell her that even now my thoughts were consumed with ways to get back. With plans and ideas about how to save Lucy's wedding. Or how, despite being very angry with him, I wanted to get back to see Andrew again. I hadn't even mentioned who I'd seen on the ship after he left. *Er*, after I pushed him out.

"I help people, Ari," I said quietly. It was the only truth I could say. "Isabella broke her foot." *Well*, maybe *broke it. Maybe I'll never know for sure.* "In fact, I *wasn't* even there to comfort her when it happened because Andrew pushed me out, but that's beside the point." I shook my head.

"She was in so much pain," I continued, "and at one point she wanted to throw herself overboard, but I was there to help her fight to live. And now she was well and was happily engaged to Nathan. Hopefully." It occurred to me much later that it only took me one try to save Isabella. I didn't have to go back and fix it like with Carly. I was getting better at this gig with practice. But I didn't think bringing up Carly's death and then not-death was appropriate.

"See?" Ari's tears continued to flow. "How can I argue with that? Suddenly I sound like a horrible person because I want your dreams to end."

"Lucy could be sent to a mental hospital because of me!" I said in a frantic shout. "Remember when we watched that *Ghost Adventures* episode about how bad the mental asylums were back then? She might be one of the ghosts that haunts asylums because of me."

"There were *several* episodes," she said, softly agreeing.

"Exactly, which means the asylums were pretty consistently awful."

She wiped her eyes and straightened her spine. "But you were in a *coma,* Emily. How is that good? Even if you're out there saving the world?"

"What do you expect me to say?" I asked. "They don't have me on medication anymore, you know that. There's nothing preventing me from remembering the memory dreams."

"Well, they should do something. How do you even know that you are actually traveling to the past and don't have some serious brain-illness?"

The knife to my heart stuck fast and deep. So much that I clutched my chest with the pain of it. "I thought you believed me."

She lifted her shoulders. "Could you please, *please,* just live *your* life? Live in the now?"

I pulled the door handle, letting in a whoosh of cold air. "I was going to ask you about Duncan, but clearly you're keeping some secret about him."

"You wanna talk about Duncan? Let's talk about Duncan!"

Her smile from the bathroom returned. "What do you want to know?"

There were things I did want to know, but I couldn't let this go. Dream-walking was a huge part of my life. I felt that I was exactly the version of Emily I was meant to be because of the good I did while traveling and being a guardian angel for people. And Arianna wanted all of that to stop.

"Maybe if you focus on your life here," Arianna said, then sucked in a deep breath. "Then maybe you won't get sucked in again like you did."

"It doesn't work that way and you know it," I said, letting the bitterness lace my tone. "But you have your wish anyway. I haven't had a single dream since I woke up." I got out of the car, crunching the ice as I shuffled and slammed the door.

living in the present

"About this morning," I began upon meeting Ari in the lunch line. I'd cooled down since my door slam. As I implemented my action plan, I took a greasy pizza slice and milk carton.

"I'm sorry I said I didn't believe you," she said, "I know your dreams are real. I was just... scared."

"I know," I said and gave her a half hug with the hand that held my milk. She returned the hug with a head lean. "But I also realized that you were right about something."

"Oh?" She sounded surprised. "What was that?"

We paid for our lunches and made our way to our usual spot near the tall windows. None of the regulars who sat with us had arrived yet, so we'd have a few minutes alone. "I *do* need to live in the present," I said as we sat next to each other on the metal bench. "So I intend to do that. Plus"—I paused; I had practiced this part in front of the lipstick-smeared mirror in the girls' bathroom on the third floor during second period—"the dreams might not return." Good, no sign of shakiness in my voice. My rehearsal had paid off. "Maybe I am done having them. It would be best to focus on what I can control." My voice hitched at the end, not because of what the words meant, but because of the formal words I'd used and the lilt in my tone. Both were from Lucy's influence. Lucy. Who I might never see again.

But it worked, and Arianna smiled with relief.

"So!" I said more enthusiastically. "Catch me up! What happened while I was sleeping?"

We both laughed at the obvious reference to one of our favorite classic romantic comedies.

"Well," Ari said, pulling the tab on her Fresca and unleashing a hissing sound. "You might not want to hear this part..." She twisted her mouth to a not-quite frown.

Duncan walked into the cafeteria just then. We both watched him walk to the food line, and Ari had that knowing look again. He noticed us watching him and met my eyes with a nod hello.

I waved slow and small. Then turned back to Ari with a twist of my stomach. "What is it?" I took a swig of my milk to mask my sudden nerves.

"Duncan has been going out with Clare Pickett."

"Oh." A stinging memory flashed through my head of my other life—tentatively becoming friends with Duncan, getting my face painted with school colors at a pep rally, and being warned by a perky cheerleader not to get my hopes up over Duncan because Clare was crushing hard on him. Of course saving Carly's life had changed all of that. In this reality, Duncan was my boyfriend long before that pep rally. I shook the confusing image out of my head.

"I mean, it's not like they're officially dating or anything, but I heard that they've been on like two dates recently." She said it all in a rush, like she was ripping off a Band-Aid. The warning was déjà vu. Just via a different messenger.

Whatever. I wanted to say. *I'm still conflicted over a certain turn-of-the-century, amber-flecked-eyed, gets-more-attractive-each-time-I see-him guy who, despite doing some pretty inexcusable things in the recent past, still makes my heart flutter whenever I'm with him. Although it's not actually* my *heart that flutters. And it's not exactly* my *eyes that see him.*

No, I was living in the present. I couldn't say any of that.

Instead I said, "Well, I did break up with him. He's free to date other girls." I said the words but didn't mean them. It wasn't right to feel like I had some claim on Duncan, even if in this reality—not the remembered one where this exact thing with Clare happened months ago—he had been my pretty serious boyfriend for over six months.

Is that why he left the hospital and never visited again? Why he hasn't answered my texts? Because he found a replacement and didn't know how to tell me because it happened while I was sleeping? (And right there was the main plot to that movie.)

"Does it bother you?" Ari asked, hesitant but with a hint of hope. I had a feeling that her excitement was more about me focusing on a real-life-boy-in-the-present for a change than it was about my chances with said present boy.

"A little," I admitted. "But with my health..."

She paused, taking a bite of her pizza, and gave me a strange look.

I rolled my eyes and pointed to my temple. "Coma? Remember?"

She took the bite and nodded her head. "Right," she said with a mouthful.

"I should probably focus on not letting that happen again. And not worry so much about who Duncan is and isn't dating."

"That's probably a good idea," she agreed. "But I wouldn't count Duncan out just yet."

We both casually watched as Duncan walked toward our table. He was one of our regulars, so it wasn't out of the ordinary. Clare was trailing behind him.

"She must've cut in line. She did *not* walk in with him," Ari whispered to me.

"Probably," I muttered back. An uncomfortable feeling blossomed in my chest at seeing her next to him. *I have no claim on him,* I reminded myself, focusing on acting like it didn't bother me in the slightest as they sat across from us—next to each other.

"Em-i-ly!" Clare sang, in her fake way. I was a little surprised by my reaction to her. I remembered liking the version of her in this reality much better than the Clare in other one, but this just proved she was still the same. It all depended on context.

"Hello, Clare." My tone was icy.

"You had us so-o worried!" she gushed, apparently not at all concerned with my cold greeting. "You know the entire school had vigil for you, right? We had candles and everything! And *everyone* was praying for you." She paused for emphasis and reached across the table to grab my hand. "We were all praying for you."

That was news to me. "Thank you?" I said and shot a quick glance at Arianna.

Ari just smiled wide as she said, "Yeah, it was actually all Duncan's doing." Then we both looked across the table in time to see Duncan's neck redden slightly. "I mean, the student council provided the funds and did all of the advertising, but it was Duncan's idea. He did most of the work."

Clare gripped his arm in a possessive way. "Isn't he just a sweetheart?"

I nodded, studying his reaction. I couldn't keep my eyes off of him.

"Don't sell yourself short, Ari," he said, head ducked into his lunch. "You did half of the work yourself."

"It was a team effort," she agreed. "Plus, we had to take turns visiting you."

"So, are you going to the Sweetheart Dance?" Clare asked me, her arm still linked with Duncan's, as he awkwardly gripped his pizza slice with his left hand.

I looked at Ari. "When is it?" I asked her softly.

"Saturday."

"Are you going?"

"We didn't know when you'd wake up," she said a little guiltily, "Brian and I are going with Duncan... and Clare."

"I'm *sure* you can find a date before then!" Clare's pitying voice grated my nerves. "Or you can just come with us. Ari and I don't mind sharing our dates for one dance."

How generous, I thought, slightly resentful. "Naw," I said, feigning nonchalance. "I'm behind on my classwork. You know, coma and all." I laughed once, but no one else did. "I should probably take it easy at home anyway. You guys have fun though!" I wasn't finished eating, but I was finished watching Clare obsessively claim my boyfriend—correction, *former* boyfriend. So I stood with my tray and walked to the exit.

Arianna was quick on my heels. "I'm sorry," she gushed as we dumped our half-eaten trays. "I should have given you a heads up. I don't have to go to the dance. I can stay home with you." But I could tell that she really wanted to go. No doubt she had already found the perfect dress and given Brian detailed instructions on what type of corsage to get.

"No, you should go," I said and meant it. "Don't cancel on account of me."

"Then you should come!"

We were walking down the second-floor hallway, safely out of sight of the cafeteria, and I stopped. "I'd love to go with you and Brian, but I'm not going as the third wheel to *that.*" I pointed in the direction of where we'd left Duncan and Clare.

"We'll cancel then," she offered. "We'll tell them we're just going as the three of us. Surely they'll understand."

"I really don't want to go."

"Scott doesn't have a date yet!" She paused. "I mean, I *think* he doesn't. You can go with him if you don't want to be the third wheel."

I raised an eyebrow. I hated that I was actually considering going. Even worse, Ari could tell.

She very nearly squealed, but knowing that would have the opposite effect, she said casually, "I have Spanish with Scott next. I'll ask him if he has a date yet."

I smiled. Scott was the poster boy of an all-American sports jock. Sure, Duncan was the starting quarterback and Scott was second string, but Scott was also one of the basketball stars for our school. There were plenty of girls after him. This late in the game, there was no way he didn't have a date.

"So that's a yes?" she asked, misinterpreting my smile. I let her.

"Sure," I said. "I had fun with him on my birthday," I added to sell it.

She linked her arm through mine, and we resumed walking to our respective classes. "Now that I think about it," she said, "I remember something about Scott being jealous of Duncan when you two were dating."

My carefree feeling sunk. "What do you mean by jealous?"

"I dunno. It seemed like a by-the-way sort of comment when I heard it." Ari was pensive as she grasped for the memory. "I don't think he'd be opposed at all to going with you." She nudged me then added, "In fact, it will probably help your getting-back-with-Duncan situation."

"My what? I didn't say I wanted..." I trailed off, knowing the argument was futile.

"Oh please. I'm not blind," she mused.

I merely shook my head. I wanted to say something to the effect of *and this is why I prefer dream-walking. Other people's drama is so much easier to handle than my own.* But that would go against my new plan to live in the present. And it probably wasn't so great for my mental health anyway.

"Let me know what Scott says," I said instead and broke from Ari, making an excuse to get to class early.

moving on... sort of

"I'm starting to think maybe that coma was good for you," Mom said on Thursday morning while I ate my cereal.

I raised a who-are-you-and-what-have-you-done-with-my-mother eyebrow while I chewed my Lucky Charms.

"I know that seems strange, but those nightmares you used to have..." She paused, searching for the right word. "They *consumed* you."

She wasn't wrong.

"And now you haven't had one since..."

Since I woke up from my super-long nap otherwise known as a COMA. Yeah, I know. I nodded. "Yep. Haven't had any since then." Not a single one.

"You seem so... normal." She didn't even try to hide her smile.

"And that's a good thing?" A stereotypical normal teenager usually being a negative way to describe a young person.

"Yes, it's a good thing. In fact, it's a *great* thing. You're studying so hard to make up what you missed, I've never heard you laugh so much with Arianna, and I heard you got a date for the dance Saturday." Her voice changed when she spoke about the dance.

"Yeah, I'm going with one of Duncan's teammates, Scott."

"Not Duncan?"

I shrugged. "Don't ask."

"Okay, away from the Duncan topic. Got it." She winked at me. "What I'm saying is that you seem more free now that the dreams have stopped. It's like you are finally living your life."

Well, that's good news, I thought as I swallowed some of the milk from my bowl, leaving a bit on the bottom and carrying it to the sink. *So far I've got two fans of my action plan of living in the present: Ari and Mom.* "I'm going dress shopping with Ari after school if that's alright," I said before heading back upstairs to brush my teeth.

"Okay!" I heard the jump of excitement in her voice even as she tried to mash it down. "Let me pay for it. You can take my MasterCard."

"Thanks, Mom," I called down the stairs. At least I was making everyone else happy.

Was I better off without the dreams? I was acing this living-in-the-present thing because it was the only option. I had no choice. Mom was right. I'd thrown myself at all the makeup work my teachers had given me. Most of them had offered to give me a pass, but I'd insisted. I needed the distraction.

When I wasn't studying, Arianna and I were giving each other manicures and talking about all things boys, specifically Brian and usually Duncan. Ari had started a get-Duncan-back campaign, involving all sorts of espionage leading up to the dance. I hadn't put my heart fully into it. I still wasn't sure if me not wanting him to date Clare translated into me to wanting him to date *me* again. And until I knew the answer to that, I couldn't let Ari get carried away. So far I had nixed any and all suggestions of sabotage. But it was getting harder and harder to come up with a good reason to veto.

Besides, I reasoned with her, it wouldn't be very nice to Scott —who was more enthusiastic to go with me than I'd ever thought possible, given his level of popularity—if I spent the entire dance in pursuit of another guy.

Distractions. They were all great distractions, and for that I was grateful. But as my consecutive dreamless days increased, I began to worry my dreams would never return.

I was committed to not talking about—and mostly not thinking about—getting back to Lucy (and Andrew). And during the day I was doing okay. But each night as I climbed into bed, the idea consumed my thoughts. Every night I made sure the Harker ring was securely on my finger, and I concentrated on getting back to them. I tried to remember exactly how I had done it with the fire. Every night I fell asleep with thoughts of Lucy and Andrew and Charles, even Betsy and Drake and Hannah and Aunt Penelope and Uncle Harry, in hopes that I would be transported back.

But the instant my consciousness drifted, my eyes opened again to the next morning. And I was only Emily.

I tried not to let it bring me down, but part of me despaired that I'd never return or experience another memory walk again.

"I HEAR YOU'RE JOINING OUR GROUP FOR THE DANCE," Duncan said behind me while I shuffled through my locker after the last bell.

I shut the door deliberately, steeling myself before turning to face him. My heart did a little lurch hearing his voice so close.

"Yeah," I said with more enthusiasm than intended. "Thanks for letting us tag along."

"The more the merrier," he said with a smile splitting his face. Being in close proximity for the first time in a while, I suddenly noticed that his hair was slightly longer than it was when we broke up.

I leaned closer and smiled slyly. "I hope Clare is okay with your former girlfriend being in the group," I teased.

His smile widened with his eyes. "Hey, she was the one who suggested you come!" He laughed, but then the smile faded. "She obviously wasn't too worried."

My smile fell slightly too. *Seems like there's nothing for her to worry about,* I noted.

"And everyone knows that Scott is cute." The words flew out before I could stop them, and I stupidly kept going. "She probably thinks that I'm moving on."

"She probably does," he agreed, then looked down and seemed intent on scraping an invisible substance from the toe of his shoe on the bottom of my locker. "He'll be glad to hear that you think he's cute," he added. "He asked me if he could ask you out a few days after we broke up."

"Oh yeah?" I kept my voice upbeat, like I was interested in hearing this information. Like I wanted to hear what Scott had said about me. "What did you tell him?"

He looked back at me again and shrugged. "It doesn't matter. It all worked out in the end," he said. "You ended up asking *him* out after all." He winked at me in that best-friend way, implying that he was happy to see me finally getting a date with someone I'd always wanted to go out with. Maybe that was true on Scott's side, but we both knew that wasn't true on mine. At least I assumed he knew.

I wanted to clarify that it was actually Arianna who had asked him out for me. But since I'd given her my blessing to do it, I guess it was a moot point.

"Well, I'm excited," I said. "It'll be fun."

"I think it's great that you two have remained friends," Clare said strolling up to us. She cozied up to Duncan and linked arms with him immediately.

He didn't shrug her off or seem to mind, so I didn't comment.

"Ready to go?" Ari asked coming from the other direction. I was grateful for her timing. She linked arms with me, mirroring Duncan and Clare so I wouldn't feel awkward.

"Yep!" I said.

"Wanna come, Clare?" Ari asked.

What are you doing? I shot a glare at her from the corner of my eye.

Ari retorted with a look that asked me to trust her.

"Come where?" Clare asked fakeily sweet.

"We are on the hunt for the perfect Sweetheart Dance dress for Emily. Something sure to make Scott go weak in the knees. Not to mention the rest of the guys at the dance."

I looked straight at Ari with wide eyes and what felt like a beet-red face, not daring to see the reaction on Duncan and Clare, or let them see mine full on.

Ari merely smiled at me before returning her gaze to Clare, who huffed.

"Sorry." Clare attempted to keep her previous sweet tone, but I didn't fail to hear angry bitterness lace the edges. "I've got my own dance preparations. It's only two days away," she sang. "But I do hope you can find something on such short notice." Her tone turned pitying, and I couldn't help but look back at her. "I found mine weeks ago, and the pickings were slim even then. Walk me to my car, Duncan?"

I dared a look back at the couple, feeling their eyes were on each other and no longer on me. Clare's bottom lip was pushed out as she gazed up at Duncan.

"Um... yeah," he said as she pulled him away. He glanced once more at us over his shoulder. "See you two at lunch tomorrow."

"You'll get him back," Arianna said quietly, pulling me in the other direction to stop me from staring after them.

I still wasn't sure about my feelings toward Duncan. Did I even want to get back together with him? But I my mind was crystal clear on one point: I definitely didn't like him being with *her*.

mean girls

The next several hours at the mall were disappointing. It quickly became obvious that Clare had been right about the available selection. Since I was an average size, every dress that caught my eye was completely sold out. Nothing but extra small and extra large was left on the racks. Even if I knew a master seamstress, two days didn't seem like enough time to alter anything enough to *make Scott go weak in the knees, let alone the rest of the guys at the dance,* as Ari had put it.

"Don't get discouraged," Arianna said as we walked out of another department store empty-handed. "We haven't looked everywhere."

"Maybe I can wear something from my closet?" I offered, cataloging all of the dresses I owned in my head. *My blue silk might do if—* Then I remembered those were Lucy's dresses, not mine. The hopeful feeling left.

"No way," Ari said. "I've seen your closet, and no offense, but your Sunday dresses are way too casual for a formal dance. Besides, didn't you say your mom gave you her card?" She nudged me. "Don't let her generosity go to waste! We'll find something."

I wasn't so sure. "Does Carly have an old dance dress I could borrow? She only graduated two years ago."

Ari actually seemed to consider that. I wanted to speak to Arianna's sister anyway. I hadn't seen her or talked to her since waking up in the hospital. It was a little strange that she had been the one to help me wake up and yet she hadn't made any effort to even call me. I suppose I could call her.

"Carly might have one or two options. She'll be our backup if we get desperate."

With each passing minute, desperation was looking more and more likely.

"This is the one!" Arianna squealed after a few minutes of browsing at the next store.

She held it up. And my heart sunk along with my face.

"What's wrong?" She looked at the dress she held and scrutinized what could possibly be wrong with it. She checked the tag. "You haven't even seen the price, but it's a good deal and it's on sale. It's perfect."

She wasn't wrong. The dress was full-length cream satin, overlaid with a burgundy lace that melted from light at the bodice to a dark rich color as it met the floor. It was beautiful and I loved it, but, "It's strapless," I said.

"Oh come on, you're not *that* flat."

"Mom would never let me wear it. And besides, isn't the dance at the capitol building? It's drafty in there. I'll freeze!"

She handed it to me. "Just try it on. Carly has a fancy winter cardigan you can wear over it that will be perfect."

I'd never liked the cardigan-over-dress look, but I did love the dress and I was nearly out of options. So I took it from her and headed for the dressing room.

"I CAN'T BELIEVE THE WAY CLARE WAS *THROWING* herself at Duncan today," Ari said as we walked up her front porch steps to her house an hour later. "I mean, it's not like she didn't know you two were practically writing your wedding vows last month. It was totally mean girl of her to do that in front of you."

I shrugged as she unlocked the front door with her key.

"That's it?" she asked incredulously, suddenly not opening the door.

"What do you want me to say?" I asked.

She huffed, then turned the knob and pushed the door open.

I followed her in and up the stairs. "Yeah, it bothered me, but some girls are just mean and Clare is far from the worst." I decided it was probably okay to mention Jenny. "A few weeks ago, I walked a girl named Jenny."

We'd reached the landing, but Ari didn't continue. Instead she folded her arms across her chest and stared me down.

"C'mon, this is relevant."

She waved a hand, mock-urging me to continue.

"Jenny got a nasty note from a girl who was supposed to be one of her best friends," I said in a rush. "It basically told her that she and another girl couldn't be Jenny's friend because they were on the cheerleading squad and Jenny wasn't. Like it would hurt their chances at making cheerleading friends. And hurt their chances with certain guys if they were even seen speaking with her."

"That's stupid," Ari said, thawing slightly.

"It is, which makes it even more awful. It's a stupid reason to tell someone you didn't want to be friends with them."

"How is it relevant?" Her abrupt iciness reminded me of another version of Ari I hadn't seen since Carly was dead.

"I—" It caught me off guard. I puffed air through my lips making a *pfft* sound. "Clare likes Duncan," I said rolling my eyes dramatically. "Sure, I don't like her shoving her status with him in my face, but girls fighting over guys has been happening since... I don't know, since the *dawn of time*. Adults do it. Kids do it. It's not nice, but it's not a stupid reason to be nasty to someone."

"Wow. That's big of you."

I couldn't tell if she was mad or annoyed or something else, but she didn't say anything as she walked down the hall toward Carly's room. I followed.

"Are you mad at me?" I asked.

She stopped just outside of Carly's door, but didn't turn to look at me. I heard a hitch in her voice when she said, "You promised."

"Promised?"

"You promised to live in the here and now." When she turned, tears rimmed her eyes. "You can't talk about the dreams. You can't wish to go back. You can't go into another coma." Two tears streamed down her face that she hastily wiped away.

"I haven't been back," I said, raising my hands in exasperation. "I haven't walked a single dream since the hospital. You *know* that."

"I know."

"And the Jenny dream, I told you that happened *weeks* ago. *Before* the coma." I gripped my friend's shoulders. "But in the dreams, I *helped* people. I *helped* Jenny."

"How?" Her face twisted with a frown.

I thought a moment before answering. "I was there with her when she felt more alone than she ever had in her entire life."

"And what happened to her after? Did she find new friends? Did she tell the old ones to go to *H-E*-double hockey stick?"

I shrugged. "I haven't walked her since, so I don't know. But I was there when she needed me."

Realization seemed to dawn on Ari, and she pulled me into a hug. "Like with Carly," she whispered.

"Like with Carly," I repeated and squeezed her back. My friend was back.

nostalgia

Carly's door opened when Ari ducked into the bathroom. She stepped out all sleepy-eyed, hair aflame around her head like a bright red halo.

"Oh hey!" I said a little surprised to see her. I figured she'd be on campus. Not in her bedroom.

"I heard you talking about Jenny," she said, crossing her arms. I guess sleepy-eyed didn't mean very recently asleep.

"And you don't want me talking about the dreams either?"

"No." She shook her head. "I just don't want you talking about them with Arianna." She unfolded her arms, looking toward the closed bathroom door, and gestured for me to follow her into her bedroom.

"But she's my best friend!" I exclaimed when Carly pushed the door partway closed. "How can I not tell her the things that matter to me, the things that make me... *me!*" Bottling everything up for the past few days and pushing everything about my curse—wow, I hadn't thought about it that way in a long time—deep down was too much. I couldn't just ignore a major part of my life. "I feel like I'm... exploding, Carly. And I can't talk to Duncan about it, he's with *Clare* now. And besides, it's probably not good to talk to a guy I'm interested in about another guy who stars in my dreams! Wow... that sounded so cheesy and Hallmark-TV-movieish."

Carly sat calmly on the edge of her bed as I vented. She smoothed her wild curls—or attempted to tame them—with her right hand and took a deep breath. "I told you that you can talk to me," she said. "Anytime. You have my number. Text. Call. Whatever. You can talk to me."

I blew out a breath and leaned against her closet door. "I know, and I should call," I said closing my eyes suddenly feeling exhausted.

"It's just not the same as telling your best friend?" she guessed.

I opened my eyes and nodded a little guiltily.

"I get it, but seriously don't hesitate to call, because—" She stopped.

I stepped away from the closet, standing straight again. "Because what?"

She sighed. "Because Ari can't handle it," she reiterated. "I wish you could have seen her while you were in the hospital." She pushed a lock of hair away from her eyes and held her hand to her forehead, keeping it pinned.

I gave her a knowing look. "I did see it," I said, "for the first few months after you died. She pushed me out of her life and she tried to mask it at school, but I still saw it." I looked over to her window that still had remnants of duct-tape around the edges. I shuddered internally, remembering the rock-bottom depression she had been in when I walked with her. Similar to how Isabella had felt in that storm. The windows then had been blocked out by dark paper, held there by duct tape. I was glad to see that Carly had let the light in again.

"Then you understand what I mean when I say she can't handle it."

I nodded again and nearly jumped when Ari barged in.

"Did you get it?" she asked, but seeing that I only held my new dress limply over my arm, she pushed me out of the room.

"Put your dress on then come back and we'll see how perfect the cardigan works.

I did as she asked, and when I came back, Arianna held out the short-sleeved burgundy jacket out to me. I don't know how it was possible, but it was the exact color and shade as the bottom of my dress.

And it hit me.

The color reminded me of the dress Lucy had worn to her engagement ball. Funny how something that looked so different could hit me so hard with nostalgia.

Slowly I threaded my arms into the sleeves and turned to look in Carly's full-length mirror that hung behind her door.

The jacket was perfect. Normally I didn't love the look of a cardigan or jacket over a formal dress, but this looked like it belonged together. The lighter lace at the top of my dress was hardly covered by the jacket that gathered at a single button just below my bra line.

I glanced at Ari in the mirror. Her eyes were wide. "It's perfect!" she said, grasping my shoulders to turn me toward them. "It's the perfect get-Duncan-back dress!"

I almost mentioned that it was short-sleeved and that I still might freeze, but I loved it enough not to criticize. Instead I said, "I'm going with Scott."

"Exactly! And when Duncan sees you in this with another guy who likes you, he'll be itching to ask you to dance and when you're in his arms..." She held her arms over her chest and closed her eyes, swaying back and forth like she was dancing.

Carly and I eyed each other. I rolled my eyes, and she covered her mouth in a laugh. But then Carly sobered. "If you want to get Duncan back, *this*"—she waved a hand at me—"is definitely the dress to wear."

I looked back at my reflection and was hit again with how much it reminded me of another dress I wore—or didn't wear. I blinked several times when I felt the prick of tears. *Not the time to cry*, I chided myself. But I missed her. I missed *him*. It felt wrong wanting to get-Duncan-back when I was still pining after someone else. Even if it was impossible for me to ever be with that someone else.

"I'm going to change back," I announced, "I assume Ari asked if I could borrow the jacket?" I asked Carly.

She nodded and smiled. "You can borrow it."

"Thanks," I said, but before I turned to leave again she gestured behind Ari's back to *call her* if I needed to talk.

I nodded another thanks.

CHAPTER 37

just crying... a lot

I woke up crying Saturday morning. Not a sobbing or screaming kind of cry, more of a tear-streaming down the face, whimpering cry. Quiet enough that my parents didn't come running. I didn't know why I was crying. It wasn't because of a memory dream, because I hadn't had another one yet.

And maybe that was why.

Maybe my subconscious was coming to grips that the memory walking was over. That I'd never help another person again while they experienced their bad days. That I'd never rejoice with someone on their happy ones.

That I'd never be with Lucy again.

She was one of my closest friends—possibly my best friend. I shared everything with Lucy, all my hopes and dreams. So much more than I shared with Arianna these days. That was enough to make me sad and want to cry.

Maybe that was why.

If I'd been taking the dream-blocking drugs, I could assume I was sad because of what happened in a specific dream I didn't remember. But Dr. Shew hadn't prescribed them since before the coma, so I knew that couldn't be the reason.

I laid in bed, looking at my textured ceiling for a while. It was Saturday, so no school, and though the dance was tonight, Ari and I didn't have plans to get ready until later that afternoon. So I laid there and allowed myself to grieve.

Mom came in about an hour later to check on me. I slammed my eyes shut so she'd think I was sleeping in, but it was too late and I heard her walk to my bed and felt her sit on the edge.

"Everything okay, sweetie?" she asked, moving a lock of my hair behind my ear.

I sat up and burst into tears. "What if I never have another dream?" I sobbed. "What if I never get back to Lucy? What if her wedding is ruined and I'm not there to help her fix it?" I put my face in my hands and cried.

I felt Mom's arms wrap around me. "Those dreams weren't good for you, Emily," she said softly, carefully. "Anything that takes my little girl away is not healthy. It's not good for *anyone* in my book." It felt like she wanted to say more, like the fact that Lucy wasn't real or that I wasn't really helping real people in my dreams, but she stopped herself.

I didn't agree with her, but I knew she meant well. She didn't believe the truth about the dreams, so of course she would be against me going back. Still, I let Mom comfort me.

"Arianna is downstairs," she said when I calmed down.

"She is?" I sat back and wiped my eyes on my sleeve.

Mom gave me a small smile. "She said something about getting your nails done this morning for the dance?"

I grabbed my phone from my nightstand and saw several texts from my friend.

Are you awake? one said.

Mani-pedi this morning? was the next one.

My treat? with a bunch of red hearts.

"Maybe she knew you needed some cheering up this morning," Mom said. "It's funny how best friends can sense when we're down sometimes."

I nodded but wanted to cry again because even if Ari had sensed that I was sad, I could never tell her why. "Tell her I'll be down in a minute."

Mom smiled and patted my leg. "I know you're sad now, but in time you might be glad that the dreams have stopped," she said. "Now get dressed and go get pampered!" She said the last part a little too enthusiastically and part of me wondered if Mom had heard me crying earlier and concocted the whole thing.

"Wow, Em, you're a knockout," Scott said when I greeted him at the door several hours later.

"It's the bling on my fingernails," I teased showing off my gel-painted nails, complete with bedazzled jewels on my ring fingers. I was in a *much* better mood. Seriously, the therapy of mani-pedis and time with Ari that ended in curling each other's hair and creating elaborate updos before donning our dresses had done wonders. I hadn't thought about the dreams. Our conversation had consisted exclusively of Ari's boyfriend Brian and the get-Duncan-back plan, which I had successfully twisted into a have-fun-with-Scott plan by the end.

"No, it's the whole..." He waved a hand up and down from my head to my feet, "The dress, the hair, *and* the bling on your fingernails." He winked and took my hand to study it like he was a girl admiring another girl's engagement ring. "Shall we?" he asked, keeping my hand in his and gesturing to his still-running car.

I smiled. I was genuinely excited to go with Scott, even though I didn't know him super well. "Let's go!" I grabbed my coat after Mom took the mandatory dance pictures of us in front of the fireplace and we left.

We met Ari and Brian for dinner, but Duncan and Clare had backed out at the last minute. Clare wanted to be with a few of her cheer friends, but they promised to meet up with us at the dance. I guess we should have felt slighted that they backed out of our original plans, but I was okay with it. The less I saw Duncan with her, the better.

Dinner was fun and I caught myself flirting with Scott a little, but I was careful not to give him the wrong idea. When we arrived at the capitol building, Scott went for my hand, but I took his arm instead. Walking in holding hands felt more *together* and not just a date. He didn't protest.

"Props to the decorating committee!" Ari gushed when we walked in the doors. The rest of the committee had taken over the actual decorating process so Ari could focus on our pre-dance best-friend duties, but Ari had been the mastermind. It was amazing. Silver garlands hung from the balconies, scalloped perfectly with twinkle lights. Tea lights and white-and-red flower centerpieces sat on every surface, and a black arch covered in more twinkle lights was in the far corner where the photographer had set up. "Let's go up!" Ari exclaimed, pointing to the balcony.

The guys didn't protest, so we walked up the grand staircase, holding tightly to our dates so we didn't fall in front of the entire school in our heels. When we reached the top, Ari rushed to look down at the crowd, pulling my hand to drag me along.

My heart fluttered in my chest as we got closer, and my stomach felt like a rock when I touched the railing.

Clusters of prettily-dressed classmates were scattered all over the dance floor. Some dancing and swaying to the slow song playing, others in groups with clear plastic cups filled with apple cider and red punch.

It was exactly like Lucy and Charles's engagement ball. Yet vastly different. Not many ball gowns or tuxedos, but between the A-line and mermaid skirts, the full-lengths and a couple of minis, similar colors filled the room in contrast to the men's dark suit coats and blazers. My insides ached at the similarities. The twinkle lights set off the same glow as the chandeliers, and about the same number of people were gathered.

And I stood in the exact same spot, looking down with a guy who wasn't *the guy* I wanted to be with. Poor Scott. He had no idea...

And then I saw him walk in. All gorgeous and looking so much like... *him*... with someone else on his arm. She even wore the same color of dress that Margaret had worn that night. Tears welled in my mascara-framed eyes. Ari had let me use her super waterproof mascara, but I still blinked several times to banish the tears—I didn't want to explain them to anyone.

"May I have this dance?" Scott said in my ear, and a shiver went down my spine. I hadn't heard him come so close.

I whipped around with a mostly real smile plastered on my face and nodded yes. I thought he'd walk me back down to be with the crowd, but he took me in his arms right then and there and held me close. Arianna and Brian were already dancing next to us—or rather swaying while they had their arms wrapped around one another, completely oblivious to the world around them.

I bit my lip. I felt my heart strings pull from my chest and throw themselves off the balcony to where they wanted to be.

Where they wanted to be.

Of course. If I couldn't be with Andrew because my dreaming had halted or was somehow banned, I wanted to be with the next best thing. The person who looked similar to and might possibly be related to the person I truly wanted to be with. With Duncan.

I missed Lucy so much in that moment. I wanted to talk to her in my thoughts and think through all of my swirling, painful feelings. I wanted her to tell me to stop pining after someone I couldn't have. I wanted her to remind me that he was engaged to her friend and that I shouldn't encourage him to keep stringing her along. But I also wanted her to contrive a special meeting for me and Andrew, like she had done so many times when things had gone wrong.

Dancing with Scott felt like dancing with Charles. Like I was with the person I was supposed to be with in that moment, but not the person I wanted to be with in that moment.

After the song ended and a new one started, I excused myself. I had to get away and collect myself. At least that's what I told myself as my lower lip trembled slightly.

"Do you want me to come with you?"

"To the bathroom?" I asked, thinking of the one place he really couldn't follow me. "I'm okay going by myself."

"Are you sure?" he teased, but then waved a hand to shoo me away.

I looked at Ari, ready to tell her not to come either, but she was melting in Brian's arms and didn't even glance at me, so I nodded at Scott, then quickly walked away.

Certainly there was somewhere I could hide for a few minutes on the upper floor. Otherwise, my emotions would be on full display as I went down the staircase and across the dance floor. I didn't think I could make it that far anyway before bursting into tears, so I shuffled down the hall along the balcony as quickly as my heels would allow.

I passed by several shallow alcoves before finally finding another hallway that led away from the dance. Probably offices, but tucked away enough that when I collapsed into a bench several feet in, I was certain no one would bother me if I kept quiet.

The tears flowed steadily down my face, certainly wrecking my makeup—only the mascara was waterproof. I wished I had gone to a bathroom. At least then I would have been able to put myself back together. How could I return to Arianna and Scott when I didn't know how badly I looked? That made me cry harder and a little yelp escaped as once again I wished Lucy was in my head to tell me what to do or take over.

"Em?" a tentative voice said walking slowly toward me.

I wiped my eyes as best as I could before turning to look at him. Dread filled my chest as I expected to see *her* next to him. Probably holding his hand or hanging onto his arm.

But when I turned, he was alone.

He sat next to me. Without another thought, I threw myself into Duncan's arms and burst into tears.

CHAPTER 38

foreign object

He held me for several moments without speaking a word. It felt comforting and warm to be in his arms again. Scott was nice and dancing with him had been okay, but being back in Duncan's arms just felt better. It felt right.

I wiped my eyes again and frowned as I pulled away.

"What's wrong?" Duncan's eyebrows knit together.

I frowned again, ready to spill the whole pathetic reason I'd been crying, but in that moment I realized how pathetic that reason really was.

I missed my dreams. How stupid was that?

I missed being *other* people. Sure, I missed some people more than others, but what was the point of that? They were either well over a hundred years old or dead by now. When would I ever learn to live and be happy in the present?

The way Arianna wanted me to be.

So many days in a row without a dream had given me some perspective.

"Where is..." I paused, not wanting to say her name. "Where is your date?"

He shrugged like her whereabouts didn't matter. "She's dancing with Matteo, I think."

"Does she know you're... with me?"

He shook his head like it was none of her business. *Was* it any of her business? "You and I are still friends," he said, "I'm allowed to comfort a friend."

"Are you saying that to convince me or yourself?" I asked, a hint of teasing in my tone.

He didn't take the bait. "What's wrong, Em? Is Scott treating you okay? I saw you two dancing earlier. Do I need to have a chat with him?"

I shook my head. "No, it's not him. He's been great, really."

"He's not getting too handsy?" He raised one eyebrow to break the tension, but looked about ready to attack my date if I set him loose.

"Scott has been the perfect gentleman," I assured him. Talking about *my* date made me a bit guilty for sitting here with Duncan. "I should probably get back to him, in fact."

Duncan's face fell slightly. "Are you okay to go back?" he asked. I suddenly realized that we'd been holding hands because he gave my fingers a squeeze.

I squeezed back. "Yes, thank you, Duncan." I allowed a genuine smile to rise. I had the slightest impression that Duncan *wanted* me to keep him longer. Maybe he wasn't in a hurry to get back to Clare.

Duncan moved his hands up my bare arms, making goosebumps skitter up my skin. "Are you cold?" he asked, rubbing his hands up and down.

My face flushed. "No, I'm fine." *It just felt nice.* I was about to open my mouth and say something dreamily lame when Duncan's face changed. He gripped my upper left arm so tightly it hurt.

"What's this?" he asked gesturing to my arm, his expression rigid and a little panicked.

"What's what?" I asked, looking at the arm. He was clutching tighter and rubbing his thumb along the inner part of my arm. It hurt like a bruise. "Ouch," I said, moving my arm to release his grip.

He loosened his fingers, but didn't let go. Instead, he turned it outward so the inside of my arm pointed up. With his other hand he pushed a thumb across the sore part. I tried to move away again, until I saw it. My skin lumped into what looked like a small cylinder-like shape. Something hard was just beneath the skin.

My eyes widened as I grasped my arm. "What is that!" I practically shouted. I scratched at it, making it hurt more. I looked at him, then back at the foreign object inside of me, panicked and my heart racing. It looked just like one of those trackers injected like in the dystopian novels or sci-fi movies. Like it was monitoring my vitals or sending a GPS signal to some government agency.

When I met his eyes again, he looked even more concerned. "You mean you don't know what that is?"

I shook my head swiftly. "Do you think..." I paused. "Do you think they put it in me while I was in the hospital?"

Duncan frowned. "Em, if you don't know what this is, you need to have a serious talk with your parents. Now." He pointed at my arm. I could feel the fury emanating from him. He seemed to think for a moment, then grabbed my hand again. "C'mon, I'll take you home," he said determined, pulling me back down the hallway.

"Wait." I gently yanked my arm to stop him and backed away to lean against the wall behind me. He didn't let go of my hand and we were only inches apart.

"Don't you want answers?" he asked. He looked so angry I half expected steam to spout from his ears like in the cartoons.

"Yes," I said softly, placing my free hand on his chest. The touch seemed to calm him slightly, and his face relaxed. "But you and I both have dates here, remember?" I loved that I had to remind him of that. I mean, again I felt a little guilty for saying it because I was having a good time with Scott up until the waterworks, but I loved that Duncan seemed to have entirely forgotten that he'd arrived with a different girl. "We didn't come here together." I emphasized. But as soon as I said it, I regretted it. Would he run back to Clare? Would he escort me to Scott and insist that *he* take me home? Would we ever be together like this again?

Now that I was back in Duncan's presence, and so close in proximity, I realized something. I didn't like Duncan because he looked like Andrew, or because he might be related to Andrew in some distant way, I liked Duncan for who *he* was. Sweet and attentive, a good friend... a good kisser. And most importantly, he was in *my* time. Not Lucy's. Not Isabella's. *Mine.* And for some unknown reason, he liked being with me too.

Now that I was back in Duncan's presence, I didn't want to leave. Not when there was something so big hanging over my head. I'd give anything to keep him from rushing back to Clare right now.

He seemed to consider my face for a moment too, a myriad of emotions racing across his features as he contemplated the next move. Wait until after the dance? I knew I wouldn't be able to do that, not after finding something *injected into my arm!* What was he thinking?

He moved closer. Part of me wanted to close the gap between us and kiss him right here, in this magical lighting. It was the perfect scene: Duncan looking very dapper in his blue suit and me in a dress that was fancy enough for me to feel like I was in some princess movie, about to kiss the prince.

But there was too much hanging over my head. There were too many complications to consider.

"You should get back to Clare," I suggested, regretting the words the moment they left my lips.

He snapped from a momentary daze—*was he about to kiss me?* The moment was over, the spell broken. But he didn't move even a step backward. "Don't you want me to take you home?"

I bit my lip. How badly I wanted him to. I wanted him to ask me to dance, to hold me close while we blocked out the world, while I forgot about whatever secret was injected into my arm. To forget Lucy and fixing her wedding, and forget worrying why I hadn't entered another dream, to forget about how I felt about the prospect of never walking another one ever again. Forget the fact that Duncan and I had ever broken up. Forget Andrew.

"It can wait a few hours," I lied. "I'll talk to them tonight."

Duncan studied my face a few more seconds. He was gauging something. I met his stare steadily, making sure my eyes were daring him to kiss me. But he never moved closer. Instead he said, "Let me know if you change your mind. But I suppose Scott could take you home just as easily." He backed away quickly, wiped his thumbs underneath my eyes—hopefully getting any escaped eyeliner, and disappeared around the corner, back onto the main part of the balcony.

I held my now empty hand to my chest, pushing back any suspected return of tears. Taking one last deep breath, I pushed away from the wall.

CHAPTER 39

cowardice and confrontation

O kay. *I'll just tell Scott I'm sick and ask him to take me home,* I thought to myself as I slowly walked back to my group.

I found them back down the stairs in the main crowd of the dance. Scott looked slightly worried when I returned, but I smiled at him and his shoulders relaxed. Ari and Brian were huddled around a smart phone with another couple a few feet away, laughing.

"Where did you disappear to?" Scott asked.

"Just needed some air," I lied, then opened my mouth to execute the plan. "What are they watching?" Execution failed.

He rolled his eyes. "Some cat video montage." He held out a hand, wordlessly asking for a dance.

"Here? Why?" I asked, taking his hand and letting him pull me to him.

He shrugged, but didn't answer.

What's the rush, right? I thought, second guessing my original plan. *I mean, I've had that thing in my arm how long? What's a few more hours?*

Okay, not second guessing. Chickening. I wasn't ready to face my parents.

I considered pulling Arianna aside to show her my arm and ask her what to do, but part of me wondered if she knew about it. What if my parents told her in case I asked her to help me remove it?

Chickening again, I didn't tell her.

I should remove it, but I can't do it here. Digging it out with my newly manicured fingernails sounded a little extreme and even if I could find one, a knife or razor blade didn't sound much better. But my hesitation didn't prevent my paranoia. Was it tracking me? Was it recording every word that escaped my lips? I kept glancing at the balconies for CIA operatives to scale down and carry me away after listening to my conversation with Duncan.

No, I'll worry about it later. Whatever it is. It'll keep until later.

Coward.

I seriously needed to get home. And where was Duncan? He'd insist on taking me if he noticed that I was still here. He'd scold me first. Ask why I hadn't left, maybe while dancing to cover our conversation. Just one dance. The thought made me smile. Where was he?

By some miracle I survived the night despite my cowardice. And I never did see Duncan again. Scott finally drove me home.

"Thanks for being my date," I said when Scott walked me to my door. The dreaded awkward-doorstep scene.

"Thanks for asking Arianna to ask me to ask you." It broke the tension, and we both laughed nervously. "We should do it again sometime."

"Um..."

"No pressure, just as friends," he said quickly. "I just mean we should do more together. As friends," he repeated.

I met his eyes, silently asking if he meant it.

He shrugged and held his hands out. "A guy can tell when a girl is hung up on someone else."

"Am I that transparent?" I covered my face with a hand, lamenting.

He pulled me into a side hug. "You should talk to Duncan," he said into my hair. "Hey, and if he's moved on, I'd love a second date."

I pushed away from him, eying his expression.

Scott was being completely genuine. "I highly doubt it though, the way he was looking at you all night..." He whistled low.

He was watching me? Since I never saw him again, I figured he'd made an excuse to leave, or was at least avoiding me. He'd been watching me?

"I probably should've shared you with him," Scott continued, "but I was afraid I wouldn't get you back." He shrugged and gave me a half smile with raised eyebrows. "And I figured it was my only chance at a date with you so..."

"I had a nice time with you, Scott," I assured him. "Really."

"Oh, I know," he said bounding down the porch steps. "And when he screws up, I'll be waiting in the wings."

I highly doubted that, as I knew he'd had more girlfriends than I could count. He'd be onto the next one by morning.

When I walked in the door, I suddenly wished I could talk with Scott longer. I was home. Which meant I needed to have the dreaded conversation with my parents. My stomach twisted with anxiety as my imagination ran wild with horrible possible reasons for the *thing* in my arm. Really, most of my guesses were nothing compared to what I truly suspected: that it was somehow blocking the dreams.

"How was the dance?" Mom would ask.

"Great, except I finally noticed there's this thing injected into my arm."

"Oh, that?" Mom would give Dad a look. "It's for the best, honey."

"What is it? What's for the best?"

"You've drawn suspicion from the FBI. They wanted to track your whereabouts..."

Okay... imagination running wild. I took a deep breath and shut the door quietly behind me, subconsciously not wanting to attract attention. Maybe my parents had gone to bed and I could sneak up to my room and postpone the inevitable until morning. *Stop being such a coward, Emily.* I needed to know. I wouldn't be able to sleep until I knew.

"How was the dance?" Mom asked, looking up from the novel she'd been reading in the recliner in the front room.

"The CIA are recording your conversations. They want to know what you know..."

Stop it.

"It was fun," I said truthfully and went into a recap of my night. I was all jittery as I described dinner and how the capitol was decorated, and the drama that broke out when Sylvia Mack caught her best friend, Ginny Reynolds, kissing her boyfriend in one of the upper-balcony alcoves. Apparently they hadn't found that side hallway.

"Are you okay?" Mom asked when I'd finished. "You seem a little keyed up."

"Because if you find out about the cylinder in your arm, we're just going to have to admit you to the hospital. Dr. Shew's orders..."

This is getting ridiculous. Get a grip, Emily.

I steeled myself and took a deep breath. My cowardice vanished. I was ready to shout. I was ready to demand what the injected foreign object was in my arm. I was ready to question what she and Dad had let them do to me. I was ready to stomp and fume and threaten to dig it out myself if they didn't take me in to have it removed immediately.

I wasn't ready to cry. But I couldn't say I was surprised when the water works started up again. *Seriously?*

"What's this?" I held up my arm as the tears streamed down my face.

I watched her expression for the guilt to appear. If not guilt, then at least anger or frustration at getting caught. But neither showed on her face.

"What's what?" she asked like she was looking at some invisible mark. I supposed from where she sat, it looked like nothing. Her reaction infuriated me. She didn't even move closer to pretend to care that there might be something there.

"This tracker, or whatever it is in my arm!" I called over my shoulder. "Dad!" Hopefully he was just in the other room watching TV and not upstairs asleep. "DAD!" I shouted louder.

Mom stood to approach me, and I stood too, backing away from her. Dad's heavy footsteps rushed from the back room. He looked bleary-eyed like he'd been asleep when he staggered in.

"What's wrong?" he asked. *Good, he sounded panicked.* "Did that boy do something?" His voice turned to anger.

I held out my arm for him to inspect. "There. Is. Something. In. My. Arm." I said each word slowly, gritting my teeth. Luckily the tears had stopped.

Mom looked at Dad in silent conversation.

"What is she talking about?" Dad asked Mom aloud.

Mom shrugged, but didn't come closer.

Slowly, Dad took my arm in his hand and turned it back and forth. "I don't see anything, sweetie."

With my other hand, I moved it to push up my skin. "You don't see that!"

His eyes widened, and he looked back at Mom.

She joined us, looking at the bulge in my arm. Her eyes widened too.

"Do you think... at the hospital?" Mom held a hand to her mouth after she spoke.

"They didn't say anything about..." Dad trailed off and studied the bulge again.

I jerked out of his grip. "It's to stop the dreams, isn't it?" The tears came again. "You think they need to be stopped by any means possible. Even if it means *injecting* me with chemicals without my knowledge! I was doing just fine living in both worlds. I felt more alive walking with other people in my dreams than I do here. But it's more than that. I *help* them. I'm *needed!* Grandma Grace believed it, why don't you?"

"Emily," Mom said softly. "Calm down, honey. Maybe we need to call Dr. Shew—"

"Will she take it out?" I was hyperventilating now.

"Sweetheart," she said, like she was trying to calm a spooked animal, or negotiate with a criminal in a hostage situation, or talk someone off of a ledge. I hated that tone. "Let's get you to the hospital so they can help you."

"Will they take it out?" My voice flipped high and I darted for the front door. No way I was going back, not after they *injected* a foreign object into me.

Mom looked slightly panicked, but kept her voice calm. "I'm sure it's nothing."

But it was too late. She'd already threatened to take me back to the hospital. I couldn't hesitate even a moment. I threw the door open and ran outside without grabbing my coat.

I couldn't run far in my heels and had no idea where I would go, but I slammed the door behind me to slow them down. Fortunately I didn't have to think long because there was a familiar car sitting in the driveway. I threw the back passenger door open and clumsily climbed inside before the front door of my house opened again.

"Drive!" I shouted between my sobs.

paranoia

"Where to?" Duncan asked after he'd driven a few blocks away. "And should I worry about your parents calling the cops?"

"I don't know," I said, my arms wrapped around me to keep warm. The heater in Duncan's car hadn't warmed the back seat yet. He probably wasn't at my house long before I came running out.

He took a left at the next stop sign.

"Where are you going?" I asked.

"Ari's."

"Why?" I shrieked. "She's probably in on it!"

"She's your best friend," he reminded me, "and a teenager. How could she be in on it?"

"She always takes their side," I muttered.

"So... did your parents know about the... whatever is in your arm?"

"I don't know. I think they lied about not knowing what it was."

"They *lied?*"

"Yeah, they pretended they didn't know anything about it."

"How do you know that they *actually* didn't know about it?"

"Because doctors don't just inject you with things without permission," I argued. "And since I'm a minor, they wouldn't have to ask *my* permission. Just my parents."

I saw Duncan raise an eyebrow at me in the rear view mirror.

"Can we not go to Ari's?" I pleaded. "She'll just call my parents, and then they'll drag me to the hospital to be *sedated* or whatever they think will make me less *delusional.*"

He pulled into Ari's driveway and put the car in park before swiveling to look at me. "They think you're *delusional?* Doesn't that prove that they didn't know about the arm-thing?"

I shrugged. Okay so they didn't actual say they thought I was delusional. And maybe I was being irrational, but I wasn't about to admit that to anyone. "I just don't want to go home."

"Fine, let's just go inside and talk to Ari," he said. "You can use my phone to tell your parents you're okay. And please ask them not to send the cops after your getaway vehicle."

I rolled my eyes. "They know your car, Duncan. They aren't going to call the cops. They know I'm with you and not some lunatic serial kidnapper or something."

Ari met us on her doorstep with her phone in her hand all lit up when we'd barely shut the car doors. "Your parents are looking for you, Em," she said, clearly confused. "What's going on?" She'd changed into her pink pajamas and was no longer wearing makeup, but her strawberry-blond hair was still in an updo of curls.

Duncan held a hand out, blocking me. "If we come in, do you *promise* not to turn us in?" he asked, wholly serious. His protectiveness warmed me. I wanted to wrap my arms around him and kiss him right then and there.

"I promise," she said, though she didn't sound so sure. She didn't sound like she was lying, just confused.

We rushed in out of the freezing air. I shivered violently in the warmth of the house.

Carly lounged on the couch with a movie paused when we walked in. Seeing my state, she stood and folded her arms with a concerned look. "What's going on?" she asked with the broken-record phrase of the night.

"Em ran away from home," Ari answered, "Her parents have been texting and calling me to ask if I've seen her."

"Why'd you run?" Carly asked.

"Should I tell them you're here?" Ari interjected.

"No!" I said quickly. "I mean, not yet." I hung my head. "I don't know. I can't go home."

Carly grabbed a blanket from the couch and walked over to wrap it around me. "Ari, take Emily upstairs and loan her some of your pj's. I will call Emily's parents and let them know that she's safe."

My head shot up. "No! You can't let them know where I am! They'll come and get me!"

"It'll be okay, Em. I'm just going to *talk* to them," Carly said. "I won't let them take you anywhere. Go upstairs and get warmed up. Maybe jump in the shower even. It'll help you calm down."

I nodded and followed Ari upstairs.

Ari didn't say anything as she rummaged through her dresser for her purple plaid flannel pajama set and handed it to me. I followed her to the bathroom and started the water, waiting for it to warm. She stood, leaning against the doorway.

"What happened, Em?" she asked quietly when I pulled the lever on the faucet to switch the water from tub to shower.

She helped me unzip my dress, then turned around so I could step into the steaming water and close the curtain. The heat felt amazing. I hadn't realized how cold I was until I let the hot water stream down my back and thaw my skin. I stood still for several seconds with my eyes closed, letting the water defrost my toes and fingers and allowed my mind to go blank.

"What happened?" she repeated.

I opened my eyes and stared at the tan-colored tiles. "My parents lied about something. I don't know what it is, but it's in my arm. I think they injected it into me."

"Like what? Like a medication?" Her voice sounded shocked.

Maybe she didn't know about it?

"How do you even know something was injected?"

I stuck my arm out of the curtain with the inside facing up.

"I don't see anything," she said.

With my other hand, I reached out to poke the cylinder so she could see it.

I heard her gasp and pulled both arms back in.

"What is it? When did you notice it?"

Okay, so maybe she sounded appalled, I noted. And I knew she wasn't good at faking that. "Tonight. At the dance," I said. "Duncan noticed it."

"Duncan? When did you see Duncan?"

Good thing she couldn't see my face because it was certainly a shade darker. "He found me crying and..."

"Did he kiss you?" She practically squealed. "While you were on a date with another guy?"

"No."

"Wait, why were you crying? Because of Scott?"

"It's... complicated," I said. She wouldn't approve of me grieving about not returning to the dreams. It was the reason I left to cry in the first place. "No, he was hugging me and noticed it," I said, changing the subject back.

"So you think it's some kind of drug?" she asked. "Was it put there while you were in the hospital?"

"I don't know," I said, "but my parents want to take me *back* to the hospital." I paused, considering how much more I should tell her. "Maybe it's something to..." I paused again. "To stop the dreams."

She was so quiet I almost wondered if she'd fallen asleep. Or left the room.

"Ari?"

"Maybe it's for the best," Ari said in a rush. "I mean, if it is drugs to stop the dreams and they're working, maybe you should leave it."

"How can you say that?" My voice was barely a whisper. I

couldn't believe I was hearing this from her. I felt trapped. I needed to get out.

"I mean, now you can live in the *now*. You've really settled into life so much better than you ever did before, especially since you aren't distracted by some dream guy you could never have. Besides, isn't it better if you never experience another death, or heartbreak? It's hard to ace your math test when you were *murdered* the night before."

How wrong she was. I'd been faking settling into the *now*, as she called it, because I didn't dare talk to her about how much I missed the dreams. I couldn't tell her how unfulfilled I felt because I wasn't helping people every night. I couldn't tell her how much I missed not only Andrew, but Lucy too.

"And hey," she continued, "Duncan is downstairs waiting for you, and he comforted you at the dance. I think you two are on the verge of getting back together. I think Clare is a thing of the past. I mean, he dropped her off only to rush over to your place?! What was he doing at your house anyway? Did you call him?"

"No." I was crying again, but I didn't want her to hear, so I kept my voice steady. "He was just in the right place at the right time."

She sighed. "He's so perfect for you."

"He is, but I think he's just being a good friend." It was probably the truth too. After all, he hadn't sought me out after that one time, even if Scott had noticed him watching me. It probably meant he was happy being with Clare all night. "Hey, could you ask Carly what my parents said when they called?" I asked. "I'm a little bit anxious about everything."

"Sure. Hopefully she told them you're staying the night," she sounded giddy. "I wanna tell you about Brian. He's just the sweetest!"

As soon as I heard the door click closed, I tiptoed out, dripping all over the floor and locked the door. I left the shower running so Ari would think I was still in and quickly dried off. I had to get out. I didn't know what I'd say to leave or where I'd go, but I couldn't stay at Ari's either. Even if I trusted Carly.

But first, I had to get the thing out of my arm.

Now.

Hastily opening drawers, I looked for something that would do the job quickly and effectively before I lost my nerve. There was a pair of scissors in the second drawer down that Ari kept for whenever she felt the need to have bangs. I pulled them out and shut the drawer.

The scissors were a way to keep Ari's bangs trimmed between hair appointments, but she usually let them grow out after only a month or so, meaning they were hardly used and very sharp.

Perfect.

I stepped back into the shower and held my arm up. Then took a deep breath.

adrenaline

Cutting into my arm hurt way worse than they ever portray it in the movies. They should add warning labels to those scenes. *Don't try this at home. It hurts way worse than you can even imagine.* I had to bite my tongue hard to keep from crying out as I dug into my skin. I didn't want anyone to see what I'd done until it was out and dressed, so I couldn't scream and have everyone in the house come running.

Hopefully I didn't cut into anything vital, I'd never taken an anatomy class to know where the major arteries were. I just hoped that whoever put it there placed it far away from anything that would be lethal to nick.

It was a lot of blood. It looked like the murder scene from Psycho—I'd never seen the movie, but I imagined it might look similar with all of the blood in the shower. Fortunately the water washed it all down the drain. I rinsed away whatever was left with the removable shower head.

It took forever to get the stubborn thing out, especially since it was slippery with my blood and the water, but it was close to the surface of my skin, so I managed it. I probably mangled my arm much more than was needed, but I got it out and it clinked onto the porcelain floor of the tub. I grabbed it with my foot to keep it from going down the drain. I wanted it as evidence.

I left the shower on when I got out the second time, all macabre, and wrapped my arm in the towel sitting next to the sink to staunch the blood. Pinching it under my arm, I quickly dressed one-handed. It was a hundred times more difficult to do since I wasn't able to dry myself as thoroughly the second time. It was frustrating trying to get into the flannel with wet skin that kept sticking to the fabric, but I eventually succeeded.

Getting the shirt over my head and keeping the towel on my wound was trickier and I gave up after only two tries. I'd need something that zipped or buttoned up front. After rinsing the rest of the blood with the shower head—and slipping the metal cylinder—which looked much smaller than I imagined now that it was out of me—into my bra, I turned the shower off.

Now what? Do I sneak to Ari's room for a jacket? Do I waltz downstairs half-naked in front of the guy I like and advertise my self-inflicted wound for them all to see?

I wanted to talk to Carly. If anyone would believe me, it was Carly.

Someone tried the handle, then knocked at the bathroom door before I could make a decision.

"Need anything?" Ari asked outside the door.

"Could I... could I talk to Carly for a sec?" I tried to sound casual, but my arm was really beginning to hurt. I must've had a course of adrenaline rushing when I cut into myself and it was wearing off quickly.

"She ran out for some ice cream."

My heart sank. "In the middle of winter?"

"Oh right... um... She ran out for tampons."

Something wasn't right. Mistaking tampons for ice cream? She was lying about something. "Is Duncan still here?" I had to grit my teeth each time I talked to push back the pain.

There was a pause. "He wanted to make sure you're okay, but I think he's leaving soon."

"Could you ask him to wait until I can tell him goodbye?" I asked. *He'd help me escape again, right?* He was my only hope. I was stranded otherwise if Carly was gone with the car. *Where had Carly gone?*

"Yeah, hold on." I heard her footsteps retreat back down the stairs.

I opened the door quietly and tiptoed into Ari's room. Grabbing the biggest sweatshirt I could find that zipped in front, I carefully slid my injured arm—towel and all—into the sleeve, then quickly put the rest on and zipped it up.

Walking downstairs, I resisted the impulse to keep a hand on the wound and held it tightly against my side, hoping it was enough to stop the bleeding.

Ari was the only one in the room when I walked in.

My heart stopped. "Where's Duncan?"

"Oh, you just missed him," she said, like everything was normal. "Why are you wearing that sweatshirt? Was the flannel top not warm enough?"

At the mention of my shirt, my hand automatically went to the bulge of the towel underneath.

Ari's eyes went wide. "What...?" She walked to me quickly.

I heard a car door outside and sprinted to the front door throwing it open. Duncan's car was running, and he'd just closed the door.

"Duncan! Wait!" I called as I ran out, barefoot on the ice-cold steps, praying I didn't slip on the scattered ice that hadn't melted with the salt laid down. He didn't hear me and began to back out.

"Where are you going, Em!" Ari called, sounding panicked, but trying to sound as normal as possible.

The car stopped. He'd heard her yell and put the car in park before opening the door.

Seeing my dripping hair and wearing only a sweatshirt, pajama pants, and no shoes, Duncan got out quickly. "What's going on? Ari said you wanted to go home," he said when I ran into his arms. "She sent Carly to get your parents..." That was when he pushed back to look at my bulging arm. The towel must've shifted and blood was soaking through Arianna's sweatshirt.

She must've seen the blood.

"She lied!" I cried and ran around to get in the passenger seat of his car. "Get me out of here!" I said as he repeated the scene from my house and peeled out of the driveway. "Do you have your phone?" I asked holding my good hand out.

He handed it to me.

I dialed Carly's number. It was a miracle that she had a number that was easily memorized.

"Hello?" she answered.

"Don't get my parents!" I cried. "I don't know what Ari told you, but they want to take me back to the mental ward or something. They think I'm delusional and want me back on meds." When she didn't respond right away, I said, "Please tell me you haven't talked to them already?"

"I haven't," she said quickly. "It was a little odd when Ari said you wanted me to get them."

"Please, Carly," I said. "You know the truth. You know the dreams aren't some mental illness that I have. You've been there. But they're doing things to me to stop it. Please."

"Okay," she said slowly, "I'm turning around. But, Emily?"

"Yeah?"

"You can't run away forever."

"I know. I'll talk to them tomorrow," I promised. "I just need some time to think."

Another pause. "Where will you stay?"

I looked sideways at Duncan. It was dark in the car, but I could see his tight jaw even in the darkness and his gray eyes were narrowed. He looked worried and furious. "Duncan's, I think," I said. "We'll see," I added when Duncan didn't make any sign that it would be okay. "Don't tell Ari though."

"I won't," she said and hung up.

I stared at Duncan for several heavy seconds. "Look. I know you probably have a girlfriend or whatever—"

"You're staying at my house," he interrupted, his voice pitched. He sounded angry. "You cut it out, didn't you?"

"Yeah, I had to. Mom and Dad—"

"I get it," he said, cutting off my words again. "Lucky for you, my mom's a nurse. You'll let her take a look?"

That one question spoke volumes of how much he knew me. My trust in the medical community was at an all-time rock-bottom low. My trust in *anyone*, even my parents and my best friend, was at an all-time rock-bottom low. But I trusted Duncan. He'd saved me twice tonight. Having something injected into me without my knowledge or consent felt enormously intrusive. But he asked if she could look at it. It was probably a good idea. I'd done a hack job and infection was very likely.

"I'll let her look at it." I said, and sank back into the seat.

CHAPTER 42

finally feeling safe

An hour later I was snuggled into the couch at Duncan's with a heavy blanket wrapped around me. My wounded arm throbbed underneath the dressings, but at least the *thing* was out. Duncan's mom didn't say a word about me digging it out in the shower while she cleaned and stitched me up. I'd probably have a nasty scar, but she almost sounded like I'd done the right thing taking it out. Especially considering the fact that I didn't know what it was so I'd obviously not given my consent—even though I was a minor.

When I began to hyperventilate at the mention of contacting my parents, she promised I could sleep on their couch. She just had to let them know that I was safe. We could deal with everything else tomorrow. Fortunately, my parents agreed to the plan. I even heard my mom sobbing through the phone as Duncan's mom talked to her.

"It sounds like they really didn't know about the thing in your arm," Duncan said a few minutes after his mom hung up. He sat next to me on the couch, but not close enough to touch. Probably because of Clare. He looked weary and like he was about ready to fall asleep. I almost suggested that he should, but I didn't want to be left alone.

"Thanks," I said, "for everything." I managed a smile. "Really. You were my knight in shining armor tonight."

He shrugged. "It's what friends do."

"What about Clare?" I asked.

"Clare? What about her?" He honestly looked like she hadn't crossed his mind in hours.

"What is Clare going to say about me spending the night on your couch?"

"It isn't really any of her business," he said, and my heart lightened.

"So she isn't..." I paused, trying to hide the smile that wanted to burst out. "She isn't your *girlfriend?*"

He paused too, and I couldn't read his face. My sudden happy feeling deflated. "She wants to be."

"Do *you* want her to be?"

Duncan searched my face for several long moments. He didn't move closer, but brushed a lock of my recently blow-dried hair behind my ear. I didn't dare move and ruin the moment. Especially since he looked so sad.

"You should get some sleep," he said and stood, shoving his hands into his slack pockets. His dress shirt was disheveled, his tie was undone, and he'd slung his suit coat over the arm chair. He looked amazing.

"Yeah, okay. You're probably beat too," I said, letting him go.

Duncan looked at me for a few more seconds. "I don't mind sleeping on the couch, if you wanna take my bed."

His thoughtfulness made me melt. If I'd been standing, I'd surely go weak at the knees. Fortunately I was not standing, and he was none the wiser how his offer affected me. I shook my head, then patted the pillow that was actually an extra from his bed. "I'm fine here, thanks."

He nodded once. "Goodnight, Em," he said, holding my gaze.

"Goodnight, Duncan."

When he turned on his heel to leave, he called back, "Maybe you'll get your dreams back tonight."

I highly doubted it. I had a feeling that something injected in me, whatever it was, would surely have some lingering effects.

"Maybe," I answered quietly anyway.

CHAPTER 43

return (finally!)

uncan was right.

I know it the moment my eyes open. I'm back.
With Lucy! To her, it is merely a blink, but to me,
opening my eyes feels like finally waking up from a long coma.
Yeah, I don't miss the irony in that.

Lucy claps our hands together once. "You are here!" she
squeals.

I'm here!

"And just in time!" When she claps her hands together again, I
realize she's wearing gloves. But not just any gloves. Intricately
laced white gloves that reach all the way up her elbow. "Look!"
She turns a quarter-turn, so we are standing in front of a gilded
full-length mirror. "It is perfect!"

Her blond curls are piled high and plaited and pinned in an
elaborate arrangement. A ring of orange blossoms and ribbon
surround her head like a crown. She is wearing the most beautiful,
hand-laced, Victorian wedding gown I have ever seen. The collar is
high, the bodice is tight—but the corset beneath will keep it from
bursting, and it isn't uncomfortable. Layers of skirts start at the
waist and flow to the ground like a waterfall—but not wide like a
ball gown.

You look perfect! I agree. *I'm so happy I arrived in time for your perfect wedding.*

Lucy beams and a warm feeling surges through me. Not only can I see the happiness on her face in the reflection, but I can *feel* it from the crown of blossoms on her head to the tiny shoes on her feet. She is getting her fairy-tale happily ever after ending. "Charles is waiting," she says. "And Uncle Harry will be here any minute to walk me down the aisle."

So everything is okay? I want to cry.

"Everything is perfect."

Oh, Lucy I was so worried. After everything that happened. After telling Charles about me and my dreams. After he left, I didn't know if... I can't finish, but know she understands my meaning.

"Yes, things were uncertain for a time, but everything has worked out." She assures me. "I am glad that we decided to tell Charles. He should know about you. He left because it was all a shock to him and he needed time to think about it. But when he came back, he said everything would be okay, and there was never even a hint that he did not want to marry me."

Decided to tell him? I didn't remember her ever deciding to tell him anything, but I shrug it off. It worked out after all. *What a relief!*

A knock sounds at the door and a blond woman enters. More than that, I feel like Lucy is looking into another mirror as she walks toward us. Albeit a mirror that shows what Lucy will look like in several years, but practically a spitting image.

"Are you ready, little sister?" the woman asks. Her voice high, but warm and velvety.

Lucy holds her hands out. "Vera!" Tears prick her eyes, but she has more control over them than I had all of yesterday. "Vera, I am so happy!"

Her eldest sister takes her hands and smiles, showing all of her teeth.

"The day is finally here!"

Vera's smile falters slightly as she looks at the hidden scars beneath Lucy's gloves. "And to think you almost did not have a wedding day."

"That is in the past," Lucy takes her hands back and holds them up to prove her point. "I survived. I am all right. And I am so happy that I finally get to marry the man I love." Her tone lowers when she says the last part.

Vera stares at us for several seconds, tears of her own filling her eyes. "You truly love him? You love Charles?"

Lucy nods violently. "I know why you ask, but you have not been here to see, sister. My infatuation with Robert ended a long time ago. I was cured of it long before I even met Charles."

Vera smiles, satisfied.

"So you do not need to stay away," Lucy says. "Move back. Certainly, Robert can do the same work from town."

Vera's smile turns mischievous, and she leans closer. "I did not want to overshadow your day, but your timing is perfect. Robert and I will be needing a bigger home soon because..."

"Oh!" Lucy looks where her sister's hand has trailed to. "I'm going to be an aunt?"

Vera nods, her emotion overtakes her and she cannot speak anymore.

"Go, go!" Lucy insists. "Before you become a blubbering mess!" she teases.

"Too late," Vera says through her tears. "But do not worry; they will all think I am weeping because of how beautiful you look. And they will not be wrong." She backs away and leaves the room right as Lucy's uncle enters.

"Is it time?" Lucy asks.

Uncle Harry nods with beaming joy. He holds his elbow out for her to take. "You are a beautiful bride, my dearest Lucy." Up close I can see tears in his eyes too.

Man, there won't be a dry eye in the house. I say to Lucy, hoping to lighten the mood so she doesn't become a blubbering mess also.

She smiles. *Thank you, Emily,* she says. *I am so glad you are here. But perhaps later tonight... maybe you could... when...*

Oh, I have every intention of pushing myself out before any of that. I say, hoping I naturally leave, but fully planning to get out quickly if it doesn't happen.

Suddenly I wonder where Andrew is. I haven't seen him yet. My heart pounds a little faster as we walk out of Lucy's home and begin the drive to the church. Lucy doesn't comment on my sudden nerves because she has sudden nerves of her own. Albeit a different kind.

Obviously I don't expect Andrew to be where Lucy was getting ready for the best day of her life, but he'll be at the ceremony, right? And if so, will he be sitting next to Margaret? His engagement feels so fake after he has gone out of his way to see me —even at the expense of Lucy and Charles's relationship. Thank goodness everything worked out in that department. But is he still keeping up the farce with her? Poor girl.

Or will he stay away? Not wanting to be caught staring at the girl who houses the girl he loves?

When we arrive, Lucy's younger sister, Hannah, and several other young girls are waiting outside the church. All wear matching white dresses and the ring of orange blossoms on their heads. I assume they are bridesmaids or flower girls as we walk the short distance from the carriage to *Lucy's* chapel and waltz up to the large wooden double doors.

A gentleman outside pushes open the doors and the first two girls glide into the chapel as the organ music begins. Two more follow a few seconds later, and finally Hannah is last.

Lucy and I collectively take a deep breath. Her heart is pounding in anticipation at seeing her beloved Charles at the end of the aisle. And I pray that my desire to see Andrew doesn't over-power Lucy's feelings. Right then and there I vow to behave just as her sister Vera has.

Your turn. I urge Lucy, who immediately takes a step forward and through the open doors.

not today

My eyes immediately fly to the stained-glass windows high above. The sunlight filtering in casts a colorful, rainbow hue on everything it touches. The atmosphere is ethereal. And with the rich organ music playing a hymn or tune I don't recognize, I am hypnotized by the entire scene. Fortunately this is Lucy's day and she has full control, so I am free to absorb and daydream.

When I first walked Lucy, she brought Andrew here with the intention of sharing this very place with him. This church is one of Lucy's most favorite places in the whole world, but we never came inside. Instead we sat behind the church on that overgrown bench and confessed that we were both cursed.

I've loved this place ever since. This is the place where I shared so many memories with Andrew. And the crazy thing is that even though Andrew didn't know about me, it was there on that bench, talking about dreams and curses, that I started to fall for him.

I search for his dark hair and chestnut eyes out of the corner of my eye as we walk the aisle. I can't very well jerk Lucy's head back and forth to scan the crowd, so my vantage point is limited. I don't see him.

We draw closer to the altar.

Lucy's smile widens as she sees the look on Charles's face. It is stoic, but his eyes smile in such a way that she knows in the depth of her soul how much he loves her. As we get closer, I notice that the corners of his mouth seem melancholy and I wonder if it is residual from everything Andrew and I have done to threaten to break the happy couple apart. Fortunately that never happened.

I don't bother mentioning my observation to her because we are here. Charles and Lucy are choosing each other in this moment, and everything will be perfect.

Lucy will rub that sadness off of Charles's face with years and years of happiness. She survived the fire. She is destined to live a long life with him. I know. I've seen the dates of her grave, so I know.

As frantic as I was to return, sadly I conclude that it is time to finally say goodbye to Lucy. She is marrying her sweetheart and no longer needs me. At least for now. As much as I would like to see Andrew, there is always another dream to meet him in.

The bridesmaids and flower girls reach the end of the line and form a line near the aisle so only Lucy and her uncle remain. A few more steps and her guardian lifts her veil to kiss her cheek, then places the hand he held into Charles's.

His hand is warm. His smile too. And the priest begins the ceremony.

WE RETURN TO HARKER MANOR AFTER THE CEREMONY for a luncheon since the Eldridge home is still being repaired from the fire.

Lucy has walked on air since she and Charles said "I do." A genuine, happy, giddy smile is a permanent fixture on her face until her cheeks ache.

Guests arrive to offer the happy couple and their parents congratulations. The wedding party sits at a table, eating their pastries and meats while guests stand around the room with plates, talking and chatting. It is vastly different from any wedding reception I'd ever been to, but... well... a hundred years makes a difference.

As Lucy greets and speaks with guests, I am able to look around the room more freely for Andrew. A hard lump forms in my throat as I suspect more and more that he was not invited because of recent events. Or perhaps he simply did not choose to come. The thought saddens me. I plan to say goodbye to Lucy before her and Charles leave for their honeymoon. I would have liked to see him here in his time once more. To talk to him as he wears his own face one more time. I am afraid if I don't speak to him and patch things up, he might never try to meet me in dreams again.

Is everything all right? Lucy asks me finally.

My thoughts scroll through everything that has happened back at home since I last saw her, but I do not want to burden her on her wedding day with tales of high school drama, days and days without memory dreams and not knowing if I'd ever get back, unidentified injected objects, and cutting the said unidentified object from my skin with hair scissors.

Not really, but nothing worth ruining your wedding day over.

She greets another woman with graying hair underneath a velvety purple hat with white feathers around the brim. Her eyes are wrinkly and kind. She gushes her congratulations and then begins regaling Lucy about some courtship of two people Lucy has never met. She tunes out the woman. I take the opportunity to ask her a question.

Where's Andrew?

She doesn't answer right away.

Did you ask him not to come after... well, everything? I ask. *Or do you think he chose not to come?* The last question breaks my heart a little because it means that Andrew really does have feelings for Lucy as I feared. I've never been truly convinced that he sees me and Lucy as two different people, no matter how much he's insisted.

Another pause. Lucy is suddenly listening to the woman, and when the woman is at a stopping point, Lucy excuses herself.

What is it? I ask when we've exited the room.

But we see them at the same time.

I hadn't noticed when Charles left the room, but he's standing at the end of the hallway speaking with two gentleman dressed in attire not entirely appropriate for a wedding gathering. Charles looks agitated and is talking wildly with his hands.

What's going on? I ask, but I instantly know that Lucy has no idea. *Let's find out.* I urge her to walk quietly so we can listen.

"You will not. Not today," Charles says sternly.

"It is imperative that she gets the care she needs. The sooner we can start the treatment, the sooner—"

"Not today!" He shouts and stomps away. He suddenly sees Lucy standing only a few feet away. He walks toward us with his hands open. "Lucy, let us get back to our guests."

She plants her feet and looks at the men who haven't budged an inch. "Is one of them named Andrew?" she asks.

What?

"What are you talking about, darling?" he asks, looking over his shoulder.

"Andrew," she repeats, her head is fuzzy and she feels a little bit dazed. "Is one of them named Andrew? I have a friend who is looking for him."

Lucy? Something is wrong. Something is very, very wrong.

"No, you have never met those gentlemen," Charles says, gripping her arm to direct her back to the wedding reception.

But Lucy steadily stares at the men who stare back. One of them takes a step forward to quietly talk to Charles.

"Sir, I really think now would be best." The man is not quiet at all.

Both men converge until each flank a side of Lucy and me.

Charles releases his grip on our arm and lowers his head in

defeat. We duck to meet his eyes. I silently ask him a question because Lucy seems to have drifted off somewhere.

"Where is Andrew?" I ask, injecting as much normalness into my tone as I can. "Have you seen him?" I turn to go back to the party. "I will let you finish your conversation," I say, "I can find him on my own."

The men close in until they are within arm's reach.

Charles's eyes and mouth fall into a frown. Tears rim his lids. Firmly he grips both of my hands. "Darling, these men are here to help you."

I don't dare release my gaze on him to glance at either man.

"I need help?"

He nods and the men gently grip both of my forearms.

"Where's Andrew?" I ask once more, tears forming in my own eyes as I connect the pieces. I have an inkling who the men are and why they are here.

I've seen the documentaries.

They're from a sanitarium. An insane asylum. A place where they took people who were mentally ill.

I need Andrew. "Your cousin, Andrew Harker? Where is he?" My voice is barely a whisper now.

"Lucy, darling." His voice is also low. "We are not acquainted with anyone by that name. I do not have a cousin named Andrew Harker."

regret and relief

"No!" I shot straight up from the couch and nearly fell off. I managed to catch myself with my injured arm—which caused all sorts of intense, radiating pain. I grabbed my arm and gritted my teeth against the pain, hoping I didn't rip out any stitches.

When the wave of pain passed enough for me to think clearly again, the devastation returned with a different kind of pain that hurt even more.

Andrew was gone.

Worse, he was nonexistent. I knew what Charles meant when he said those words. He wasn't *pretending* he didn't have a cousin by that name, he meant that he'd *never* had a cousin by that name. He was gone. Erased. Never-existed. And if Charles's reaction didn't convince me, the fact that Lucy didn't know him either did. She could feel the need for me to find him, but she didn't know who he was to find.

Because of me she was taken away to a mental hospital—worse, a sanitarium—in the early nineteen hundreds, a place where tuberculosis ran rampant and people died more often than they ever got out.

The only good that came of it was that my goodbye to Lucy

was indefinitely postponed. She needed me now more than ever, and I would get back to her as soon as possible. Hopefully since she was rich, she would be taken to a less disease-infested hospital. I could only hope and pray until tonight when I could get back to her.

"Emily!" Duncan rushed out of his room and to my side on the couch. His basketball shorts looked twisted and his shirt was on backwards which told me that he'd quickly thrown them on only seconds earlier. Meaning, he would have been at my side sooner if he slept with more clothing. I tried to banish that image from my mind before looking at him. "What happened? Are you okay?"

I managed a weak smile. "I had another dream," I said. "A memory walk. With Lucy."

His face brightened at that, but when he saw my sullen expression it dimmed again. "Isn't that a good thing?"

"Yeah, except that she was taken away to a nut house, and I'm pretty sure it's my fault."

His eyes widened in surprise, a little bit more than I'd expect since he didn't know Lucy.

"I have to get back to her and be with her. Maybe I can get her out somehow," I added, I guess trying to ease his mind on the matter. Though I wasn't sure why he needed assurance. I held up my taped-up arm. "With the *thing* gone, I can get back to the dreams. Just like you promised." I smiled weakly again. "What time is it?" I asked, yawning and looking around.

Duncan looked over his shoulder at a wall-clock. "Almost seven," he said. "Do you want to go home?" He sounded disappointed to be asking that question.

"Not yet," I said pulling the blanket tighter around my shoulders with a sudden shiver.

"Well, you can stay all day if you'd like," he said. "It's Sunday. Things are pretty chill around here on Sundays."

"Thanks. I should probably talk to my parents soon though. I put them through quite a lot last night."

"Em, I think they understand that you were pretty freaked out," he said.

We were both silent for a few seconds.

"So, do you believe that they didn't know about the *thing?*" he asked.

I shrugged my shoulders. It was amazing how differently I felt after some sleep. "It doesn't seem like them to keep something so big from me. But I can't stay away forever." I bit my lower lip. "If it turns out that they did know, if they threaten to commit me, could I come back here?"

"Yes!" he said a little loudly for not-quite seven on a Sunday. "Yes," he whispered again, shushing himself.

I searched his eyes a moment, letting the gratitude for his friendship fill me. "You're the greatest, you know that?" I said, then felt my cheeks color for sounding so dumb.

He brushed his fingers on the sleeve of his shirt, then blew on them. "I try," he teased. "I've gotta impress the ladies somehow."

I laughed, then sobered quickly and looked down at the patterns on the afghan covering me. I traced the greens and browns with my eyes when I said, "It must've worked on Clare." I shouldn't be digging again, especially after Duncan's nonanswer last night. But I was a glutton for punishment. I didn't even know what I wanted the answer to be.

"About Clare..." he said slowly. I dared look up, my gaze more hopeful than it should have been.

"Sorry," I said quickly, stopping him from continuing. "It's really none of my business." It felt like I wanted him to say that she wasn't his girlfriend, and he was ready for me to have that title again. But my subconscious certainly was aching for a distraction now that I knew Andrew was gone. No, I wasn't going to lead Duncan on or use him as a rebound or whatever because I might never see Andrew again.

It wasn't fair to Duncan.

He cleared his throat, and I forced myself to look like an interested friend as I waited for him to talk. "I think I'll ask her out again," he said slowly, like he was trying really hard not to hurt me and letting me down easy.

"Oh yeah, you should," I said with more enthusiasm than I felt. "I mean, if you like being with her and all... you should definitely go out with her again." I nudged him. *I nudged him?* I wanted to die, but kept going. "Have you kissed her?" Internal facepalm. I wanted to facepalm for real, but fortunately I had enough self-control not to. "Sorry," I said, shaking my head. "None of my business." I looked at the clock over Duncan's shoulder even though I knew it would only read a few seconds later. "Could I borrow your phone, actually?" I asked. "I think I should call my parents."

"Sure," he said and left to get me his cell.

DUNCAN WENT BACK TO BED AFTER HANDING ME HIS phone, probably so I could have some privacy—or maybe avoid a continuation of the mortifying conversation. I couldn't blame him for that.

I wished he'd stayed though, because it would have forced me to dial immediately. As it was, I let my palms sweat and my pulse race for a full ten minutes while I wrote a script in my head of what I was going to say when Mom or Dad picked up the phone. Finally, I dialed. They were my parents. They'd assured me as long as I could remember that I could talk to them about anything. It was the reason I'd told them about the dreams in the first place, and maybe that was a mistake, but this felt a lot bigger.

Dad picked up on the first ring.

"Ems?" He let out a breath like he'd been holding it all night. He also didn't sound like he'd just woken up which made me feel a little bit guilty. He and Mom had probably been up all night.

"Hi, Dad," I said meekly.

"Listen, honey. Your mother and I had no idea that they'd put something in your arm. We are both absolutely *sick* that someone would do that to our little girl—"

"Sweetheart," Mom said. It sounded like she yanked the phone from his hands. "Sweetie, are you all right? Mrs. Stewart said that you cut that... that *thing* out of your arm?" She choked on the words and began to sob.

"Emily"—Dad again—"we called a lawyer last night. We are going to get to the bottom of this and find out what happened and who did this to you."

"Last night?" Now my voice caught. They really hadn't known about it? They hadn't secretly given consent for whatever it was to be placed in my arm? "Dad, I left the house at like eleven-thirty. What lawyer answered a phone that late?"

"It doesn't matter," Dad said. "Your Uncle Greg knows a guy. Anyway, we called, and he thinks we have a case. They said you cut it out. Did you happen to keep it?"

I'd forgotten about it, but remembered that I'd slipped it into my bra before leaving Ari's. "Yeah, I have it."

"Smart girl," he said, sounding relieved. "Good. Don't lose it."

"I won't." My whole body felt lighter. Mom and Dad didn't know a thing, and they were batting for me. They were going to find whoever did this to me. "Dad?" I asked after a few silent seconds.

"Do you want me to come get you?" he asked. "You're still at Duncan's?"

I looked down the hallway toward Duncan's room. "Yeah, I'm at Duncan's," I said torn between wanting to go home and wanting to stay with Duncan. I didn't know how much more one-on-one time I would get with him since he was clearly wanting to pursue Clare. No matter what he said about us being friends, I doubted she'd be okay with me hanging around him so much, let alone having sleepovers on his couch. But I couldn't dwell on that now. I got back to the question I wanted to ask. "Who do you think did it?"

"We think it was Dr. Shew," Dad said. There was fury behind his tone. "While you were in that coma. We even think that she might have *caused* the coma in the first place since she switched your medications right before it happened."

I nodded though he couldn't see it. "I think it was her too," I said, a little sad to admit it since I liked her so much.

"You do?" he sounded shocked that I'd come to the same conclusion, though it seemed obvious now that I thought about it.

"Who else would it be?" I said. "I haven't had a memory dream for days, but last night after I took it out, I finally had one."

There was a pause on the line and the guilt of blaming my parents came crashing down.

"Hey, and Dad?"

"Yeah?"

"I'm so, so sorry I blamed you and Mom."

"Nah." His voice sounded different. Like he was trying to hold it together.

"No, I should've known you'd never let someone do that to me."

"I'll be there in ten minutes," Dad said, then hung up.

CHAPTER 46

1925

Pushing open the glass doors to the side porch, I stumble, then giggle and hold a hand to my mouth. The cool air bites the back of my neck, shoulders, and bare legs, clearing my head a little.

Steadying myself, I grab the iron rail with the hand not holding my half-empty glass and lose my heels before descending the stone stairs to the pathway below. The tassels on my dress swish against my thighs in a pleasant sensation with each step. *I love this dress,* I think for the thousandth time tonight. It hangs in all the right places, shows off all of the right curves, and covers just enough to leave the rest to imagination.

Thoughts of my brand new black flapper dress remind me why I left the party in the first place. To find him. I begged Father to buy the dress for me *because* of him.

He's playing so hard to get, but I know he's attracted to me. I've seen it in his brown eyes. I've seen it in his half-smile and the way he twists his hands when he's nervous. I've seen it in the way he won't look at me and avoids any situation where we might be alone. He won't escape me this time.

The saxophone sings through the still-open doors and the strings of the bass play a beat in my chest and through the skin of my naked feet, even as the volume of the jazz number lowers the further I walk into the yard.

There aren't many places to hide, so although I am a little bit inebriated, I easily find him in the gazebo. His dark form leans against the whitewashed wood, his head tilted down, his back turned toward me.

I cover my hand to stifle another giggle. *Shush!* I scold myself and tiptoe even slower, absently wondering where I left my drink because it's no longer in my hand. If he doesn't hear me come, he won't be able to slink away again. I'll have him trapped! The mere thought makes me giddy.

I stick out my bottom lip as I round to face him. "Did the party not have enough to hold your attention?" My words slur slightly.

"Genevieve," he says with a sigh, running his hand through his sandy brown hair and closing his eyes.

I smile. *I've caught him!* I saunter closer, trying my best not to make any sudden movements that might spook him. "Why do you look so sad?" I ask, carefully forming my words to sound more sober. "Plenty of girls were willing to dance with you while I spent time with Father's ideas of proper suitors. But I was saving my last dance for you." I reach out and place both hands flat on his chest, careful not to caress after what happened last time.

He reached up and grabbed them both but didn't let go of my fingers. "Ginny, stop," he said sternly, meeting my gaze full on.

My heart does a schoolgirl pitter-patter after he said my name so familiarly. I lean in to kiss him, but he stiffens his elbows to keep me at arm's length.

"Ginny, I'm..." he pauses, but keeps eye contact. "Ginny, you are intoxicated."

"So? We are at a party, everyone else is."

"It's illegal, and you are only sixteen!" He releases my hands and backs further into the gazebo.

I follow him in. "And you're eighteen," I say. "Would you kiss me if I weren't *intoxicated?*" I giggle again.

His eyes narrow. "Ginny, I am in love with someone else."

"Who?" I hear the rise in my voice, the alcohol suddenly having less affect. "That little Ruth girl who always follows you around like a lost puppy?" I know I sound bitter, but I don't care.

He shakes his head in exasperation. "You wouldn't understand. She's—"

"Just tell me her name!" I cut him off, angry now.

"Genevieve..."

"Tell me or I'll tell my father that you've been acting inappropriate with me."

His eyes widened. "You wouldn't."

Good. I've got him exactly where I want him.

"I've never touched you, Ginny."

"Who do you think he'll believe? You or me?" I stick my hip out and put a hand on it, letting my mouth twist smugly in the dim light.

His shoulders slump as he says, "Her name is Emily, but I haven't spoken to her in a while."

When he says my name, it isn't like I'm suddenly unaware of myself and then instantly know who I am, Genevieve's drunken state is affecting me too. I've been in a daze as everything played out. Until he says my name.

There is no flashing purple and blinding white.

How did I not recognize him sooner?

Andrew? I think I spoke aloud, but Genevieve pushes me back. It is unmistakably him. His hair color is different, but maybe it is because we are in a gazebo after dark. I can see twinkling stars peek in every opening and want to stroll out to look around. It is beautiful tonight.

Jazz music drifts from the party up at the house—well, mansion is probably more appropriate now that I'm really looking at it.

"Why haven't you spoken to her in a while?" Genevieve asks, her tone changed slightly.

Andrew shakes his head and twists the ring on his finger.

If I could only touch him, I think to myself. *If I touch his ring, maybe I can take control.* I try to keep my thoughts to myself so Genevieve doesn't hear, but it has the opposite effect in her drunken brain. My suggestion to touch him is *exactly* what she wants to do. I take that little bit of desire and add it to my own, sprinting until I have his hand in an awkward grasp.

"Andrew," I breathe.

With his other hand he tries to gently remove mine, but I'm afraid the release of the ring will release my control. "Ginny, please let go of my hand."

"Andrew, it's me!" I cry out. "It's me, Emily. I'm here with Ginny."

He freezes and stares at me with those brown eyes which aren't the chestnut color I remember, and now that I'm up close, his hair color is definitely lighter than before.

He narrows his eyes, trying to decipher whether I'm telling the truth. I look down at our hands. "I had to grab your ring, to take control," I say. "Genevieve is very headstrong. Much more than Lucy."

Something I said must have convinced him because instantly both of his arms are wrapped around me, and he breaths something unintelligibly into my ear.

Genevieve is loving every second of this and loosens her resistance toward me.

After a few moments, he slowly pushes back to look at my face.

I give him a weak smile. "I don't know what's going on," I say. "I don't know why I'm with Genevieve and not Lucy." Remembering Lucy causes a lurch in my stomach. She needs me, but for some reason I'm here with another girl and not with her. A huge weight of guilt surges as I contemplate whether it's my fault. I should be with Lucy.

He gives me a knowing smile. "I know why you're not with Lucy."

"Oh, no. Did something happen? Did Lucy die? I wasn't

there with her!" I begin to hyperventilate and without thinking I let go of his hands and pace on the cold wood with Genevieve's bare feet. Fortunately she doesn't wrench control back again. He's suddenly paying more attention to her than he ever has, and she is eating it up.

I shiver once and wrap Ginny's bare arms around myself. It feels like spring, but Ginny is definitely underdressed to be outside.

Then I realize what she is wearing. A short dress with no sleeves, cut in a v-neck and covered in black tassels. I reach up and feel her bob haircut, and move a strand into my line of sight to look at the straight blackness of it. Smiling, I recognize that it's very close to my own color.

I look back at Andrew who is carefully watching me piece things together. But it's not clicking and only getting more confusing. Andrew looks *younger* than I remember. How is that possible?

"We're in a different time," I say, partly grasping at straws.

He merely nods, his smile widening.

"But we're further in the future."

He nods again.

"But you still look like you, and you answered to *Andrew,* so you can't be walking like I am."

Another nod.

I stop talking and march up to him with a what-the-hell-is-going-on look.

"It's nineteen twenty-five," he says quickly, suddenly surprised by my attack.

"Okay, that explains the dress and the illegal alcohol you mentioned, and the fact that I don't remember anyone named Genevieve in yours and Lucy's time."

"We aren't in Lucy's time." The way he said it, *Lucy's time* like it belongs to her and not him strikes me as strange.

"Lucy and Charles got married," I say.

"I know."

"And you weren't there."

"That is correct."

"In fact, they both denied that you even existed. They both said they didn't *know* you. Your *cousin* doesn't know who you are."

Andrew's smile finally fades, and he backs away to lean against a far post of the gazebo. "To them, I never existed."

I was right. He was erased somehow. And I went and blabbered with Lucy's mouth that I needed to speak to Andrew. Poor Lucy, she must've sounded even more crazy in that moment. I've made an even bigger mess of her life. Again.

"What happened?" I ask.

Andrew straightens and wipes any hint of smirk or teasing or smugness from his posture and expression. "My plan is working," he says and takes a step toward me.

"Your plan?"

Again he nods and twists the ring on his finger, taking two more steps until his face and lips are inches from mine again.

Genevieve swoons inside but keeps quiet.

"My plan to get to you." He says the words slowly and quietly, but with an undertone of richness and purpose.

I almost have all of the pieces, but I can't see the forest for the trees. I search his eyes, asking the question I don't have the words for.

"I've changed things, Emily," he says, "I am no longer Charles's cousin because I prevented my birth from happening in eighteen eighty-two to become his cousin."

"I... I don't understand." *He prevented his birth?* My mind reels as I try to sort this information out. *If it's nineteen-twenty-five now...* "But you're here. If you prevented you birth, how are you here?"

"I'm only eighteen, Emily," he says, talking quickly, a little bit impatient that I'm not getting it. "I was born in nineteen-oh-seven." When he reads my expression and realizes that I still don't get it, he continues, "I'm moving up in time!" he says, "I've changed my parentage. Haven't you noticed some differences about me?" He points to his different hair color. "I've found a way to move up by changing things when I dream walk."

I'm completely at a loss for words and forbid Genevieve from saying anything until he's finished.

"This Andrew is only the first stop," he says, waving a hand at himself. "I suspect it will take a few more changes and jumps before I get to you, but I will get to you."

I move forward the last few inches to kiss him. He doesn't pull away like he did a moment before with Genevieve. Instead, he responds energetically.

We pull apart briefly for a breath. "I'm coming to you."

End of Book Two

Get three FREE short stories when you join Joanna's email list at joannareeder.com

thank you for reading

Thank you for reading *Trapped In Her Dreams*!

If you enjoyed immersing yourself into Emily's world and meeting Lucy, Andrew, and Duncan, please leave an honest review! Reviews are essential to indie authors like me.

acknowledgments

First of all to my readers for reading this book! Thank you!

But seriously it never would have come to fruition without the support of my family. From my sweet husband who may not understand my need to tell stories but supports me anyway, and my crazy kids who are completely content to watch Netflix or nap for a couple hours a day so mommy can write. Also my parents, siblings, and extended family who have been my beta readers, emergency brainstorm session heroes, and for supporting me and encouraging me all of these years.

I also couldn't have done it without my amazing writer's group (Go Team Fellowship!) and critique partners, Jesse Booth and Aaron Herd who have helped me brainstorm, develop my stories to make them stronger, kept me motivated, and boosted my confidence along the way (you are my rock, Team Istari!).

Lastly, a huge thank you to my editor Katrina Beckstrand (editsbykb.com), who completely understood and visualized my vision for the *In Her Dreams* trilogy and helped polish them to make them all lovely and shiny.

about the author

Joanna Reeder is a USA Today Bestselling author who takes readers time traveling through dreams, shifting into fantastical creatures, and tossed into Faerie. Her fantasy stories always have a dash of romance, leave readers turning pages long into the night, and eager to recommend them to their daughters and grandmas and coworkers!

When Joanna isn't writing, she enjoys bike rides and kayaking with her hubby and kids, vacations at the beach (with a book to read, of course!) and learning new songs on her blue electric guitar.

She's a believer in the paranormal (seriously, she has stories) and her motto is, "A Dr. Pepper a day keeps insanity away!"

If you love fantasy romance too, you can sign up for Joanna's weekly newsletter at joannareeder.com. You can also chat with her on Instagram @joanna_reeder.